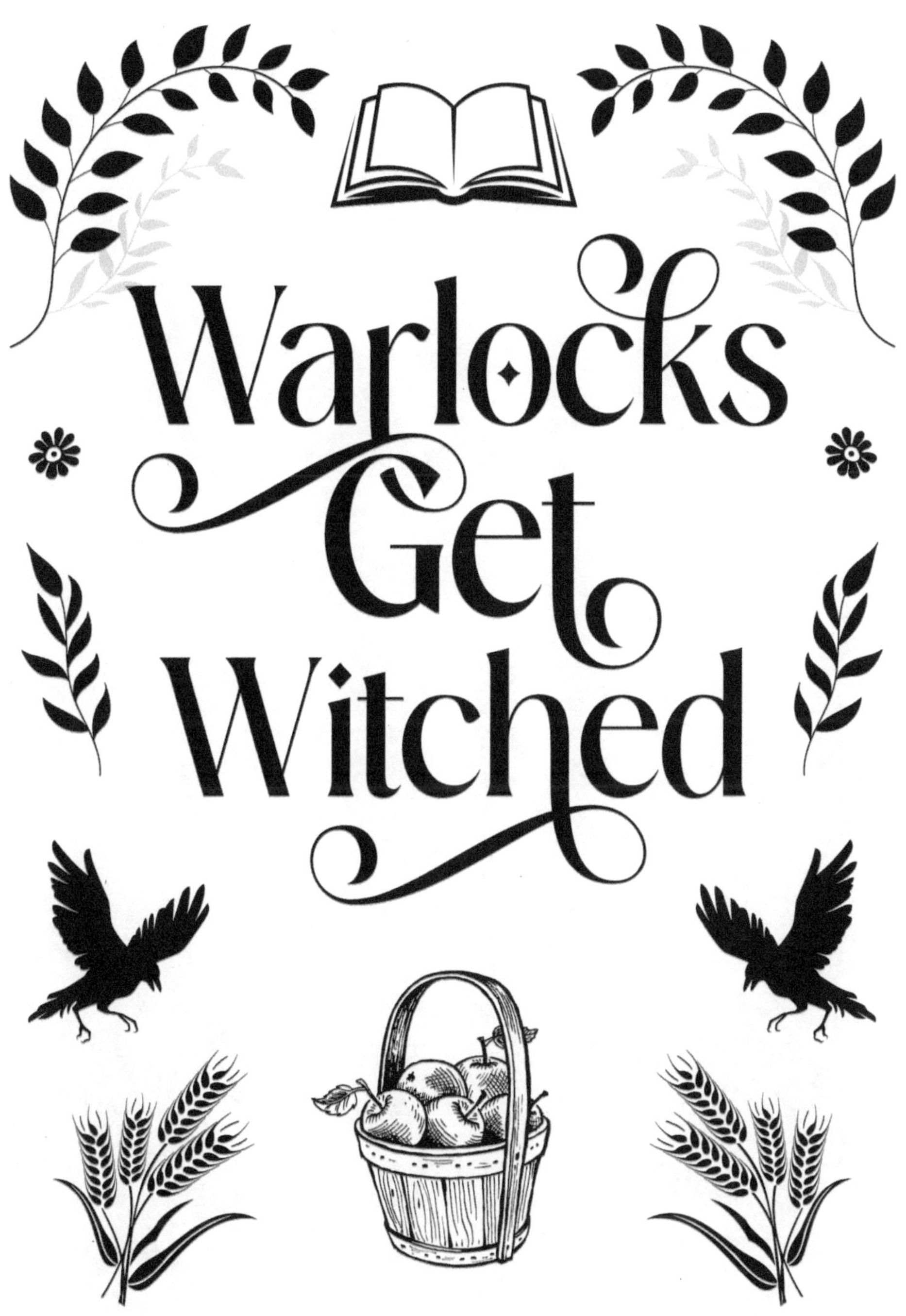

Warlocks Get Witched

COLLEEN DELANEY

COLLEEN DELANEY

This book is a work of fiction. Names, characters, places, and incidents either are products of the author's imagination or are used fictitiously. Any resemblance to actual events or locales or persons, living or dead, is entirely coincidental and not intended by the author.

WARLOCKS GET WITCHED
The Witches of Star Island, Book 4

CITY OWL PRESS
www.cityowlpress.com

Cover Design by MiblArt. All stock photos licensed appropriately.

Edited by Tee Tate.

For information on subsidiary rights, please contact the publisher at info@cityowlpress.com.

Print Edition ISBN: 978-1-64898-577-5

Digital Edition ISBN: 978-1-64898-578-2

Printed in the United States of America

To Jimmy and Brian
One of these days I'll write a book where a woman has an actual brother. I promise.

Praise for Colleen Delaney

"Delaney casts a spell with the first in *The Witches of Star Island* paranormal series. The love story is endearing and the supernatural twists propel the story forward at an exciting clip. The ending leaves many questions unanswered... but Delaney's sturdy worldbuilding ensures this series has plenty of places to go. This is a strong start." — *Publisher's Weekly*

"Family relationships, soulmate relationships, past lives, and incredibly well done magical elements keep you turning the pages of this one." — *HJ Reviews*

"*Finding His Mate* is an interesting story in a dystopian future where different paranormal creatures rule the world. The characters are so damaged and so resilient, and the next book promises more of the same. Highly recommend for fans of shifter romance with fated mates, especially if darker backstories are your thing." —*Jaycee Jarvis, author of The Hands of Destin series*

"The Hedge Witch is a fast-paced and delightful read with a heavy dash of spice as well. I recommend this to fans of a good witchy romance, particularly if you enjoy a suspenseful plot to go along with it." — *Your Book Friend Blog*

Also by Colleen Delaney

THE WOLVES OF LUVEN

Finding His Mate

Waiting for His Mate

Stealing His Mate

Protecting His Mate

Aching for His Mate

THE WITCHES OF STAR ISLAND

The Hedge Witch

Bewitching Rosemary

Hauntings and House Witchery

Warlocks Get Witched

Chapter One

In Sage Bay's not so humble opinion, the first Saturday in September was indisputably the best day of the year.

Gone were the beachgoers traipsing their sandy feet all over the island. Bachelorette parties with huge sunglasses and a greenish pallor thanks to their nights before kept their antics in June, July, and August. These September attendees were New Englanders in cozy knits, worn jeans, and casual shoes who liked going home on the ferry with a lot of island-grown fruits and veggies.

The market officially opened at seven, but Sage had gotten to her stall at six. She had a ton of produce to set up, and half the battle was a good display. That meant a solid hour of beautifying her broccoli, turnips, squash, plums, and nectarines. While she'd have more on display in a few weeks—those pumpkins, Brussels sprouts, and apples weren't quite ready—this weekend was always the big seller. Tourism would slow down exponentially, and by the time mid-October hit, the ferry only ran a few times a week and was often canceled due to weather. Sage knew that if she wanted that tourism cash, she needed to hit the ground running in September.

"Well, Sagey, you have the best-looking broccoli I've ever seen." Theo O'Doyle stepped out from behind his stall and stood with his hands on his hips in front of her. "I still don't understand how you managed it this year.

What with the aphid population decimating almost every other farmer's crop? It's almost as if that sister of yours had something to do with it."

Sage didn't bother to hide her disdain for Theo and exhaled loudly. "Maybe I'm just better at taking care of my bug population, Theo," she snapped back. She couldn't stand this man who always insinuated there was a reason her crops were better than his. First of all, yes, she was a harvest witch. She had a connection to the soil and people of Star Island he could only dream of. Second, that man had a terrible attitude, so even if he did *magically* grow better produce than she did, fat chance that anyone would pick his stall over hers.

"I'm here, I'm here, I'm here," Laurel called, rushing toward her. Sage raised her head and saw her older sister clomping over in her Doc Martens. She finished the look with a black miniskirt, fishnet tights with a hole over the knee, and a corset.

"Well, speak of the devil," Theo muttered as he moseyed back to his stall, shaking his head.

"Oh, my goddess," Sage breathed, pinching the bridge between her eyes. Farmers' markets had an unspoken uniform. Tourists came to see the sellers in their flannels and jeans. Maybe a weathered baseball cap. If you were going to wear a dress, it better be plaid. But no one here wanted a seller dressed up like they were going to meet Dracula in 1996.

"I stopped at the Immortal Cupcake," she continued and handed Sage a mug. "Chai tea with a pinch of cinnamon and a pump of caramel."

"Thank you," Sage answered. If Laurel was going to dress like a Goth teen, at least she brought a peace offering.

"I know I'm late, but I didn't go to bed until three last night, so when my alarm went off at five-thirty, I couldn't do it."

"Burning the midnight oil?" Sage prompted.

Laurel lowered her voice. "Ugh. Working on the Fortworth curse. I still can't unweave it. I thought maybe if I tried a few weakening spells first I might be able to tackle it, but no such luck."

Five months earlier, the Bay sisters learned that in the eighteenth century, an absolute asshole of a warlock and his witch sister cursed their line: if any magical being was able to collect the blood of all living Bay witches, the Bay power would transfer to the one who had their blood.

This would have been less of a problem if the Stoch family, composed of witches and warlocks all connected to the Bays in past lives, didn't know about it. Laurel, Rosemary, and Verbena had met their Stoch nemeses, and Sage and Lavender were waiting around for the oldest brother, Miloslav, to come take his vengeance on one of them for something they had no memory of doing hundreds of years ago.

"Have you tried to break it yet?" Laurel asked.

"How? By growing really good squash?" Sage wasn't exactly a powerful witch. She was a harvest witch, a skill that was extremely important in the past when famine could wipe out an entire town. Now, it wasn't a big deal that even if there was a drought or too much rain or an early frost, Sage could still produce food. Weather could be inconvenient, but not life or death.

"You might have some latent power you don't know about. Hell, I didn't know I could unweave a curse or heal myself," Laurel pointed out.

"Lots of hedge witches can do both of those things. You never felt like testing your power before. I've never heard of a harvest witch doing anything other than harvesting. It's okay. I trust the four of you to figure this shit out." Sage smirked. "Here come the crowds. Try not to scare anyone away. Or let your boobs fall out."

"That'll be twenty-five even," Sage said to a particularly ragged looking mother with a baby strapped to both her front and back. She took the somewhat sticky cash and handed her a bag stuffed full of veggies.

"If you have any big business ventures in the future, definitely add turnips to your pile," Laurel said to a buttoned-up man perusing the vegetable display. "They improve fortune and lead to success."

"Okay," the man answered slowly.

"And they're delicious," Sage cut in. "Roast 'em with some butter, salt, and lemon juice for a treat. Perfect for the crisp nights that will be here before we know it!"

The man nodded but walked to the booth next door where Lavender's employee, Hazel, sold pastries from the Immortal Cupcake.

"Come on, Laurel. That man doesn't want to hear about superstitions." She busied herself restacking the turnips.

"I'm sorry, I think you meant to say, thank you, Laurel, for giving up your Saturday morning sleeping in to work this stall with me. I appreciate your help. Especially since your hot soulmate was curled around you this morning and it was a little chilly."

"It's seventy degrees."

"Still."

"Thank you, Laurel," Sage said sarcastically. "You're an amazing sister and the perfect saleswoman, and you look gorgeous in your corset. Your boobs are almost touching your chin."

"That's enough." She peeked over Sage's shoulder. "I see a large group of women dressed head to toe in fall vibes, and yet I have no one on my books tonight." Laurel read tarot cards on Star Island, and tourists were her biggest demographic. "I'm going to go see if they want to schedule something."

"You're going to walk up to a group of strangers and see if they want their tarot cards read?"

"Yes. If I didn't, I'd never make any money." Laurel winked and pulled her corset up. "Be back in a few minutes."

Sage rolled her eyes, then turned back to her customers. Laurel might have to hunt down clients, but people had no problem coming straight up to Sage, whether she liked it or not.

In truth, the farmers' market was the worst part of her job. She didn't love interacting with strangers, and every once in a while, someone would disparage the fruits of her labor, and she'd have to quell her rage. For Sage, being a harvest witch was about growing. She loved to commune with the earth, listen to the soil and the seeds, and pry nutrition out of them. She was a provider at heart, someone whose soul worked for the community. When some rando from New York or Boston said shit about a tiny blemish on one of her beautiful veggies, well, it was a struggle not to scream at them. Or punch them.

But the work of a harvest witch had changed with the times. She'd settle for being everyone's favorite stall at the farmers' market, if she couldn't be the savior from famine. It was a lot less stressful since the fate of the entire town didn't rest on her shoulders.

The wind blew across her face, warm and lovely as the golden September sun, like it was beckoning her to leave the stall behind and go back to her roots. It was the perfect weather to run through a field, work the soil, reap the harvest...

She finished helping a young woman, then turned to face the sensation, hoping to enjoy it a little longer before the real world required her attention.

Him.

Sage froze. Her hands and feet started to tingle, and the sensation traveled up her limbs and into her torso. It felt like the time she accidentally electrocuted herself when she plugged in her hairdryer, but instead of being contained to her hand, her whole body buzzed.

Him him. That him? He was here. What the fuck—he was here? On Star Island. Here.

Her soulmate was here. At the Star Island Saturday Farmers' Market. Her soulmate was at her place of work? This was...oh, she was not prepared for this.

He was hot. Holy shit. Hot man right there.

Sage blinked her eyes furiously and tried to think what she should do next. He—ooohh boy—she could not stop looking at that man over there. Hell, Sage wanted to attack him right now. What was happening? Nope, nope. She didn't like this. What the hell was going on? She rubbed her chest a few times, wondering if the sensation would dissipate. She could not freak out in front of her customers.

"See, now I have seven women getting their tarot cards read before their dinner reservation, and that's why I walk up to strangers." Laurel brushed her shoulder against Sage's. "You are making a weird face."

"See him?" Sage said. Her voice sounded off, like she was half-choking on the words coming out of her mouth.

"You're going to have to be more specific, Sage. You are looking out at a crowd."

"Him. That guy right there. Who looks like he teaches Updike at Boston University. And has probably considered smoking a pipe."

Laurel cocked her head. "The guy in the tweed jacket? With the elbow patches?"

And the longish brown hair tucked behind his ears and a wide smile and a dimple on his left cheek. Sage nodded furiously.

"What about him?"

"He's my soulmate."

"What!" Laurel exclaimed. "Hell, Sage, lead with that. Oh, my goddess, I need a better look." Laurel went on her tiptoes. "He's cute! Got that professor look definitely."

"Okay." Sage looked at her sister. "Okay. This is fine. This is fine? I'm not going to freak out. You can handle the rest of the day, right? By yourself? Like three more hours working? Yeah. It's the busiest day of the season, but you are great. At selling vegetables. Close up at two or when we run out of food. Don't forget to lock the cash box and I can grab it from you later."

"Excuse me?" Laurel squeaked.

"Just, you know, take their money. Give them change if they need it. Um. I'll leave you my phone so you can run credit cards. It'll totally be fine. I have a soulmate to meet. I'm probably going to take him home and maybe have sex with him in the next hour so...see you later?"

"Are you fucking with me right now?"

Sage let her mouth split into a big goofy grin. Was this what it felt like to be giddy? She'd never experienced this sort of excited joy in her life.

Maybe this was awesome. Her soulmate was here. And after twenty-four years on this planet, Sage was attracted enough to someone to get naked with them. This could be a good thing.

"Nope." Sage brushed her hands on her pants and walked away. "Good luck. You'll do great. Sell fruit and vegetables and don't fuck up my business."

She had a man to meet.

Chapter Two

Will Markham was not a beach vacation person. If he were to design the perfect trip, it would be Edinburgh or Paris or Cairo. Somewhere he could get lost in libraries and museums and marvel at the history of humanity through books and broken pieces of lives lived. He wanted to stand on paths walked by the great historians of the world. Wander through the streets of cities older than the printing press.

Instead, he trudged off a crowded ferry, dragging his suitcase and holding his three-year-old niece, Tilly, whose apple juice-filled sippy cup was steadily dripping against his chest.

"Tilly, can you...let me..." He tried to wrestle the cup out of her sticky hands before giving up. There was nothing he could do, he would be covered in apple juice. He could change when they got to the house.

Behind Will and his drippy niece, his brother, John, walked carrying his one-year-old, Ryan. Then there was Cate, who was John's pregnant wife, and their parents.

It was a veritable family vacation but instead of being a salty teen, Will was a recently unemployed twenty-five-year-old man.

"Isn't it beautiful?" his mom exclaimed, gesturing at the port.

"Gorgeous," Cate gushed. "It's going to be a perfect week." She rubbed her belly a few times. The entire reason they were on this vacation was because Cate and John couldn't stop having babies and their small house needed an addition to fit their constantly expanding family. But John could only stay for the weekend since he was a teacher and school had started a week earlier, so the grandparents were called in, and Will was roped in as well.

They made their way through the port, caught a shuttle to the Centauri peninsula, and arrived at the four-bedroom coastal cottage they had for the week.

Will looked over the weather-beaten shingles and large front porch and finally conceded that this would be a pretty nice place to spend a week with the pile of books in his bag. It wasn't like he was doing anything else. He pulled out his phone and quickly refreshed his email. Nothing.

"I already picked out rooms for everyone," his mom prattled. "John and Cate, there are two rooms toward the back for you and the kids, Dad and I will take the front room, and Will, your room is off the kitchen."

He ducked into the smallest of the four rooms with a single twin bed and small nightstand. It was monastic, but clean, with a window that looked away from the water but was picturesque nonetheless with its view of a beautiful maple tree. Will dumped his suitcase on the floor, quickly changed into something not covered in apple juice, and then collapsed onto the bed.

Two months earlier, he'd been working at Harold Washington Library in Chicago, living in a small but cozy apartment in West Town and enjoying a normal life for a man in his mid-twenties. Then massive layoffs hit the library system, which included anyone hired in the last two years, his lease ended on August first, and he found himself living in his parent's basement in Cleveland, surrounded by boxes.

Will saw little need to unpack yet. He currently had applications at every major library system in the United States. There was no use in setting up his life in Cleveland if he was only going to pack up again, especially when he owned close to seven hundred books. So, his bed, books, clothes, and minimal furniture were crammed into the corner of the basement beside the furnace, and he currently slept on a pullout couch he'd frequented in high school.

His mid-twenties were not turning out the way he hoped.

At the airport this morning, Will had received two generic "thank you for applying but we've filled the position, we'll keep your resume on file for the future" emails. The first was from the Oliver La Farge branch of the Santa Fe Public Library system. Which was hardly heartbreaking as Will couldn't really imagine living in the desert. He would have taken it, hell, he would have taken anything, but it would probably have been the type of job he only stayed at for a year or two before looking for something else. The second, though, had been from the Parkway Central Library in Philadelphia and hurt his heart more than a little when it came through. A chance to work at a library in a mid-Atlantic city steeped in history? That was a dream.

"Time for the farmers' market!" his mom called. "Will, are you coming?"

Will looked around the room. He wouldn't have minded staying home to bask in his disappointment in the quiet of the cottage and cracking open *Finnegan's Wake*, which he'd been meaning to read for eight years but somehow kept pushing back in favor of less dense reads. But as if on cue, his stomach grumbled loudly, begging for food.

"I'm coming," he answered. *Finnegan's Wake* would still be there after a full stomach and a good look at the island he'd be living on for the next week. And in all honestly, his sour mood would be waiting right where he left it also. Maybe a bit of sunshine and food could shake him out of the funk for an hour or two.

Star Island was the quaintest place in the world. Almost sickeningly sweet. On their way to the park that hosted the farmers' market, Will passed a bookstore, a bakery, a preschool with stars painted all over it, a tiny maritime museum, and a few restaurants. The streets were lined with mature maples and hickories already showing hints of red and yellow at the tips of their leaves. It was like a fictional town from a cozy mystery series had been conjured up and placed in the Atlantic Ocean. When they finally made it to the park, the entire family had been hypnotized by this coastal island.

"After the market," Cate began, shifting Ryan to her hip, "I want to go explore some of the woods in the interior. It looks like Vega peninsula in particular has some nearly ancient forests. The first settlements were hit often with ergot poisoning and famine, making logging a secondary thought to surviving."

John smiled and put his arm around his wife. "Maybe during nap time? If Nonna and Pop don't mind hanging around the cottage?"

"Not at all!" his mom answered, scooping Ryan out of Cate's arms.

Will wandered away from his family, looking at the different stalls. There were farmers with produce, a few artists with paintings and photos for sale, a bakery tent, even a juggler. It was crowded, but not overwhelming. Most of the patrons had the tourist look, dressed for vacation rather than regular life. Will knew he looked out of place, but he didn't care. He liked dressing like he was going to work, and he liked to work at old libraries with special collections. And because of this, he was quickly overheating. He thought September in New England meant chilly breezes, but as the day tromped toward noon, sweat began to trickle down the back of his neck.

Will stopped at one of the art tents, looking over the tranquil landscape scenes from around Star Island. Cloudy blues, greens, and tans made up the shoreline with dots of umbrellas across the sand. Pretty, but he had always preferred classical art. While he couldn't actually own a Rembrandt or Van Gogh, his boxes were full of prints of his favorites, framed and wrapped in old newspaper until he found a place to live that wasn't a basement below his parents.

"Will!" his brother called. "You want a sandwich?" John, Cate, and their children stood a few stalls down in line. His stomach grumbled again, reminding him he hadn't gotten anything to eat yet.

"Sure," he answered and walked to stand with them. He glanced at the clapboard menu, thinking a ham and cheese sounded good. Oh! And they had giant pickles. A burst of salt would be—

Look up. Will jolted his head up and immediately caught the eye of a woman walking toward him.

"Holy shit," Will said much louder than he expected to. His hands immediately started buzzing. He shook them out a few times, then realized it wasn't going away, but traveling through his whole body.

"Will! Language in front of the kids!" John barked.

"Shit, shit, shit."

"Are you going to faint?" Cate asked. "John, he looks like he's going to faint."

His brother grabbed his arm and shook him.

Will blinked and looked at John. "My soulmate is walking over here." He stared at his big brother. "Help."

"Ah!" Cate squealed.

"Holy shit," John reiterated. "Who is she?"

"That woman in the green flannel and jeans." Will's mouth went dry. His entire body felt like a steady pump of electric shock was coursing through his veins, which made calming down almost impossible. His soulmate was here. Here. On Star Island. In the middle of this farmers' market. And she was coming toward him.

"Play it cool," John mumbled.

"Or not. I didn't and it worked out fine," Cate added. "Just introduce yourself. She obviously has her eye on you, which either means she knows, or she thinks you're cute. Either way, you're golden." She patted his shoulder. "John, pick up Tilly. No reason for our children to get between these two."

Will took a deep breath. In the next few moments, his soulmate would be standing in front of him, and he had to decide what to do.

Clearly, he would talk to her. He had no game though. None. He was the most awkward person he knew, and his sister-in-law had sprinted away from his brother the first time they'd seen each other. What would Will say? Maybe something about the island? Was she a local? Or on vacation like he was? His mind was racing a mile a minute, and he still hadn't figured out what on earth he was going to say.

She stopped in front of him and stuck her hand out. "Hi, I'm Sage."

"Oh, um." He took her hand and shook it. "I'm Will." Her shake was firm, her hand a bit calloused, and no part of him wanted to let it go.

"Nice to meet you, Will." She looked away from him at Cate, who had the biggest grin on her face.

"I'm Cate, and this is my husband, John, and these are our kids. It's so nice to meet you, Sage! What a pretty name!"

Sage narrowed her eyes and looked at Will, then flitted her eyes around the entire group.

"You all know who I am?"

"I think so," Will answered. A wave of magic crashed off her toward him.

His soulmate was a witch...or at least something magical. Relief washed over him like warm water. That would definitely make things easier.

"Cool. I have a front to keep up here. You know." She gestured at the crowd. "So, do you want to get out of here?"

"Absolutely."

Will threw a last look at John, who gave him a goofy grin and a thumbs up. Then he turned and followed Sage away from the farmers' market to wherever she would lead him.

Chapter Three

Sage led Will out of the farmers' market at a safe distance. To the casual observer, it looked like she was giving a lost tourist some directions, maybe telling him how to get to the Muse for a drink or the Immortal Cupcake for a pastry.

It wasn't immediately apparent that never-had-a-significant-other Sage Bay was taking this man home to maybe sleep with him.

Was she going to sleep with him? Eh, she didn't know yet. He was so attractive and every synapse in her brain was firing toward the cavewoman part, telling her it would be very fun to sleep with him.

But, Sage had never successfully been with anyone, so there was that to consider. Also, she couldn't remember the last time she'd shaved her armpits, and while she didn't think the goddesses would give her a soulmate who cared, she wanted to make a good first impression. He was, after all, here for the long haul.

She cast a quick glance at him. His eyes were slightly widened. Almost like he didn't expect to meet his soulmate at the farmers' market this morning and was still recovering from the shock of it all. So that made two of them.

But she liked the look of him. Sage hadn't ever given much thought to what her soulmate would look like. There were no fantasies of a mold he might fit into, nor did she regularly have anything more than a fleeting infatuation with other men. She didn't see the point in hooking up with a lot of people she knew weren't the one for her. She gave a couple a try, but she was busy with her plants. Wasting time on dead-end relationships was something she couldn't fathom.

But Will was unexpected. Medium build, long brown hair, an energy she couldn't quite pinpoint. Whatever it was, it was pulling her to him like she had a rope tied around her waist.

"This is my car," she said abruptly. "The back seat is very dirty, but the front is fine."

"Yeah, no problem." Will climbed into the passenger's seat and buckled his seat belt without another word.

Well, fuck. This was happening.

Sage shook her hands out and got into the driver's seat. She pulled away from the curb but kept eyes on the road. The last thing she wanted was to make eye contact with anyone who lived on Star Island and would later question her over a man being in her car. Especially during the busy hours of the Saturday farmers' market.

"You live here? On Star Island?" Will asked.

"Yeah. For a while."

"Cool." He sounded so relaxed. Hell, he must have gone home with tons of women before. It clearly wasn't a big deal to him. Damn it. Was she actually ready for this?

Sage got out of town and pulled onto Laxy Way toward the Vega peninsula and the Bay cottage.

"So, are you a warlock or a sonofawitch?" Sage finally broke the silence as they turned onto her street. She guessed he could have been an animan or small mammal shifter, but both of those were much rarer.

"Warlock. And you're a witch?"

"Yup."

She knew she should ask follow-up questions. What kind of warlock? Were those people with you magical too? But at the moment, she was way too nervous to make the sort of small talk someone should probably have with a person they were about to sleep with. All she could do was focus on not crashing the car and keeping herself from squealing out of a mix of excitement and terror.

She pulled into the driveway. Good, Lavender's car was gone. Either Rosemary had stopped over to borrow it, or Lavender was still at the Immortal Cupcake and the house was empty. She really hoped the latter. It wasn't like she couldn't have a man over. She was twenty-four and a full-fledged adult, but her older sister tended to be weird about relationships, even soulmates. Plus, they'd never crossed back from the guardian-child role even after Sage had turned eighteen. It would be like taking a man home in front of her parents.

"You live here?"

"Share it with my older sister." Sage clomped up the front steps, glancing to make sure Will was following. Hell, she didn't really picture herself with a guy like this, but now that he was in front of her...why didn't she picture herself with a guy like this?

He was hot as Hades, but sort of, slight? Sage was not small. Even without her heavy work, she was a bit of a rectangle, five feet eight inches, and solid. She was the tallest of the Bay sisters, and in high school, the softball coach had begged her to join the team, even without ever having played softball before. She'd ended up leading the team to their first regional championship as a stellar catcher.

Will looked like he could have been a nineteenth-century poet. But in the best, tuberculosis-free way.

"This is a very nice house," Will said, stepping inside behind her.

"Yeah, it is." Sage turned on her heels to face him. There would be time for small talk later. She could ask him his favorite color or what he liked to eat or his last name after she found out what it was like to kiss her soulmate. "So. You want to go up to my room or..."

"Oh!" Will looked around the house. "Your sister isn't home?"

"She runs the bakery in town. Saturdays are busy, even when there is a farmers' market." Sage dropped her keys on the front table beside the stairs.

Had she made her bed this morning? Probably not. Soulmates didn't care about stuff like that, right? And her pajamas were probably on the floor. Or maybe on Rosemary's empty bed. She and Asher weren't moving into their new house for another two weeks, so all Rosemary's stuff that wasn't of daily use to her still resided in their shared bedroom.

Also, she was wearing a sports bra. Sage almost always wore a sports bra, if she was wearing one at all. Was it possible to take off a sports bra in a seductive manner? She didn't think so. But she wasn't really a seductress. She was just Sage. And if Will was her soulmate, he would need to come to terms with the fact that the universe didn't give him a sexy woman. It gave him a regular woman. Who didn't own nice underwear and definitely didn't know how to take them off in a manner that suggested anything other than "about to get in the shower."

Will looked at her though, his eyes a bit hooded, the corner of his bottom lip stuck between his teeth, and suddenly Sage couldn't remember anything. She wasn't even sure her middle name was Juniper anymore. Could have been Susan for all she knew.

"Come here," she said in a voice that was way more sultry than normal.

Will obeyed and closed the distance between them. His hands went to her waist and his mouth stopped inches before crashing into hers.

"Is this what you meant?" His voice took on a husky tone. She nodded, wrapped her hand behind his neck, and kissed him.

She kissed him like he was water, and she was the desert, like the world was ending all around them and she had only this one moment with her soulmate. It was frantic and fast, a clash of tongues and teeth. His hands flew across her body now, grasping at her hips, then squeezing her breasts. He shoved his knee between her legs, and she could feel *him* against her hip. He thrust a couple times against her, his thigh hitting her deliciously.

Hell yes, she thought.

This was it. Sage Bay was going to have sex with her soulmate. After twenty-four years without a boyfriend, she was about to have an afternoon filled with mind-blowing soulmate sex.

She dragged him to the parlor, threw him on the couch, and climbed on top of him.

"Whoa," he mumbled before finding a perfect spot on her neck to nibble.

"Oh, goddess," she moaned. Now, that...that was heaven. She moved against him, trying to find some purchase through her jeans and his pants. She rocked her body back and forth, panting as she did. She felt wild, almost animalistic, like she could just let go with someone for once. Let someone into her life completely.

Finally, she got a good rhythm, hit a delicious spot as she moved over him.

"Wait, oh!" Will grasped her hips and went rigid, his head banging against her collarbone.

Sage looked down at Will. His eyes were wide with terror, his mouth slack, his cheeks pink.

Holy shit. "Did you..."

"Yeah. I'm so sorry. I don't know, that's not, I'm mean not that I'm like a Casanova or anything but that's never—"

"It's fine," she answered quickly, climbing off his lap. "Um, there's a bathroom under the stairs."

"Thank you," he answered quietly, pouncing off the couch and disappearing out of the room.

Sage collapsed back onto the couch.

Well. That was unexpected.

She should probably be flattered. Her soulmate was so into her, he came before she even had her shirt unbuttoned.

Hm.

She wasn't sure how to feel. Right now, her mind swirled with disappointment, embarrassment, and a dash of terror. Was it always going to be like this?

It looked like sex today was off the table. Sure, she could wait around for him to be interested again, but that could take a long time. And Laurel was currently running her business.

She shook her head and popped up. She straightened her shirt and quickly re-braided her hair.

What had she been thinking? None of this soulmate shit mattered right now. It was her busiest farmers' market of the year. And Laurel was a disaster at sales. She was probably bungling the whole thing, and Sage would have more produce left over than she ever had on the first Saturday in September. Hell, she needed to get back to the stall. It had only been about half an hour since she left, plenty of time to get things back on track at the market. She wasn't having sex today, so she should go back to work. It was the only thing that made sense.

After a painfully silent trip back to town, Sage let Will out a block away from the market. She couldn't face anyone she knew seeing a random man get out of her car, especially when she wanted to crawl under the seat.

Will climbed out then turned back toward her. "Can I have your number?"

Sage winced. "I'm sure fate will throw us in each other's paths again."

Will nodded and shut the door.

Sage left before he had a chance to walk away, forcing her eyes to steer clear of the rearview mirror. She drove around the corner and parked in an empty spot, then rested her head against the steering wheel.

What the fuck? She had held out hope that they'd think of something to talk about on the way back to town, or he'd at least offer some sort of explanation but...nothing. Before Sage was willing to give him the benefit of the doubt, but now, she was mad.

Was this always going to happen? Were they going to make out and he was going to finish before she really even started? What a fucking way to live her life. She climbed out of the car and headed back to the park with her eyes plastered on the sidewalk. The last thing she needed was to catch the eye of that couple who Will had been with.

"You're back! Thank goddess!" Laurel exclaimed. Her sister had a line six deep and was holding five acorn squashes.

"I can help whoever is next," Sage said quickly, picking up her apron and tying it around her waist. A man immediately stepped in front of her and handed her a pile of produce. "Let me get you a paper bag." Sage buried herself in her work, letting her mind focus on the beautiful fruits and vegetables that were her life, and not the boy who had rudely interrupted her perfect Saturday.

"I thought they'd never leave," Laurel said as the last customer walked away with their bag. In the end, it had been a good day. Only three squash, two heads of broccoli, and a handful of plums were left. They could eat the veggies for dinner tonight and tomorrow, plus Lavender could always make a tart or something with the plums.

Sage packed up the leftovers into a wooden crate, then slipped the cash box into the side. Once she'd set up her phone to take credit cards, her cash sales had plummeted, but there were always a few people who wanted to pay the old-fashioned way.

"Sage!" Laurel shouted.

"What? You can leave. We're done."

"Oh, for the love of Demeter. What happened during the forty-five minutes you were gone? Considering it's a seventeen-minute ride home...did you two hang out in the car?" Laurel put air quotes around hang out.

"Don't want to talk about it," Sage answered curtly.

"We don't have to," Laurel said quickly. "Do you have a name?"

"Will."

"Strong name. Last name?"

"Didn't get one."

"Is he...you know, like us?" Laurel lowered her voice. Keeping their witchy status secret was imperative for Sage if she wanted to continue working at the farmers' market without rumor.

"He recognized me."

"That's awesome! At least, it's been really nice to have that with Owen. You know, holidays will be easier once we have kids and all that."

Sage nodded. "I'm beat. You need a ride home?"

"No, no, no. Owen and I are going to meet at the Muse and grab a late lunch. You go hang with Will. Whenever you're ready, I can't wait to meet him." Laurel picked up her bag and slung it over her shoulder. "I'm really happy for you, Sage."

"Yeah," she answered softly.

At least someone was happy. Sage currently felt nothing but a sinking panic. And a bit of sexual frustration.

Chapter Four

"Fuck, fuck, fuck," Will mumbled under his breath. He ducked down random side streets, brushing past pedestrians, and tried to keep his voice down and the dirty looks from parents to a minimum.

How had that happened?

That had *never* happened. It wasn't like he had slept with a ton of women—one woman. Will had slept with one woman his junior year of college. But still. Why on earth did his first attempted time with his soulmate have to end like that?

Luckily, he had gotten into her bathroom before his clothes were unsalvageable. The last thing he wanted to do was explain to his parents why he needed to dry-clean his pants on vacation.

It had been so awkward afterward. Will had tried to psych himself up in the bathroom. He was going to go back out there, apologize, maybe go upstairs with her, and make the next thirty to forty-five minutes about her. Honestly, he could rally with no problem in that time period. They could have spent the rest of the afternoon together. She'd really wanted to hook up, but afterward they could have talked. Gotten to know each other.

But when he exited the bathroom, Sage's mood was completely

different. She had her keys in hand and was standing next to the open front door.

It was quite obvious she wanted him to go. And then that terrible car ride...

Will really couldn't imagine it going any worse than it had.

He stopped walking and tried to get his bearings. All these tree-lined streets looked the same, and he needed to find his way back to the rental house and come up with a plan.

"Excuse me," he asked a woman walking out of the florist. "Can you tell me how to get to the rental cottage block on Centauri Way?"

"You're almost there," she replied cheerily, her brown curly hair bouncing as she talked. "Turn around, walk toward Pluto Parkway, turn left, and then you'll be able to see the water. Pretty easy from there!"

"Thank you," he answered. He'd be in his room in a couple minutes, and he could figure things out.

"See you around!" the woman called from behind him, even though he'd rushed away from her. So far, Will had a feeling the people of Star Island were among the friendliest in the world, and he'd managed to offend the only important one.

He found his way back and tried to sneak in the front door, hoping he could throw on some shorts, grab a book, and spend the rest of the day trying to concentrate on reading but actually mulling over every poor choice he'd made in the last hour while in close proximity to the ocean.

Why did he let her climb on top of him? If he'd been on top, he could have positioned himself better—

"Will!" his mom shrieked. "Tell me it isn't true." She rushed him the moment he stepped over the threshold.

"What?"

"Your soulmate lives here? On Star Island? In the middle of the Atlantic! Of all the places in the world! I'm going to have grandchildren on either side of the country. How could this happen?" She rubbed her forehead.

"Kelly, it's going to be fine," his dad said slowly. "We can visit frequently."

"But what about when we retire? We'll have to choose if we're going to move to Arizona to be closer to John and Cate or Florida to be closer to Will and...Sage? Her name is Sage, right?"

"Considering you had to double-check her name, I wouldn't be looking at beach houses just yet." Will walked past his family, his eyes trained on his bedroom door.

"Where are you going?" his mom demanded.

"In my room. I'm going to change my clothes and stare at the ceiling for a little while. Then I'm going to think about how I'm going to tell my soulmate, who I've already managed to piss off, that I'm currently unemployed and living in my parents' basement. Oh yeah, also that I work in a really particular field in which I pretty much have to be in a city to find a job. I'm going to have to tell all those things to a woman who lives on a remote island in a beautiful cottage and I'm pretty sure runs a stall at the farmers' market." Will slammed his door and locked it.

He heard his mom take a few steps toward the door, but then his father mumbled, "Leave it."

He pulled off his jacket and button-down, laying both over the foot of the bed, then stepped out of his pants. He tossed his boxer briefs into a corner of his suitcase no one would look in and put on a fresh pair before collapsing on the bed.

He needed a plan. At the moment his soulmate probably thought he was an overeager teenager who was going to be miserable in bed for the rest of their lives. And by the way she reacted, she had no time for that.

If only...

He rolled his eyes and sat up, rummaging through his bag. If only what? He'd lied and told her he wanted to take it slow, or refused to go home with her? No way she wouldn't have been hurt. Who didn't want to be with their soulmate? No matter which way he sliced it, he was fucked.

She'd been so cold afterward too. Was that her normal personality? Jump into bed with someone and if it didn't go perfectly, ice them out?

Will pulled out his trusty tarot—a beat-to-hell Rider-Waite-Smith deck he used while traveling. It was replaceable and the Five of Wands had a coffee stain, so he didn't feel bad putting it in checked luggage. He smoothed the blanket on the bed a few times and took a deep breath.

"Sage," he whispered, keeping her face in his mind. He shuffled four times, cut the deck, then discarded four cards, picked one, discarded four more, picked a second, and set the deck to the side. He glanced in front of him.

The Five of Pentacles and Strength.

"Is this a joke?" Will rubbed the bridge of his nose. "Nurtia, please tell me I do not have to face extreme hardship to get along with my soulmate. That sounds terrible." He ran his fingertip over the card. There were two people on the Five of Pentacles, limping along in poverty and desperation. "Or we're going to face hardship together? Either way. Great. Just great." At least Strength was sitting there, staring up at him. Hopefully that meant together, they'd have some.

Will picked up the cards and placed them back in their box, then got dressed. This time, he put on shorts and a T-shirt and grabbed the slides he'd begrudgingly packed. Then he pulled out *Le Morte D'Arthur*. Today wasn't the day to start *Finnegan's Wake*. He needed an old favorite to ponder.

After three hours with Arthur and his knights, plus Morgan Le Fey, Will felt nothing other than slightly sunburned and enamored with the ocean. He had lived near Lake Michigan for the past two years and had spent his childhood staring at Lake Erie, but the vast Atlantic, especially on the beach of a small island, felt very different.

The cobalt water was dotted with white caps, and there weren't any swimmers today. It seemed to be reminding the public of its power—the ocean may be beautiful, but it was also dangerous.

He wasn't a nature warlock. His power didn't come from the water or earth or fire. He was a Zetic, a warlock whose power rested in knowledge and foresight. But he couldn't deny that the magic in his soul stirred here. And if his soulmate, a witch, lived here, Will wondered if there was something particularly magical about Star Island, like Stonehenge or Uluru.

He picked up his book and chair and wandered back toward the rental house, but only long enough to set both things on the porch. He heard quiet voices inside and wasn't ready to face the family. They would want to talk about his newfound soulmate, and he didn't have much else to say. He wasn't going to tell them what happened. He'd have to be at least five beers in to admit that to John. Probably would need a lobotomy before he said anything to his mom. No, he had other plans.

He wanted to find Sage.

Without her number or her address, he was left with a solitary option. Solaris wasn't a large place. If Sage was at the grocery store or diner or even walking around, he could probably find her if he looked long enough. So, like a man of another time who'd seen a woman once he wanted to see again, Will began his quest on foot. Sage had mentioned having an older sister who worked at the bakery, therefore he would start there.

The main drag in Solaris was quieter than it had been this morning. There were still tourists walking around, but under the slanted late afternoon September light, the whole place felt calmer. As if everyone who walked past was finding their own bit of peace on these quaint streets.

Will kept his head up, searching every face in his eyeline for hers.

Sage.

She was beautiful. She'd had her chocolatey brown hair tied back in a tight braid, but wisps had pulled free and framed her face. A spray of freckles over her nose brought out the amber flecks in her deep brown eyes. The clothes she wore hid any hint of her figure, but Will liked that.

He didn't need flashes of skin or curves pressing against clothing. He liked the mystery of a present still needing unwrapping.

And she was like a present still wrapped up tight and covered in tape. His awkwardness earlier had made sure of that. But he wanted to unweave some of that mystery. He wanted to know her favorite foods and how she drank her coffee, if she loved the sunrise or the sunset, what her favorite phase of the moon was.

And hopefully her last name.

He wandered to the bakery, but found it closed for the day. It was nearly six now, and most of the shops had flipped their signs for the evening. Will hung his head. Maybe tomorrow.

"Will?"

He looked up. Standing in front of him was...

A witch. At least, what society would classify as a witch. This woman had on ripped fishnets, a black corset, and a huge silver crescent moon necklace.

"I'm sorry, do I know you?"

"No. But, hi. I'm Laurel. Sage's older sister." She gave a little wave. "I saw you from far away today. When she noticed you at the farmers' market."

"Oh. Is Sage with you?" He looked past her, hoping his soulmate might be hiding out in a doorway.

"No, she's probably at home." Laurel raised an eyebrow. "Are you looking for her?"

"Yes. Desperately. I may have..." he stumbled. What could he say? He'd fucked up completely in the first hour of their acquaintance? "I didn't get her number."

"Oh! I'll give it to you." Laurel pulled her phone out of her pocket. "And mine. Might as well. Before you know it, you'll be on the family group text and have to contend with so many pictures of plants and baked goods." She handed him her phone. "Here, text yourself, and then I'll send you Sage's contact. Trust me, I completely understand being a little too frazzled to remember things like exchanging numbers during that first encounter. My soulmate and I met in May. And I ran away from him. Ah. And then someone tried to kill me." She smiled and gazed past him. "That sweet beginning."

"Someone tried to kill you this year?" Will asked slowly.

"Yeah, it's a whole thing. Sage'll tell you about it at some point." She took her phone back and texted him. "Now you've got her number. I have to run. I'm picking up dinner for me and Owen, he's my soulmate. You two will have to hang out soon. Have a good night!" She waved as she walked away.

Will looked down at his phone and opened a new text.

> Will: Hey, this is Will. From this afternoon. I ran into Laurel, and she recognized me and gave me your number. I really want to see you again. Obviously. I'm here for a week and I'd like it if you let me take you out to dinner or for a walk—whatever you're comfortable with. I want to get to know you.

He pressed send and then shoved his phone into his pocket and made his way back to the rental. It was all he could do right now. He wasn't going to show up at her house and demand she spend time with him. He sent the text, she could respond when she was ready.

His phone dinged a moment later, and Will whipped it out of his pocket so quickly it clattered to the sidewalk. He dove to open it and found...

An email notification from the Seattle Public Library. Another rejection.

He sighed. He would have been crushed if it had come through this morning. Living in the Pacific Northwest, close to Cate and John but not on top of them, working for one of the coolest systems in the country was a dream. But now, with a soulmate living on the other side of the country on an island only accessible by boat...maybe committing to a job that was nearly on the Pacific wasn't a good idea.

Will shoved his phone back in his pocket and headed home.

Five hours later, when he finally turned off his light to try to fall asleep, she still hadn't answered.

Chapter Five

Sage was going to punch Laurel in the face.

Probably not, but she was going to punch her boob. Really hard. And maybe mess up her tarot cards. Because her meddling sister had thought giving Will her personal phone number was a good idea.

And in turn, Sage had received the pleasure of staring at his text for six-ish hours last night, unable to decide what to do about it. Should she text him back? Delete it? Block him? She probably shouldn't block him.

But you know what she didn't want to do? Obsess over a man. She was Sage Bay, for Demeter's sake. Men had nothing on her. Not even her soulmate.

She had never, ever been the type of girl to even care about what a boy thought. Hell, in high school when everyone was trying to pair off into couples, Sage was violently uninterested. She didn't see the point in having a partner or even a steady make out person. Sure, she liked orgasms as much as the next sexually active twenty-something, but seeking out companionship? No. Thank you. Orgasms did not equal boyfriend. And so far, she had been doing just fine on her own.

She groaned and rolled out of bed. Was her apathy on love and sex due to the fact that she hadn't met Will? Had the universe decided that unlike Rosemary and Verbena, Sage would *only* ever care about a relationship with her soulmate? And then fate had the gall to send her someone who exploded moments after making out?

Fate was shaping up to be quite the bitch.

The sun was already up, and in September, it didn't matter if she only slept a handful of hours. There was a shit ton of work to be done.

Because she spent most of Saturday at the market, Sundays were jammed with every little chore that needed to be caught up on, plus her regular daily activities. She pulled on a pair of jeans and a gray T-shirt that had holes in both armpits and a frayed hem, but who was she impressing? The trees?

After a quick trip to the bathroom, she crept downstairs and scarfed down a zucchini muffin from the tray in the kitchen. Delicious. Between her perfect zucchini crop and Lavender's baking skills, this muffin was like early September in a mouthful. She filled her travel cup to the brim with coffee, added four spoonfuls of sugar, pulled on her work boots, and headed out back.

By Demeter, it was a gorgeous morning. The world was still damp with dew, the sun felt warm but not hot, and Sage felt the tension in her shoulders disappear. She sipped her coffee, leaning into the soothing river of caffeine. She wasn't going to think about Will now or how incredibly sexually frustrated she felt at the moment. It was September, and she was a harvest witch. It was her time to shine.

The morning went by quickly between picking everything that had ripened overnight, checking the irrigation system, and watering some of the smaller pots she had in the greenhouse. There were still apples to be checked and weeds to be pulled in some of the beds, but Sage was starving. She needed to eat an enormous lunch, maybe doze on the couch for a few minutes, and then she'd be back out and finish the rest before dinner.

She kicked her boots off on the screened porch and headed to the sink to scrub her hands and scavenge whatever leftovers were still around from Lavender's cooking the night before.

"She's back!" Rosemary called. "Family meeting time!"

"Oh, come on," Sage grumbled. It was Sunday. She wanted to rest a bit before heading back out. Bay family meetings were rarely quick and usually involved hashing out all the new details pertaining to the horrific generational curse set over their family. Or if there was a new witch or warlock in town trying to kill one of them.

"I made shepherd's pie to entice you," Lavender said quietly. She leaned against the counter beside the sink. "There really is a lot to talk about. Especially since Laurel mentioned you met your soulmate yesterday?"

"I did," Sage conceded.

"You didn't think to tell me while we sat in the same room for over two hours last night drinking tea?" Lavender pressed.

"Lav, I really thought you'd be the one sister who wouldn't push on the whole soulmate thing."

"Hey, I think you should take your sweet time with whoever this young man is. But I would have appreciated a heads-up. When Owen came, Morana Stoch came. When Asher came, Ivan Stoch came. When Verbena and Luke started...up, Boris came. We've got one Stoch left that we know of, and Miloslav is a freaking chaos warlock. If he's going to show up and try to kill you, I'd like to be aware of the situation."

"Right now, it's Bays 3, Stochs 0. I'm feeling good. Plus, if I betrayed him or something in a past life, I don't care. I'm not emotionally responsible for anything I did in the past."

"He might not feel that way," Lavender reminded her. "So. What's your soulmate's name?"

"Will. He's a warlock of some sort. We'll see what happens."

Lavender nodded. "Take your time with it. Long as you want. You know that, right? Your soulmate isn't your end-all. If you don't want to be with him, life isn't over. Solo living is a fine choice for a witch, too."

Hm, Sage thought. Lavender had been saying a lot of weird stuff like that ever since the soulmate prophecy last May. Lavender had always been quiet, but cryptic was a new facet to her personality. If Sage cared more, she might pry, but her oldest sister's business was her business, not Sage's. If Lavender wanted a shroud of mystery around her, so be it. She wouldn't fight her on it.

Laurel, Owen, Rosemary, Asher, Verbena, and Luke sat at the dining table, each with a plate in front of them. In the center of the table, Lavender had put out two shepherd's pies, a loaf of homemade bread, two pitchers of iced tea, and a brick of cheddar cheese, with a few slices already cut.

Sage's stomach growled so loudly, everyone turned to face her.

"What? I'm hungry. I don't see any of you spending your Sundays on manual labor." She took her place between Asher and Verbena and helped herself to a heaping plate of all the offerings. She looked up at Laurel. "I owe you a boob punch."

"What!"

Sage shoved a forkful of shepherd's pie in her mouth, somewhat calming her mood. "You gave Will my phone number without checking with me."

Laurel looked around the table. "And that is a problem because…?"

"Laurel!" Rosemary interrupted, "Sage should be the one to give her phone number to her soulmate. When Owen asked me for your phone number, I did not give it to him, if you remember correctly."

"That's true," Owen said slowly.

"But you had…you know…spent time with him already? I figured it had just slipped your mind."

"Nope." Sage shook her head. "And I know we aren't having this family meeting so everyone can hound me about my soulmate. What's the agenda?" She reached for another slice of bread and piled it on her plate.

"Actually, I called it," Lavender said, taking her spot at the head of the table. "I've made some headway with a North American Witch's Council."

Since the spite between the Stoch and Bay families had reached dangerous levels, all the sisters agreed that a true council was needed. They existed in several European, African, and Asian countries, plus there was a rather large one based in Brazil for South America.

"There are a pair of sisters based in Northern California, Paige and Sierra Romano. They're both earth witches, from an old line. They've agreed that one of them would sit on the council, once it was settled. I like that they are from the West Coast. I think the general community will be more inclined to accept a witch's council if the representatives were not only different kinds of witches, but from around North America. The Gagnon family in Quebec City and the Tremblays in Calgary are our best bets for Canada, Laurel has already spoken with Elena Lozano in Mexico City. In other words, it's coming together pretty nicely."

"Great news," Verbena said.

"So, what happens if this witch council decides we're all in the wrong for transgressions in our past lives?" Laurel asked. "I did seriously curse Morana in medieval France."

"I don't think a witch can be held accountable for something that happened hundreds of years ago. Plus, the Stochs have been the aggressors in this life. Not us," Lavender pointed out. "But after Verbena and Luke had to kill a literal ghoul, I think we need some support. And now," she continued, "since Sage's soulmate is here, we can assume Miloslav will show up. He's probably unhappy about both his siblings being incarcerated by The Collective. He knows where we all live, he knows where we work. So ever vigilant, as always. No walking down wooded paths alone, no opening the door without looking through the window. Verbena—"

"I'll reinforce all the boundary spells around everyone's work. Plus, I can do Rosemary and Asher's new house as soon as the paperwork goes through."

"First day in our house and we'll need a protection spell," Rosemary said wistfully.

"Better to be safe," Asher said, bringing her hand to his mouth and kissing her knuckles. "I don't want anyone related to Ivan anywhere near you."

"I pulled a picture of Miloslav, which wasn't difficult since it's a mugshot, and he looks like Ivan but slightly healthier." Lavender passed her phone around the table. Like his brother and sister, Miloslav had ice-blond hair, piercing blue eyes, and a permanently menacing scowl.

"Keep an eye out for someone who looks like they might murder you, got it," Sage grumbled.

"Especially you," Lavender added. "There's a pattern, and if it follows... well, you're about to have a terrible month."

Sage snorted. Miloslav or not, it already looked like Sage's favorite month was taking a turn for the worst. For the time of the year she was usually most excited for, September was looking like it might swing shitty. Sure, her soulmate was here, but their first encounter was anything but enchanting. And now a chaos warlock who wanted her blood and her power was most likely going to try to kill her.

Sage ripped off a piece of her bread and shoved it into her mouth.

Well. He could *try*.

Chapter Six

It had been over twenty-four hours since Will texted Sage, and she still hadn't answered. Yesterday, he had tried to distract himself at the beach, but it was impossible to focus on his book when he couldn't help looking up at every person who passed by. It was ridiculous, really. He doubted Sage, a resident of Star Island, spent her Sundays on the touristy beach. But that didn't stop him from searching for her. It was a compulsion.

Monday morning, he felt adrift. He knew soulmates could start out rocky; hell, John and Cate had gone on five dates before they'd clicked. But if Will and Sage wanted to have five dates before his time on this island was up, they needed to start tonight.

And she wouldn't even answer his text.

"You look pensive," Cate said, bumping her shoulder against his. She sat on one of the counter stools in the kitchen.

"Where's everyone else?"

"Your parents and John took the kids to pick up donuts. I think John is starting to feel guilty he's going home to work tonight. Isn't it nice and quiet, though?" Cate sipped her tea. "Did you hear from Sage overnight?"

"Nope."

"It's okay. Everyone figures it out in their own way," Cate reminded him.

"Sure. But...I...I don't think I reacted the way she wanted me to." Will liked his sister-in-law a lot but they didn't have the type of relationship where he could tell her he came in his pants while making out with his soulmate.

Cate shrugged. "She doesn't know you. And you don't know her. But, if I might give you some advice, you sort of have to rip the Band-Aid off. I was terrified of John. I mean, he's your brother, but he's got that whole popular kid vibe. Something I definitely don't have."

"Me neither." Will laughed. No one would believe he and John were distantly related, let alone brothers. John took after their dad: tall, big, good at sports. Will took after their mom: medium build, medium everything.

"You need to talk to her. Once I found out more about John, saw that he was like me, nervous about meeting his soulmate, it became a lot easier. And you know how long that took. We left a trail of confused café and restaurant workers in our wake."

Will nodded and took a mug off the counter, then filled it with coffee.

"She doesn't want to text. That's okay. Pretend it's 1850 and go find your soulmate. You know she's on this island, you know her name and her sister's name."

"I know one of her sisters works at the bakery," he added.

"Yeah! You've got a lot of leads. Don't be weird, don't break down her door or throw rocks at her window. But look for her. What else are you going to do, read *Le Morte d'Arthur* again?"

"Hey!"

"Oh, come on. I love folklore as much as the next witch, but the pages are falling out. Plus, Sage didn't look like a damsel in distress in need of saving. She looked like a witch who lives in the modern world. Put the book down, get out there onto the rough streets of Star Island, and track down your slippery soulmate."

Will rolled his eyes, but headed back to his room, coffee in hand. Cate was right. Wallowing in his mistake wasn't going to change anything. If he wanted Sage to have a better opinion of him, he needed to give her a reason for it, and that wasn't going to happen with him sitting around the rental house. He was going to find her, and this time, she was going to get to know him. So help him, Nurtia.

Two hours and several stops later, while Will stood outside the bakery, Sage stepped out, like a gift from the gods surrounded by the scent of cinnamon.

"Sage!" Will called immediately and loudly, soliciting a small jump from her. "Sorry," he followed up.

"Oh. Hi." Sage nodded her head once, then turned to walk away.

"Can I walk with you?" he nearly shouted again.

"Sure," she answered slowly. "Were you going to get something from the Immortal Cupcake?" She motioned toward the bakery.

"No. Just...looking for you. In a non-creepy way, I hope." Hell, it had been less than two minutes, and nothing was going how he wanted it to go.

But, instead of looking horrified, she smirked. "Well, let's walk then." Sage held a coffee mug in one hand and a small paper bag in the other.

"What did you get?"

"Black coffee, three sugars, plus two brown sugar donuts."

"You like sugar."

"It's a non-negotiable," Sage answered.

"I have no problem with sugar." Will quickly recovered. "I'm partial to banana cake."

"My sister makes a good banana cake. She makes a good everything, though." Sage turned the next corner, and Will followed.

"What's your sister's name?"

"That one? Lavender. You've met Laurel. There's also Rosemary and Verbena."

"Wow. Any brothers?"

"Just the five of us."

"Are they all...like you?"

Sage snorted. "If you mean magical? Yes. If you mean a farmer with a sparkling personality? Nope."

"I have one brother. He's like me insomuch as we are both warlocks. But he is a huge former football player, and I am a librarian."

"Librarian?" She looked like she was mulling it over, then nodded. "I get it that siblings can be different. You saw Laurel. I'm hardly a goth in a corset at a farmers' market." Sage glanced at him for a moment, just long enough to catch his eye before looking away. "Want to have a donut at the park?"

"I would love to." A huge wave of relief slid down Will's chest.

They turned down a few more streets until Sage brought them to the place the farmers' market had been two days earlier. It was a lot quieter today; the stalls were taken down, and other than a few families at the playground, it was empty. They found a bench under a lush maple tree, and Sage handed him one of the donuts.

"You don't have to share if you really wanted two."

"It's okay. I live with the baker. I get a lot of treats. It's a stipulation."

"This is really good," Will said the moment he bit into his donut. It was the perfect mix of brown sugar and cinnamon. Almost as if someone had conjured autumn and mixed it in with butter, sugar, and flour.

"Lavender is a kitchen witch. It's kind of her thing."

"Makes sense." Will took another bite. "What kind of witch are you?"

"Harvest. My powers are a little old-fashioned. I can guarantee a good harvest, which was awesome when whole communities depended on a solitary field. Now, it just means I always have apples and veggies to sell, no matter what sort of rain or heat or frost situation happens." She broke her donut in half, then bit into it. "Not that cool."

"I don't know. Seems pretty cool. What's your favorite thing to grow?" Will took another bite of his donut. He wanted to keep her there as long as possible. If he wanted Sage to give him another chance, he needed to dazzle her, and right now all he could think to do was figure out what she loved.

"Impossible to choose. I'll give you a top five. Apples, squash, radishes, strawberries, and herbs. I won't narrow it down from that."

Will grinned. "I love that you threw in herbs. Just an extra one hundred or so plants thrown into your fifth choice."

"It's like asking a genie for more wishes," she mused. She took a long drink of her coffee, then a bite of her donut. "I have a lot to do today. Harvest season, you know."

"I get it. I'm on vacation, you're in real life."

"The busiest month of real life," she added. "There are apples and veggies to pick, bugs to banish, irrigation lines to check. While Star Island isn't really a tourist destination in January, I would have had a lot more free time to hang with you if that's when you came."

"Can I see you tonight? When you're done with your work for the day?"

Sage screwed up her mouth. "What do you want to do?"

"Dinner, the beach, another walk—I'll do whatever you feel good about." Will felt like she was a deer. He was doing everything in his power to stop her from bolting into the woods, never to be seen again.

"Beach," she answered finally. "I haven't been in September in ages. Usually too busy."

"Perfect. Which beach?"

"Vega. I'll pick you up. Where are you staying?"

Will pulled out his phone and looked up the exact address of the cottage he was staying in, then handed the phone to Sage.

"Um, about the text," she said slowly.

"It's okay."

She shook her head and took a deep breath. "I'm not a texter. And I was a little mad at Laurel for giving you my number."

"You don't have to say anything else. Thanks for this," he said and lifted the donut, "and agreeing to tonight."

Sage nodded. "I should go. The tomatoes aren't going to prune themselves." She paused. "Do you know how to get back to your cottage from here?"

"Yeah."

"Okay then." She stood up and he followed suit. "See you tonight." For a minute, Will thought she might lean in for a hug, but a moment later, she turned and power-walked away.

Will stood completely still, watching until she disappeared from sight.

That went better. Not great, but better. It looked like small steps were going to be the way to go. Which wasn't ideal, with a departing flight breathing down his neck.

By the time Will came home, John was packed and saying goodbye to Cate, who was crying.

"It's just a few days," he said softly to her. "And when you get home, our room will be completely dust free. The kids too. And I'll make sure they haven't taken the weekend off from working."

"I know, I know." She sniffled. "Love you and miss you."

"Love you and miss you," his brother answered.

"Will! Did you find her?" Cate called once she saw him.

"I did. We're going to the beach tonight."

"Yay!" Cate cheered. She turned back to John. "I'll be okay. I'll throw myself into Will's business. I'll keep you updated with every soulmate development. Get ready to silence your phone at school because it's going to be nonstop."

"Wonderful," Will said, shaking his head. "Have a safe trip home, John."

"Thanks, man. Call me when you know where you and your soulmate are landing."

Will nodded and headed inside, going straight to his bedroom. He dumped the entire contents of his suitcase on his bed and looked over every stitch of clothing he had brought.

He wanted tonight to be perfect. He wanted Sage to see him as her soulmate, the person she could pour her heart out to, not just a man who accidentally came after five minutes on her couch. He wanted to look like the perfect man for her.

Did shorts say that?

Chapter Seven

Sage stopped the car a few houses early to take a couple deep breaths. She fiddled with her swimsuit, which she wore beneath a plain white tee and jean shorts. She didn't think they'd swim, but she wasn't in a skinny-dipping mood. Plus, the cops were getting tired of finding naked Bays at the beach. Sage had only been caught once in her life, and she wasn't looking to double it.

She smoothed her hair, then nearly slapped herself across the face. Sage Juniper Bay did not care what people thought of her appearance. She did not. It was a lesson learned at twelve and never forgotten. If her soulmate didn't like what he saw, well, looked like the fates had fucked him.

Sage was pretty sure Will liked what he saw. At the very least, he liked what he felt. Hell, she'd been a sweaty mess after hours working at the farmers' market, and he'd still...

No, no, no. She wasn't going down that road.

She shook out her shoulders and drove the remaining few houses, parked in front, and waited. If he thought she was walking to the door, where there could be other people waiting to attack her with questions... well, she wasn't.

After a few moments, he exited the house, almost looking like he was peeling himself away from whatever was going on in there. As he jogged to the car, Sage couldn't help but notice all the front curtains swishing against the windows.

"Hey," Will said as he slid into the passenger's seat. "You look nice."

"Thanks," she answered, a little taken aback. "You too." She tried not to ogle him, but he did look good. His hair was tied up and away from his face, giving her a better glimpse at his dimples and deep brown eyes.

"My parents are probably watching us pull away."

"Wait, your parents are here?"

"Yeah. I'm on a family vacation. My brother left today to work, but my sister-in-law, niece, nephew, mom, and dad are all in there. Spying on my soulmate."

"Shit. That's a lot of people." No wonder the curtains were moving.

"Yeah. Do your parents live on Star Island?" he asked.

Ah. Here it went. The sob story that had defined Sage ever since moving here. In Ohio, she had been a person before the accident. A kid with hobbies and a specific personality. Here, she was always the youngest Bay, little orphan girl raised by her older sister. Nothing more, nothing less. At least once she opened the stall at the farmers' market, she was the orphaned *farmer* raised by her older sister.

"My parents died in a car accident thirteen years ago. They'd been to Star Island once to visit my great-aunt. That's whose house I live in. I was raised by my oldest sister, Lavender. She's the one who owns the bakery. Until recently, all five of us lived in the cottage together, but in the last few months, everyone's soulmates have come to the island. So, Rosemary, Laurel, and Verbena have all moved in with their significant others." She spat it all out, impatient for Will to have all the information and be able to move past it.

"Whoa," he breathed in response. "That's a lot. Sorry about your parents."

"It was a long time ago," she answered. Sage pulled away from the curb and drove out of Solaris. They headed away from the touristy Centauri peninsula and back to Vega, her favorite part of the island. Sure, their house was closest to the Vega beaches, but more than that, Sage thought they were the most beautiful. They were quiet, not desolate, sandy, not rocky, and very few tourists wandered this far north. The waves were rougher here, the Atlantic more her moody self than on the golden beaches in the south.

"Still. How old were you?"

"Eleven."

"Wow. How old was Lavender?"

"Twenty. It was a group effort, from the moment they died, but she really took the reins. Probably a better parent than half the kids in my class had. Really strict too. Not much of a problem for me, but she was a pain in Rosemary's ass."

"How old was Rosemary?"

"She was eighteen, but Lavender had all sorts of rules. No boys overnight until everyone was over eighteen, no alcohol other than a glass of wine until everyone was over twenty-one. I think she was always worried DCFS would take us away." Sage kept her eyes on the road, surprised how easy it was to say all these things to him. Hell, Sage had never told any of her friends about this stuff.

But there was this unfamiliar sort of ease with him today. She hadn't noticed it before. Probably because her other emotions, like lust and anger, had been elbowing it out of the way.

"And now everyone has a soulmate?"

"Not Lavender. But there's a prophecy that we'd all find our soulmates between Beltane and Samhain. I'm fourth."

"Really?" Will grinned and laughed a little. "My mom will be happy to know our vacation here was predestined. She's always wanted to go, and my dad complained a ton that we weren't just going to Traverse City."

Sage smirked. "Let her know the fates were going to get her to Star Island no matter what."

"It's crazy, sitting here next you." Will turned to face her, but she kept her eyes on the road. "I have to be honest, I hadn't started looking for you."

"Me neither. Until I heard a goddess or something call down the prophecy last May, I didn't really have any interest in finding my soulmate. No offense."

"None taken." He paused for a beat. "How old are you?"

"Twenty-four. You?"

"Twenty-five. I'm relieved you're age-appropriate. Makes things easier."

"Yeah. The fates aren't always so nice. My sister, Verbena, met her soulmate for the first time when she was seventeen and he was twenty-two."

"Holy shit. What did they do?"

"He's a regular human so she sort of drugged him for ten years to not be into her. He was so pissed when he found out." Sage laughed. Thankfully, Luke forgave Verbena and now they were cohabitating happily next door.

"Please don't drug me without telling me," Will said slowly.

"No worries. I'm not a big spell witch. And I don't do potions. Just me and my plants, feeding the population of Star Island but mostly my family." Sage risked a grin in his direction, her heart thumping against her chest.

Ugh, why was he so hot? And so easy to talk to? It would be easier to handle this if she didn't want to kiss him every time she saw him and if the sound of his voice didn't settle in her soul like a missing piece.

Sage pulled the car right up to the edge of the beach, another perk of the Vega coastline. There were no droves of tourist cars to contend with or overcrowded parking lots ruining the view. The main drag along the water here had a skinny lane for parked cars and that was it. She grabbed a large beach blanket from the back and led Will toward the water. It was a perfect night, warm and windy, the sun hanging low in the sky behind them. Ahead of them, the ocean was an expanse of purples and blues, moving like an ancient being with all the power in the world.

They found a spot of warm sand and spread out the blanket, then sat beside each other.

"It's beautiful here," Will commented. "I've never lived by the ocean. Must have been a cool place to grow up."

"Yeah. I didn't really appreciate it until about three years ago. I always thought life would have been a lot easier if we stayed in Ohio. But Lavender didn't want us to have financial stress on top of the regular mental strain of losing parents. Easier to go live in a house that's been bequeathed to us rather than a place in the suburbs with a mortgage and high taxes."

"Ohio?"

"I lived in Geneva, Ohio, until my parents died. Our great-aunt left us the cottage in her will a few years before. Lavender sold our house, which my parents still owed a bunch of money on, and we came here. It was ours outright and the taxes are criminally low considering it's never been sold, only inherited."

"I'm from Ohio," Will interrupted. "I grew up in Cleveland. I know where Geneva is."

"No shit," Sage breathed. "That's weird. I could have run into you at a Browns' game."

"If I was with my brother, you definitely could have."

Sage looked at Will. For the first time in her life, sitting beside her was someone she wanted to know more about. "You said you're a librarian. Where'd you go to school?"

"I went to University of Michigan for undergrad and my master's. Then I moved to Chicago right after school and started working, but we had massive layoffs a couple months ago, so I'm living at my parents' until I get a new job." Will looked down. "Sorry, I assumed I'd be more established before I met you. I've been trying to find a new job, but it's been rejection emails pretty much non-stop."

"Don't say sorry. I didn't go to college, I've never lived anywhere other than my childhood home and the cottage you saw. I've been to Boston a few times, New York once. You lived in a different state from your family. Hell, you have a master's. That's amazing. I haven't done much with my life besides grow food."

"Do you like it that way?"

Sage shrugged. "I don't know. I think that if I didn't lose my parents, I would have tried out the college thing. Majored in something absolutely ridiculous just for fun. I think it could have been a good life experience, and all. But I never wanted to stress Lavender out any more than she already was, you know? It was easier to jump straight into my career. Plus, what eighteen-year-old has a paid-off five acres?"

"Good point. I got a partial scholarship, and my older brother got a full ride. My parents helped me out, so I don't have student loans. I love books so much I would have buried myself in debt to go to school, but I'm glad I didn't have to."

"Since there probably aren't any ears nearby that can overhear," Sage began, "I never asked you what kind of warlock you were. I'm guessing not harvest."

"No." He laughed. "I'm Zetic. It's a weird line. My mom is a storm witch. My dad is a Zetic warlock. It can manifest differently, but for me, I can absorb the contents of a book in about five minutes."

"Five minutes?!" Sage gasped. "Holy shit. I could have used that in high school."

"It's a nice trick for a librarian. I have to lie about how many books I consume a year, or else people would think I was exaggerating. I also have some prophetic gifts."

Sage raised an eyebrow. Laurel was a psychic. Sage had never been interested in that path of magic.

"Do you know what our future looks like?" she asked.

"Nope. It's very unhelpful. I read cards, which can help organize it, but a lot of times, I'll bump into someone and then see them eating dinner later that night. The only reason I figured out it was seeing the future and not simply hallucinating was that I saw my brother John at his future college. After that, I really started to notice visions with people I knew. Then, I could see it all coming to fruition." He paused for a beat. "I did read the cards about us."

"Don't tell me," Sage answered quickly. "I'd rather be surprised."

Will nodded. He inched his hand toward hers across the blanket until just the tips of their fingers touched. Sage felt the nicest rush of warmth in her chest. This was good. It wasn't ripping each other's clothes off or unbridled passion, but it was nice. She liked talking to him, telling him parts of her that had been held close to her heart her entire life. Hell, she couldn't remember the last time she talked about her parents with someone who wasn't a sister. She'd spent the last decade going further and further inward, afraid of what the world might throw at her. But Will was a pretty nice thing so far.

"Hey! Is that Sage Bay?"

Sage turned around and saw Officer Mulligan, the new sheriff.

"Yes. What?"

"The beach is closed," she called to them, her hands on her hips.

"We're just sitting here, Claire," Sage complained. "No alcohol or anything."

"It's public property, and it's closed. Plus, the rumors about the Bays and the beach are still circulating."

Sage rolled her eyes and turned to Will. "We gotta get out of here. Several of my sisters have been caught naked on the beach." She left out that she also had been caught.

"No problem," Will answered. He stood, then reached down to help her up. She slipped her hand in his and stood.

"Thanks," she mumbled. They folded up the blanket and headed back to her car. She was a little bummed the night was already coming to an end.

"Have a good night," Officer Mulligan called after them.

Sage grumbled. "You too."

They climbed into her car as Claire watched them drive away.

"Hey," Will said quietly. "Can we go back to your place for a little while?"

Sage blinked hard.

"Yeah. We definitely can."

Chapter Eight

It was imperative that Will did not embarrass himself tonight. The evening had been going too well.

After the disaster of their first moments together, Will wanted the physical to take a backseat for now. He wanted to listen to her talk and learn everything he could about his harvest witch. Maybe he would hold her hand or kiss her at the end of the night. His return flight to Cleveland had been breathing down his neck, but for now he needed to ignore it. He wanted quiet moments with Sage in a private place, not a loud bar or a crowded street. Or gods and goddesses forbid, the rental he was sharing with his family. He wanted Sage alone.

The sun dipped below the horizon, casting a blue glow over the world as Sage expertly drove around wooded corners and down gravel roads. They ended in front of the cottage he'd visited two days earlier, but now anxiety didn't course through his veins.

He only felt anticipation and excitement of the path ahead. He and his soulmate. They would get to know each other slowly until he had to go home. Maybe she would come to Ohio once her growing season ended. Maybe he'd get a job in Boston. He already had an application in at the Adams Street Branch. It was close enough for a weekend trip to see her often, or the other way around. Plus, she was a harvest witch. Once her plants went dormant for the winter...maybe she could come stay in Boston with him? It was going to work out. They were still young. A lot of life still had to unravel.

This time, there was another car in the driveway, which Will assumed belonged to...Lavender. Sage had a lot of sisters to keep track of, but he would do his best.

"Do you want to show me your farm?" Will asked hopefully as the car crunched to a stop. There was something cool about seeing where a harvest witch grew her food. He wondered if he would be able to tell it was magical.

"Not tonight. It'll be too dark to see in five minutes. I'll take you back there during the day."

They got out of the car and walked up the front steps. Without using a key, Sage walked through an open front door.

"Lavender! I'm home and I've brought Will. I'm taking him upstairs. Leave us alone." She turned to face him. "She's the only sister who actually listens to my requests. Do you want anything to drink?"

"I'm okay." Will rubbed his hands on his pants. How were they already sweating? In the car he had been so focused on taking things slow, talking and getting to know her, but as he walked up the stairs behind her, he wasn't sure he had the fortitude to resist her. Plus, would she be mad if he turned her down? All he wanted was for things to go smoothly, but he didn't know which was worse: turning down her advances or making a fool of himself again?

"So," Sage interrupted his thoughts, "it's going to look like I'm taking you to my bedroom to seduce you, but I'm not."

Crisis averted. "Where are you taking me?"

"Our library. You should feel really special. I don't think Asher or Luke have been up here and they are already solidified parts of the family."

"A library!" Will couldn't disguise the excitement in his voice. Now, he couldn't wait to see what she was about to show him.

Will followed her up the stairs and into a bedroom with a twin bed on either side.

"This is my room. I shared with Rosemary but now she lives with Asher in an apartment in town, and they're moving into a house. But the cool part is this." She opened the closet and revealed a hidden set of stairs.

"Whoa," Will breathed. "This really is a witch house. I'd love to find out what these were originally used for."

"Probably what we use them for today: hiding our witch shit from people passing through." Sage flicked a light switch on the wall and looked back at him. "Come on up, warlock. I don't even have to warn you." She flashed a devilish grin.

Damn, he was so happy his soulmate was a witch.

He followed her up the creaking stairs, trying to stay focused on not falling down said creaking stairs and making a fool of himself in front of Sage. But between the overall magical atmosphere and Sage's very sculpted butt less than two feet in front of his face, he was having a difficult time.

They made it to the top, where Sage flicked another light, and the room illuminated.

"Holy shit," Will said, taking in the room in front of him.

It was an attic, with sloped ceilings and two dormer windows. There were huge pillows in jewel tones on the floor, a pair of velvet chairs, a large table covered in books, dried herbs, and a few glass jars, but the real eye-catcher was the enormous bookcase.

There had to be close to a thousand books in this room.

"Do you have a magical library?" Will asked, his eyes trained on the mountains of books.

"I do," Sage answered. "You're going to hate it."

"What?" He whipped his head toward her. "That's impossible. It's a magical library! I'm a librarian!"

"Yeah, it's not organized." Sage plopped into one of the chairs.

"What do you mean? Like you don't have the topics divided, it's just alphabetical?" Will took a few steps closer to the shelves and squinted.

"No, I mean if I take a book off the shelf, I put it back wherever."

"You do not." Will ticked his eyebrow up.

Sage nodded. "We all do. Lavender had some grand plan to organize it, but at this point if we need something, it's really a matter of going spine by spine to find it. Now, the *Compendium of North American Magical Families* we keep out. We've been needing it. A lot lately. And *The History of Bay Witches*. But everything else, we just pop in wherever there's room."

Will couldn't stop the heavy sense of unease crawling up his spine. This was an invaluable asset to the Bay family...and yet it could take hours to find what they needed. The horror.

"Would you please allow me to classify this library for you and your family?" he asked slowly.

"Yes," she answered, popping out of her seat. "I thought you'd never ask. We've had Owen, Laurel's soulmate, fixing all the quirks with the house, Luke, Verbena's soulmate, makes us all delicious mixed drinks, and Asher, Rosemary's soulmate, used to be a cop, which was very helpful. But no one's soulmate is as helpful as mine. Because you are going to make this library more useful. The most important task of them all." She grinned widely.

"Where did they all come from?" he asked, moving toward the shelves. His hands itched to begin the work right this moment, start pulling down every book, making piles...oh, he needed to get his laptop so he could create a catalogue. He could even go old school and create a binder that functioned like a card catalogue. That might be more helpful. They wouldn't have to drag a computer up here and ruin the atmosphere. Maybe the Bays would take the time to mark how often they used each title, and he could create a heavily used shelf...

"My great-aunt June collected most of them. This house has been in the Bay family for over two-hundred years. A lot of the really old ones came with the house. Some of those haven't been opened since we moved in. We did bring ours from Ohio, though. Anything on house witchery was my mom's. Plus, Lavender and Rosemary have compiled some of their spells and tucked them up here."

Will ran his hand over a few of the spines. "Do you have any books in here?"

Sage shook her head. "Nah. I hate to break it to you, but I'm not really a book person. Harvest witches tended to be lumped with home and hearth witchery, but I've never really felt like it was the same. I'm probably closer to an earth witch when it comes down to it. I like growing food and that's about it."

"No easy feat. As you said, a hundred years ago, the entire island would have depended on you to get them through the winter. But this library is amazing. Really. What a collection." Will could spend weeks up here. Maybe him getting fired was fated. Sure, this job didn't pay, but classifying a magical library? That was a dream job.

His mind flitted about, thinking he could move his flight, if Sage was cool with him staying here, so he could get the work done sooner rather than later. They should add another bookcase, also. Most of the shelves were jammed full, with stacks resting on top of the shelved books. Hm. He should probably scour the marketplace for some cheap but sturdy shelves to add onto the side. There was a lot of open wall space up here.

"You look like a kid on Yule morning," Sage said.

"Sorry." He turned away from the shelves. "I work in special collections, which are basically weird library materials. This will be by far the coolest collection I've ever worked with. Thanks for letting me organize it."

Sage smiled. "I'd be lying if I said you didn't look hot as hell right now staring at those books."

"Really?" Will's voice pitched a bit. He grimaced. "Never been told that before."

"Nothing like seeing someone with whatever makes them passionate." Sage leaned against the wall and looked down. Some wisps of her hair fell out of her braid and over her forehead, and Will felt a lovely warmth spread through his chest.

She was beautiful.

"I'm really sorry about what happened a few days ago," he started. "I'll make sure it doesn't happen again. Or at the very least I'll handle it better."

"I...didn't handle it well either," Sage admitted. "I shouldn't have thrown you into that position. Literally."

"Maybe having a gorgeous soulmate is going to make me lose any control I've ever possessed." He risked a small smile.

"Thanks," she said quietly. "Never been called gorgeous before," she quipped.

"Should have been." Will turned away from the bookcase and took two meaningful strides toward her. Going slow flew out the attic dormer window. He reached his hand out and set it on her waist.

"Sage," he breathed, leaning to her. His hand went to her chin, tipping it slightly toward him. He didn't tower over her—there was probably only an inch between them—but her brown eyes looking at him nearly undid his soul.

"Shit!" she yelled, pushing him against the wall and jumping in front of him.

"What? Sorry," Will stammered before looking past her.

There were three ghosts floating in the middle of the room.

"What the fuck?" he yelled and grabbed Sage, pushing her behind him. Will didn't have a lot of experience with ghosts, but whenever they showed themselves unannounced, it was usually a bad sign.

"It's okay, I know them!" Sage yelled, stepping out from behind him.

"You know them?" They were not friendly looking ghosts. Their dresses were burned at the edges, their fingertips were blackened, their hair looked like fire.

If ghosts took the form of their most recent body, these women were burned to death.

"Are they...cool?" Will asked slowly. Ghosts came in all shapes, sizes, and personalities, ranging from harmless to downright malicious.

"They might be mad at me," she whispered.

"Sage Bay," the middle ghost howled, raising her hand to point at his soulmate. "You have an unfinished task."

"Okay, I know, I know. Been a little busy. Harvest witches can't really fuck off in the midst of harvest season to go to Baltimore."

"We want our price," the middle ghost reiterated. "Bind Jonas to the ground. Keep his soul from walking this earth again while we languish in our pain!" The flames on her head brightened with her screams.

"Fine! Fine. I'll go."

"You will leave now," the ghost gasped.

"I will not. It is dark out, and the ferry isn't running again until tomorrow morning. Plus, I need to pack." Sage paused. "You don't understand any of this. I'll leave within the next two days, okay? He'll be bound in no time."

"We will return if it isn't done," the ghost warned, her flames sparking again.

"It will be. Trust me, binding the soul that cursed us is something I've been looking forward to."

The ghosts shifted their focus from Sage to him.

"You are not a Bay," the middle one snarled.

"Oh, fuck," Will mumbled. The ghosts trained their eyes on him, floating closer.

"He's my soulmate. Leave him alone and, I mean this as politely as possible, fuck off? I'm going to take care of it. But it's hard to concentrate with the three of you around. Out of my house, please?"

The ghosts narrowed their gazes, then vanished. Will stared at the empty air where the three of them had floated, now jarringly empty.

"Well. Looks like I'm going to Baltimore tomorrow," Sage said, then blew out a breath. "Damn it, I have a lot of harvest related shit going on this week. I was really hoping they'd be cool with me going in November. I have to see if Rosemary will take care of my plants. Shit." Sage prattled on as if three terrifying ghosts hadn't been floating in the middle of the attic moments ago.

"I'm sorry," Will interrupted. "What the hell is going on?"

Sage stopped for a moment, then crossed her arms. "Everyone always freaks out. I'm not freaked out. Know that going in."

Will nodded.

"There's a curse on our family. If any witch or warlock collects the blood of every living Bay, they get imbued, or whatever, with all of our powers. But it's all or nothing. And my sisters and I are the only living magical Bays. Plus, there is an annoying as fuck family that knows this and is connected to us through past lives. Or at least three of them have been so far. Those witches, the ghosts, were the originally cursed and murdered group, and I promised I would bind Jonas Fortworth, the warlock who convinced his sister to curse our line, to his grave so he couldn't be reincarnated. His grave is in Baltimore. All this shit took place in the 1700s."

Will swallowed. This was a lot. His family didn't get involved in a lot of magical problems, but it looked like his soulmate's did. A curse from the 1700s? That was no short-lived curse. Breaking it and binding the soul that cast it...those were big spells. Huge. Almost unthinkable.

"Okay. What time do you want to leave?"

"Well, the ferry leaves at ten, so I'll be on that."

"Sure. I need to run home and pack a bag. You want to spend the night in Baltimore? How far of a drive is it?"

"I don't know, seven hours? And what do you mean you have to pack a bag?"

"Obviously, I'm coming with you."

"Why? I mean, we just met, and you want to go on vacation?"

"I don't think binding a soul to a grave is a vacation. And I saw in the cards—I know you didn't want me to say anything—but I saw we'd be going through a hardship together. I'm not going to abandon you to the hardship. You know, we're a team and all that. Even if we did just meet."

Sage screwed up her mouth and tapped her foot. "Fine. Suit yourself. Let's get out of here. I need to get you home so I can figure out who's picking and watering for me. Ugh. Rosemary is going to be so annoyed."

Will allowed himself a small smile. Road trip to bind the soul who cursed the Bays? It wasn't the same as a romantic weekend at the beach, but it was something.

Chapter Nine

"I thought the two of you were taking it slow?" Lavender asked, rubbing her temples. She sat at the dining table, her notebook of recipe ideas for the Immortal Cupcake spread in front of her. Sage spied notes for something with pears, brown sugar, and allspice that sounded amazing.

"We are. We haven't fucked." Sage set her bag on the table and opened it.

"I...don't need to know that. But going on an overnight isn't taking it slow. In case you are confused. That is jumping into a relationship. Sleepovers out of state are things people in a relationship do," Lavender chided.

"What do you want me to do? He's a card reader. He saw that we're supposed to go through some hardships together, which, duh. But he wants to come and honestly, it'll be nice having someone with me. It's a long drive for me to do alone." Sage was making excuses, but with Lavender, she felt like she had to. They were the two last holdouts, the sisters with no interest in soulmates. And now she was leaving with hers.

"Are you okay?" Sage asked.

"Yes, why?" Lavender snapped her head up.

"I'm sort of your baby, right? And now I've got a soulmate."

Lavender sighed. "You aren't my baby. You are my youngest sister. Our relationship...it got muddled somewhere between sibling and parent. But we were a team, we are a team. I was in charge, but your life is yours to do with what you please. I'm not going to tell you what to do. If you want to go to Baltimore with your soulmate, if you want to go to Baltimore with some guy you met off the street, it's up to you." Lavender closed her book. "I'm not anti-soulmate. As far as I can tell, Laurel, Rosemary, and Verbena are very happy. But I know it doesn't always end that way."

"You mean with our past lives?" Lavender had created a spell that allowed couples to look into the lives they had shared before, and so far, not one had ended well.

"More than that. Even this life. Soulmates are tricky. It doesn't always lead to a happy life." Her sister sighed. "I hope you and Will have a nice time together. I hope binding Jonas Fortworth is simple and you don't run into anything crazy. Have Verbena ward your car before you leave. If you see a Stoch—"

"It would be crazy if one of them found me in Baltimore," Sage interrupted.

"Or it would be fate. These past months, it's all been fate. Laurel had been in the Hedge World a hundred times before she ran into Morana there. That's what started it all. A prophecy and an end date. We've been living easy, but not anymore. It's a final chance for all our pasts to catch up with us, our enemies from lifetimes ago to come forward. Be safe. Please."

"I will, Lav."

"I'm serious. I know you aren't afraid of anything. This is scary. The curse is scary. Be afraid of Miloslav. We don't know what a chaos warlock can do. Three Stochs have tried to kill three of my sisters. I don't want it to be four."

Sage nodded. "I didn't mean for Will to come. To Star Island. I always thought you and I would be living here together, just the two of us, until we were old crones." Sage felt this pressing need to apologize to Lavender. Like she had conjured her soulmate out of nothing to abandon her.

"Nothing you could do about it. It was always coming. The moment we heard that voice on Beltane, I knew you'd all be whisked away."

Sage snorted. "I do not think anyone could whisk me away. I'm far too solid for that sort of thing."

"Either way, I don't want you to feel like you are leaving me. I always knew we'd come to this point. You were going to grow up eventually. And while I didn't think I'd be worried about you running into a chaos warlock in Baltimore, I did worry about normal things. Like what if you wanted to move to Kansas? But I did all I could, and now I have to, begrudgingly, trust you out in the world without me. Don't get killed. Don't kill anyone."

"No promises on the latter. I'll be fine. I'm going to Baltimore, not a war zone."

Lavender smiled. "That'll have to do. Now. Since it isn't going to be just the two of us much longer, let's eat the entire sweet potato pie I have in the fridge."

Sage: Can you take care of my plants tomorrow and the next day?

Rosemary: Sure! What do they need?

Sage: Pick any ripened veggies or fruit, especially the apples, check the irrigation lines to make sure they are dripping, water the pots, maybe throw a prayer to Demeter. But if you think that would make Idunn mad, skip it.

Rosemary: She is not a jealous patron, as far as I've been able to tell. Are you and Will getting a hotel? A little time alone??? Do you have something sexy to wear?

Rosemary: You don't need anything sexy—you could just do the whole T-shirt and panties thing. That totally works. I mean, anything will work. He's your soulmate. Are you nervous?

Sage pinched the bridge of her nose. She loved Rosemary, dearly. She was the sister who got her through those first two years after losing their parents. She was a bundle of comfort and so damn caring.

So, she told the truth.

Sage: Yes.

Rosemary: Oh!! It's going to be okay. I know it's a big step. But you can handle it.

Sage: We don't know each other. What if he doesn't like me when he gets to know me?

Rosemary: That's ridiculous. He is going to fall in love with you. But he does need to get to know you first. Sure, I wanted to rip Asher clothes off and he sort of did rip mine off, but I had to get to know him before I fell in love with him. I didn't look at him and know exactly how our relationship would work. Hell, I thought he'd never accept me for who I am. But we worked it out, after we got to know each other.

Sage: If you say so.

Rosemary: I do say so! And I'm your big sister so what I say is always right. Go to a hotel with Will and have fun. As much fun as you want. Or as little. Be a good judge of the level of fun you are ready for.

Sage: We're actually going to Baltimore to bind Jonas Fortworth to his grave but we'll spend the night so we don't have to drive there and back in one day.

Rosemary: Well, that's not as romantic, but good luck. Hope you both have an orgasm in Maryland.

Sage: I'd settle for a successful kiss.

Rosemary: Oh! Now, that's romantic.

Sage slipped her phone into her pocket and looked at the piles of things in front of her. She'd go to the market tomorrow and grab snacks for the trip. She had two outfits, which was more than enough, a pair of pajama pants, and a T-shirt. No matter what Rosemary said about wearing something sexy, Sage couldn't picture herself seducing anyone. She had no moves or game. Hell, her first attempt at seducing her soulmate had been batshit crazy and gone very badly.

"Fuck," she mumbled. She was so wound up. The small part of her brain that wanted a soulmate to show up was entirely for physical reasons. Sage didn't date. She didn't do random hookups, either. And she'd be lying if she said the first thing she thought when she saw Will earlier tonight wasn't "could you lay on top of me?" She wanted to feel the pressure of another body on hers. Yes, an orgasm would be really, really appreciated, but more than that, she craved the physical touch of someone else. Someone who might find her attractive. She just wanted to bury her face against his neck and breathe. Was that too much to ask?

She grabbed two pairs of beige underwear and added them to the pile, plus two pairs of socks. And a hoodie.

Who was she kidding? This wasn't going to be a romantic trip. She was literally binding a soul to the earth. It was some pretty metal shit. They probably weren't going to have a moment to look at each other.

"Sage?"

"What!" she shrieked.

"I didn't mean to scare you," Lavender said, standing in her doorway. "I wanted to remind you to get to the ferry thirty minutes early to load your car." Lavender cocked her head and squinted. "Something is stuck to your butt."

Sage looked over her shoulder and brushed the seat of her pants, knocking something to the floor, which fluttered under the bed. She got down on her hands and knees and reached for it.

A tarot card.

"What the hell," Sage muttered, flipping it over. "The Two of Cups." She shook her head. "It must have fallen out of Laurel's deck onto one of the chairs and stuck to me when I sat down."

It was a flimsy explanation. Laurel didn't leave cards behind. They were basically an extension of herself. Plus, Sage didn't recognize this deck. She didn't know much about tarot, but this card had two people staring at each other and looking like a couple.

Hell, was this one of Will's cards? He didn't show them to her in the house. Or even have them as far as she knew. But weird things had happened in the Bay Cottage. Sage slipped the card into her bag.

"Thanks for the reminder," she said to Lavender. "I'm going to finish packing and get the supplies ready for the binding spell. Then I need to hit the hay. Long day tomorrow and the day after."

Lavender nodded. "I'll leave you to it. Yell if you need anything. I'm going to be working on a new recipe. I'm off tomorrow so say goodbye before you leave." Lavender disappeared downstairs.

Sage looked back at her bag. She had a lot to do before she went to sleep tonight. Preparing for a spell to bind an evil warlock's soul to this earth was no small feat. Neither was spending the night with your soulmate for the first time.

She threw in a pair of black underwear and took out one of the beige pairs.

Chapter Ten

Will wasn't sure what he should bring on a road trip with his brand-new soulmate to curse someone, but he thought snacks were a good place to start.

He wandered down the chip aisle, which at the tiny Star Island market was more of a shelf than an aisle, and grabbed a variety.

"Will?" his mom called from a few rows over. "Do you remember if there was milk?"

"Nope," he answered. He had come to the store this morning to attempt to contribute something to this trip other than his warm body. He'd made the mistake of announcing he was going to the market, and his mom had insisted she needed to grab a few things too.

"No, there wasn't, or no, you don't remember?" his mom called back.

Will grimaced and turned around the corner and nearly ran into Sage.

"Sage!" he yelped.

"Sage?" his mom shrieked. She dove out from her aisle and ran to stand right beside them. "Oh, my goddess, Sage!" His mom grinned so hard her face could have split. "I'm Will's mom! Kelly. That's my name. And you can call me Kelly. I'm so happy to meet you."

Sage flicked her eyes between his mom and him, assessing the situation before saying, "Nice to meet you."

An awkwardness crackled through the air as Sage looked at the space between them and his mom stayed still, smile plastered on her face.

"Why don't we step outside for a minute," Will started, setting his basket on the ground. "So we aren't taking up the only standing space in this market."

Sage nodded tersely and beelined it for the door.

"She's not usually this excitable," Will mumbled as they slipped out the door, his mom out of earshot. "She's been wanting to meet you."

"Yeah. Makes sense." Sage rolled her neck a few times, but Will could see the discomfort hanging onto her.

His mom pushed out of the store to follow them. Damn, he was hoping she would stay inside. "How are you feeling about the trip?"

Sage eyed Will.

"It'll be fun, going down to Baltimore to pick up the book for Sage's sister. Plus, there are so many good museums there. We'll make a nice overnight of it," he spat out as quickly as possible.

"Well, well, what do we have here? The best farmer on Star Island taking the morning off?" A middle-aged man Will didn't know sidled up next to Sage. "Shouldn't you be working tirelessly in your fields? After all, you manage to produce more food than anyone else."

Sage scowled at the stranger. "You're not at your field either, Theo."

"And who do we have here? A boyfriend?"

"Fuck off, Theo," Sage spat. She turned back to his mom. "I have a lot to get done." She nodded and looked at Will. "See you in a bit," she added, then walked back into the market. Theo laughed as he walked away.

Will stood dumbfounded, and in silence, until two minutes later when she exited the market with a large, iced tea and nodded at them again, with a little half wave, then disappeared around the corner.

"She seems nice," his mom said slowly. "Maybe a little shy? And that man was certainly brash."

"Yeah, I guess," he muttered. His mom was being respectful. After all, that woman was his soulmate. But he didn't quite understand why she'd been so rude to him. More than that, why she'd been so rude to his mom. A simple hello and handshake would have done wonders.

"Let's go back in. You can grab whatever you want for the trip and get back in time for her to pick you up."

Will nodded and followed his mom. But his mind was jumbled. He'd thought the two of them had made strides the night before. Apparently not.

Will checked his bag again and tossed his tarot cards in on a whim. He knew Sage wasn't into cartomancy, but at the moment he didn't care. He wanted to bring them, so he would.

His hands itched to pull some cards about the overnight and how it would go, but she'd be here any minute. He should be focusing on leaving for the trip and not what could potentially happen on the trip.

Another alert went off on his phone. Probably another rejection.

Will grabbed his phone and opened it, surprised that it wasn't a rejection, but an alert of a job posting.

Special Collections Librarian, Charleston County Public Library, available immediately...

Will scanned the listing. Great pay, cool position. A week earlier he would have dropped everything to fill out the application and find a contact in the system. But now he was about to leave on a soul-binding road trip with a soulmate he couldn't figure out. Working in Charleston, South Carolina was not in the forefront of his brain. He saved the link, then shoved his phone back into his pocket.

He collected his things and said a quick goodbye to his family. After how things had gone the market, Sage coming in and talking to everyone wasn't a good idea. He didn't think he could handle her being rude to his entire family in one day and then getting in a car with her for hours.

He sat on the stairs, fidgeting with his fingertips. It was a trick a doctor had recommended whenever he felt anxious. He was supposed to say some vaguely new age words while doing it, like peace or relax, but his doctor didn't know he was a warlock. So, instead, he said *Seshat, Athena, Ogma, Mímir* with every tap of his thumb against a fingertip. His small devotions were woven into a calming regiment recommend by someone who thought magic existed only in stories.

Will's family didn't have any particular gods or goddesses they were devoted to. He favored those who stood for knowledge or wisdom, while his mom loved a good storm deity. It was an interesting amalgamation on holidays. An offering for Athena, another one for the Cailleach.

The soft hum of an approaching car tore Will from his meditation.

Sage. She stayed in her car, her eyes forward and hands gripping the wheel.

Will exhaled, grabbed his bag, and opened the car door. She still didn't turn to look at him, or say hello, or anything. Just silence.

Will slid into his seat and buckled his seatbelt, then pulled out his phone. It was going to be a long ride if she insisted on doing it in silence. But as the moments stretched into minutes, Will decided to open his NYT app and play a few word games.

"I have a hard time with new people," Sage said, as she pulled her car onto the ferry. Will jumped a little. He'd just settled into the anagram game. "Especially if I don't know I'm going to meet them. And fucking Theo. That guy is such an asshole. He's constantly trying to undermine my work as a farmer because I'm in my twenties and have a vagina. Seeing him this morning made everything worse." She shrugged. "I know I'm not what a witch would want for her warlock son, but I should have handled it better. I thought I'd have more time before I had to impress your mom. And, you know, not be wearing a T-shirt." She moved to exit the car, but Will grabbed her forearm.

Mine, my love, the only one to warm my frostbitten heart. Our icy skin pressed against each other. Stars in the sky, stars in your eyes. Rime on your eyelashes. My fingertips brushing the snow from your hair. A tangle of warmth in a frozen solid world. All we have are moments in the chaos. Speckled flashes of embraces.

"Will. Will!" Sage shook him. "Are you having a seizure? Shit, where's my fucking phone..." she mumbled, rooting around her bag.

"I'm not having a seizure," he finally managed to say. "My water." He pawed over the cupholders until Sage handed him the bottle. He couldn't open his eyes. Not yet.

"Thank you," he said after taking a gulp. "Not a seizure. Just a vision." Will settled against his seat and rubbed his forehead, trying to pull the pain off his brain. The headaches weren't as bad now as when he'd been a kid, those were skull-splitting migraines that lasted hours. Now, he'd have some water, rest for a minute, and be right as rain.

He hadn't a vision like that in years. He had no control over when they came and went, only hoped they didn't happen at work. But that...that wasn't dinner tonight or her pulling weeds a week from now. It was somewhere else entirely.

"Do I want to know what you saw?" she asked warily after a few moments of silence.

He shrugged. "It was from a very, very long time ago. You weren't alone. I was with you. A night lit only by stars. A frozen land. Doubt it has much to do with us now." He took another sip of water. It had been Sage, in his arms, or some version of her. But it was them. So terribly long ago.

"It might." She groaned. "The whole curse thing—all the Bays, so far, have been connected to a Stoch through a past life. Did you see anyone else there? Anyone menacing?"

"It was just us."

"Where were we? When were we?"

"For someone who doesn't want to know the future, you are sure interested in the past." Will took another sip of his water and draped his arm over his eyes.

"Don't be a dick, tell me what you saw."

"We were wearing furs. There was no light. Not even candles. Just stars in the sky. We both had frost on our skin. We were dying."

"Were we...cave people?"

Will laughed. "Probably. We weren't speaking. I don't think I had all my teeth. Or toes."

"Fuck. How gross. Rosemary got to go be a Viking and murder a man, and I'm going to freeze to death in Paleolithic times." Sage crossed her arms over her chest.

"It was one of our past lives. I'm sure there are lots of other ones, maybe even one where you got to be a Viking."

"I already know I got to be a kitchen wench in Ireland. Which sounds boring and like a lot of thankless work and trying to escape attempted assault." She blew out an exasperated breath. "Let's go sit on the deck. I'll get seasick if we stay down here the whole time." Sage pushed open her door and slammed it shut.

"Wait!" Will called, struggling to get out and catch up with her. Damn, his head was pounding. "What did you say before? When I grabbed you?"

"I'm not what...*mothers*...want for their sons." She rolled her eyes. "I have no preconceived notions on what other women think of me."

"What the hell is that supposed to mean?" His mom had been perfectly nice to Sage.

"Will. You don't have a sister, so I won't fault you for being blind. Look at me." She gestured at her body. "No one wants this for their son."

Will looked at Sage. She looked cute, in her gray T-shirt and jeans. Her thick brown hair was pulled back in a braid, which was the only way he'd seen her wear it so far, but it suited her well. Her shoes were a little scuffed, but who cared?

"I have no idea what you are talking about," he finally answered. "My mom wouldn't want me to be with someone...who wears jeans?"

"Keep your voice down, there's a lot of non-tourists on the ferry. People I know." She pulled him toward the staircase to the upper level. "I'm not feminine. You know. Not a girly-girl? Don't give off any sort of maternal vibe or lady-ish vibe at all."

"So?"

"Look, my whole life people have ridiculed me for this. If I had known I was meeting your mom I would have...well, I don't own any skirts, but I would have maybe thrown on some mascara and a nicer shirt. I definitely would have put on a real bra."

"Are you not wearing bra?" he asked, his voice lowering. He couldn't help but let his eyes wander down, maybe catch a glance of her nipples through her shirt.

"Yes, I'm wearing a bra. Like a sports bra. For exercising. Not a fancy bra."

"Sage." Will closed his eyes. "I am very confused why my mom would care what kind of bra you were wearing."

"Never mind, you won't get it." She turned and walked up the stairs.

"Sage!" he hissed. "Don't walk away from me!"

"Uh, I can go wherever I want," she snapped.

"Just, fuck, just stop for two seconds." She did, standing two steps above him, her expression like a stone.

"Thank you," he said. "I think you are hot, and it doesn't matter to me what anyone else thinks about you. You're hot, I like your face and your body and that's that. You. Are. Hot. The end. I would have thought my performance a few days ago would have displayed that. I don't care if my mom thinks you are feminine enough for me, and you don't know my mom. Honestly the thing she is most worried about right now is that I'm going to live on Star Island while John lives in Oregon and she's going to have kids on both sides of the country, okay?"

Sage was quiet for a few beats, then blew out a breath. "I'm sorry I was rude to your mom. I promise I will do better the next time I see her. I just don't like getting caught off guard when meeting new people."

"It's not a big deal. When Cate, my sister-in-law, met us, she canceled four times before actually doing it. And she could barely talk to John when they met. We all have our things. Now can we stop talking about my family and look at the ocean? I never get a chance to be by the ocean. And it's our first trip. If you could refrain from talking about anything that includes my mom and what kind of bra you are wearing from now on that would be preferable."

Sage blinked a few times, then nodded.

"Yeah," she finally answered, letting her arms drop.

"Thanks. And for future reference, when I have an...episode, it comes with a headache. If we could save fighting for at least an hour afterwards, I would appreciate it." Will pushed on his temples with his fingertips.

"Do you want me to get you something to eat or drink? I have a bunch of stuff in the car," she offered.

"No. I want you to sit next to me and say things like, oh, there's my favorite red house on the coastline and oh, the oak trees are already orange. Treat me to a tourist experience on our way to Baltimore."

"I haven't been to Baltimore since I was fifteen, but I can definitely tell you about shit in Massachusetts."

"That would be nice." Will followed Sage up to the deck and they grabbed a pair of seats away from everyone else. The ocean was a blue gray that morning, with clear skies above it, to Will's delight. Having always lived in the Midwest, there was a part of him with a healthy fear of anything controlled by the tides. And hurricanes. He was really afraid of hurricanes.

"I didn't take the ferry for three years after we moved here," Sage began. "I don't really like boats. I'm very much an earth person, you know? The harvest, my birthday is January tenth so I'm an earth sign. I'm not crazy into astrology, but Laurel told me I only have earth and fire in my chart, so the ocean and I have been at odds a lot. Plus taking the ferry that first time felt like leaving our planet." She chuckled. "I had swum in Lake Erie as a kid but never seen the ocean. Our line isn't water-based at all."

"Yeah," Will answered softly. "My mom's a storm witch, but there's no seawater in her line. She loves Ohio. Tornados are kind of her thing."

"Your mom is a tornado witch? And I was rude to her? Shit, she's never going to like me."

"She doesn't create tornados, but she can control them, make them jump over buildings. When I was in fifth grade, a tornado was heading for our middle school. I was scared shitless. My mom is a storm witch, but I'm book guy. She knew though, jumped in her minivan and drove straight at it. It ended up destroying some corn crops, but all the kids were safe. Pretty good trade-off."

"Your mom is a badass." Sage shook her head. "I've always felt like a badass witch stuck in a harvest witch body. I wish I was a fire witch, or tornado witch. Something that had supreme power. The kind of witch other witches were afraid of." She leaned back in her seat and kicked her feet up against the railing. "Does she hate me?"

"No. Neither of us thought I'd be meeting my soulmate on our family vacation," he quipped.

Sage smiled. "And that I'd be dragging you to Maryland to do the bidding of a trio of ghosts."

"According to my mom, it's an overnight to get away from our families. My parents get it. They met on vacation."

"Really?"

"Yeah, I don't ask a lot of questions because their vacation was three days long and John was born thirty-nine weeks later."

Sage laughed, hard and loud.

"Now. Give me a tour, Harvester."

Chapter Eleven

Damn it, Will was so fucking hot.

He looked hot eating corn chips. No one looked hot eating corn chips! But here she was, gazing at him—when she was supposed to be keeping her eyes on the road—shove corn chips in his mouth, and all she could think about was slamming on the brakes and climbing onto his lap.

And more than that, he was so damn understanding. When Sage had walked away from meeting his mom, she'd known she had messed up. She had this weird thing in her brain that defaulted to rude, and no matter how old she got, she couldn't turn it off. It was like her default setting was cold bitch and there was nothing she could do about it. And the way he handled her apology had her waiting to grab his face and kiss him right this minute.

She wasn't going to do it—they were on the Interstate, and it'd be extremely dangerous—but that didn't mean the cavewoman part of her brain wasn't screaming at her to do exactly that.

"You've got about a quarter tank left. Should we stop and get gas?" Will asked, breaking the spell he had over her.

"Yeah." She could splash some cold water on her face and snap out of it.

"I could drive for a bit also. If you want a break."

"I don't mind driving." Keeping her hands on the wheel was probably the only thing keeping her hands off him.

Ugh, what the hell was wrong with her? She squirmed in her seat. She should have been prepared for this. Hell, Rosemary told her everything, and she meant *everything.* She knew this soulmate shit could make people crazy horny. Her sister had gotten naked in the Star Island Police Department. This wasn't a feeling for amateurs.

But that's exactly what Sage was, an amateur. She couldn't seduce Will; she'd never seduced anyone! She kissed four people between the ages of fourteen and eighteen, one of whom touched her boobs. Another who told the entire school she was a terrible kisser and probably gay. Which led to the one girl Sage had kissed. Myra was the only person who was nice to Sage after the rumor had spread like wildfire through their entire school. But Myra knew she was definitely gay and not interested in being an experiment for Sage, someone still figuring out their sexuality. Which, in hindsight, was extremely mature for a seventeen-year-old.

Sage pulled off the Interstate and found a gas station before thinking about her disappointing sexual history caused a car accident.

"I'm going to run to the bathroom," she said quickly, leaving Will to fill up the tank. She sprinted toward the building and beelined it to the restroom.

Once inside, she locked the door and exhaled.

What the hell was wrong with her?

She washed her hands and gave herself a once-over. Her braid was messy, loose with wisps around her face. She pulled it out and re-braided it quickly, then looked over her face.

She looked tired. Light purple patches under her glassy eyes told how little sleep she had gotten the night before. Her actual farmer's tan peeked out from the neckline of her T-shirt revealing shockingly white skin compared to the nutbrown complexion she rocked from June until early October when it started to fade.

She looked like...herself. Normal Sage. Who apparently was enough for Will.

Damn, that made her even more attracted to him.

She pulled out her phone and tapped out a text to Rosemary.

Sage: Everything going okay with the garden?

Rosemary: All the plants were in tip-top shape when I swung by an hour ago! Irrigation lines look good, and I picked about fifteen apples and a whole basket of tomatoes. I'll peek in again around dinner. Asher and I are going to eat with Lavender. I don't want to talk about plants, HOW IS IT GOING?!?!

Sage sighed and blew out a breath.

Sage: Okay, but he's so...attractive. I don't know how I am supposed to take things slow with him.

Rosemary: You don't have to take things slow.

Sage: I can't take things fast when I'm driving 70 MPH. Plus, there's a lot to do in Baltimore. I don't think I can just take off all my clothes the second we get to the motel tonight. And I have no moves to warm him up to that idea.

Rosemary: There are so many ways to seduce a man that have nothing to do with touching him. You're staying at the motel tonight and then doing the spell tomorrow, right?

Sage: Yes.

Rosemary: Perfect. When you get to the hotel, unbraid your hair really slowly in front of him. Sleep in just a T-shirt. Stretch your arms over head a lot. If you have lotion, act like moisturizing your legs is something you do every night before you go to sleep.

Sage: I only brought sunscreen.

Rosemary: Then do that in the morning. Act like you are going to be at the beach for twelve hours.

Sage: Even though I brought pants to wear tomorrow?

Rosemary: I truly doubt he's going to notice that you are putting sunscreen on your legs. He's just going to be looking at your legs.

Sage: Okay, thank you. I need to wrap up this bathroom visit before he thinks I actually poop.

Rosemary: Lol. He seems like a smart guy. He already knows.

Sage slipped her phone back into her pocket. She could do this. She could wait two more hours until they got to Baltimore and then be sexy adjacent.

She peed, figuring that if she had to stop in an hour because she had sat in the bathroom and texted her sister, Will might be confused. She washed her hands again and then went back out to face her soulmate.

She found him leaning against the car, his face turned toward the sun and his eyes closed. He looked like a man out of history. A poet or medieval professor. A trusted advisor to a just king. Someone who had a way with words and paper.

Sage! Snap out of it.

"You ready?" she asked, brushing past him. Her forearm collided with his, and before she could sneak around the car, he reached and grabbed her hand.

"Hey," he said quietly, pulling her back toward him. "You are a badass witch. More than any fire witch or even my mom. You're going to bind the soul of an evil warlock. You have the power to feed a population. That's badass shit." He ran his thumb over her knuckles and leaned in closer. "My soulmate is an extremely scary witch."

"You're just saying that," she stuttered, her entire brain focused on his grip on her hand. It was firm. His hands were drier, rougher than she expected. She hardly had dainty hands. She wore gloves most of the day, but even with gloves, growing food took a toll.

"I'm not. If I didn't know you were meant for me, I'd be scared of you. I'm still a little scared of you." He smiled and for a moment, Sage didn't think she could walk away from him. There was nothing like listening to a man say you were scary—it was all she had ever wanted.

She loved it.

"We should get back on the road if we want to get there before dark. Let me drive for a little while. You've been going all morning."

"Thanks," she mumbled, shaking her head a little. She dropped her hand away from his and slid into the passenger's seat. Will climbed in to drive and adjusted his seat and mirrors.

Suddenly her exhaustion hit her like a train. Barely sleeping the night before...and every night since meeting Will was catching up with her.

"I might try to nod off for a bit," she said quickly, tucking her arms over her chest. "I didn't sleep well."

"You should sleep if you can. I'll wake you when we get close." He plugged his phone into her charger. "Do you mind if I play something quiet?"

"Go ahead. I can sleep through anything," she lied. Usually, to fall asleep in the middle of a September day, Sage would need an eye mask, white noise, and a potion from Lavender. But she was curious what he was going to put on.

A moment later, a solitary piano softly filled the car.

"Is that too loud?" Will whispered.

"No, it's perfect." Sage leaned against her seat and shut her eyes. She took a steadying breath.

A librarian who called her scary, picked out quiet piano music for when she wanted to sleep, and had the best dimples she'd ever seen? Sage had never dreamed up a perfect man, but here he was.

Lovesick was not the way she wanted to approach Jonas Fortworth's grave. That man deserved the worst curses in the world. Sage needed to reclaim a bit of her metal before she attempted to torture that man for eternity.

She needed to lean into her badass witch self.

Chapter Twelve

For the next two hours, Will followed the nearly silent directions and exited the Interstate. He drove down a few side streets, then pulled into the motel parking lot. He carefully avoided a pothole in the middle of the lot and found a space.

"Sage," he whispered, running his hand over her shoulder. "We're here."

She jumped a bit, her hands flying up and smacking against the window and dashboard.

"Did I fall asleep?" she demanded, looking as if she'd been woken up in the middle of a battle rather than a quiet car.

"Yeah, about an hour ago. But we're here now. I didn't think you'd want to sleep in the motel parking lot when there's a bed not too far away."

Sage nodded and ran her hand over her face.

"I'll get us a room," he offered and ducked out of the car. He could come back for the bags and Sage. Plus, it would be good to give himself a moment to collect his thoughts. He'd spent the end of the drive trying not to stare at Sage and keep his eyes on the road, but if she didn't look absolutely beautiful while she slept...her chin tucked against her chest, eyelashes spread over her cheeks. Gorgeous.

Will walked into the check-in area. It didn't feel right calling it a lobby.

There were fluorescent lights, an overflowing trash can, and a solitary employee blowing a bubble the size of his face.

"Uh, hello?" Will said at the moment the bubble popped and covered his beard with gum.

"What's up?"

"Um," Will stammered, caught off-guard by his nonchalance. "I need a room for two people."

The guy pulled gum out of his beard. "You want a queen or two fulls?"

"Oh." Will looked back toward the car, where Sage was slowly extracting herself. She stretched her arms overhead and rolled her neck.

"Sage?" Will called, holding the door open. "One bed or two?"

"Whichever is cheaper is fine." She leaned back into the car and pulled her bag out. "Or immediately available."

Will turned back to the front desk. "Which is less expensive?"

"The queen."

"We'll take the queen." Will's heart thudded against his chest. He was sharing a bed with Sage tonight. Cool. Cool. He could share a bed with Sage tonight. No big deal. Will was an adult—he could handle it.

Five minutes later, they were in their room. Their bags were on the floor, the food they'd gotten for the trip spread on the bed, and they sat beside each other watching a slightly fuzzy rerun of *I Love Lucy*.

"Should we go get food?" Sage commented, fishing a few corn chips out of the bottom of the bag. "I'm not starving, but do you need a real meal?"

Will shook his head. "I'm fine finishing all this up. What about you? Are you a person who needs a protein, starch, and vegetable for dinner?"

"Nope. But I will need a big breakfast. I'm spoiled living with Lavender. There's always something delicious waiting for me."

"Big breakfast it is," Will agreed. He pulled his phone out to search for nearby diners. "After you bind Jonas to his grave, could we go to a museum?" Will knew he should be focusing on the insane spell Sage had to do, but he couldn't visit a major city for the first time and not at least try to go to a museum. Plus, when his parents peppered him with questions when they got back, he could really lean into details on the solitary museum they squeezed into the trip.

Sage paused, a handful of popcorn halfway to her mouth. "Which museum?"

"We could go to the Baltimore Museum of Art? Or the American Visionary Art Museum? Or the Walters Museum of Art?"

"Any that aren't art?"

"Yes. The Museum of Industry, the B&O Railroad Museum, the Edgar Allan Poe House and Museum—"

"That one. I liked his sad boy poetry in high school."

"Nice." Will was secretly overjoyed. Going to the Edgar Allan Poe House in September? It was a Zetic warlock's dream.

Sage brushed her hands on her shirt. "I'm going to get changed." She hopped off the bed and grabbed her duffel. "Be right out."

Will nodded and looked back at his phone. Perfect, they'd seal that soul to the earth, take a quick trip to the museum, maybe have time to hit up a branch of the library. They could even make it back for the evening ferry. Will wasn't sure how long it took to curse a soul. Could be ten minutes, could be three hours. Spells were finicky like that.

Warlocks tended away from spell work and toward simple innate power, though he and John were a little odd for the Zetic line. There were tons of spells with books. Hell, basically every weird medieval priest journaling about chanting in Latin was either a Zetic warlock or had happened upon some Zetic warlocks and was attempting to copy their rituals. But being raised by a storm witch and a Zetic warlock meant things in their house were a little unique. His mom didn't use spells, and his dad had sort of retired from magic ten years earlier.

As Will opened up the Edgar Allan Poe House website to check on opening time, he heard Sage leave the bathroom.

"Hey, how long does it take to—" Will looked up. Sage was unwinding her braid, so slowly, picking out those strands of hair one by one. She had on a white T-shirt also. Only a white T-shirt. And it was a little see-through.

"How long does what take?" she prompted.

"I...never mind." Will's brain was short-circuiting. Sage's legs...hell. Those were some really good legs sticking out from under that T-shirt.

She slunk down and sat on the end of the bed, one knee tucked under her seat. She worked on her braid, her eyes roaming over the room. She finished with her hair, then combed it out with her fingers.

Will swallowed hard. He shifted on the bed, nervously piling the snacks on the small bedside table.

"Should I get ready for bed?" He eyed the clock. It was only nine, but Sage looked very ready for bed.

Whether she wanted to sleep or do something else, he had no idea.

She shrugged casually. "If you want." She shook her hair out a bit.

Will nodded, grabbed his bag, and took it to the bathroom.

He tried to regain some sense of calm. His soulmate was sitting on the bed they would share. No big deal.

He rifled through his bag and pulled out a pair of shorts and a T-shirt to sleep in and his toothbrush and toothpaste. He set to brushing his teeth, looking fondly at Sage's toothbrush already on the side of the sink. It was so small, but it felt like a cementing of their connection. He was on a trip with his soulmate. He was with the woman he was going to spend the rest of his life with. It was their first overnight, maybe even the first time they—

"Shit," he exclaimed through the bubbling toothpaste.

"You okay?" Sage called.

"Fine," he answered quickly. "Forgot...my...facewash."

"There's some in my bag in there if you want to borrow it," Sage said.

"Thank you."

Will shook his head. Now he needed to wash his face when in truth he forgot something completely different.

Condoms.

In his defense, he wasn't really in the sex headspace at the market this morning with his mom. And while she wasn't a prude by any means, buying a pack of condoms with his mom in tow was far beyond Will's comfort level.

He finished his teeth and washed his face, then changed into his pajamas. It was okay. He wouldn't have sex with Sage tonight in this questionable motel. It was clean-ish, but he was a pretty romantic guy. In a few years, he'd probably wish they had their first time somewhere a little nicer.

He took one last look in the mirror, then exited.

Sage had moved up the bed, her head on the pillow and her bare legs stretched out down the bed. Her T-shirt barely covered an inch of her thighs, and Will couldn't help staring.

"The face wash work out?" Sage asked.

Will nodded his head. "Yeah. Great. Thank you." He tucked his hair behind his ears and walked around to the other side of the bed. Sage wasn't under the blankets, so he lay on top of them and tried not to stare at her.

"Are you nervous about tomorrow?" he asked, hoping that their extremely dangerous mission at hand might quell a bit of the lust he was overcome with.

Sage sighed. "Not really nervous. Part of me is excited. I get to be the Bay to fuck over the warlock who murdered a bunch of my ancestors. He was a really bad guy."

"I believe it. Cursing an entire line isn't good warlock stuff."

"Yeah, beyond that though. He did it all because Eliza Bay wouldn't marry him. So basically, this is all happening because one of my ancestors wouldn't sleep with some guy. And he murdered her entire family and cast a shadow on her line over it. What a dick."

"But now you are here to bring down vengeance."

"I guess I am."

"That's stuff a badass witch does," he added.

She cracked a smile. "One step closer to becoming the badass witch I was born to be."

"Do you want me to read your cards for tomorrow?" Will asked.

Sage grumbled. "You sound like Laurel. What's going to happen is going to happen."

"True," Will countered, "but I find it helpful to focus sometimes. Look at the cards more like a guide than a fortune."

"Fine," she conceded. She moved to sit cross-legged. Will grabbed his cards out of his bag and sat across from her on the bed, shuffling them over and over again.

"So, what's your thing?" Sage asked.

"My thing?"

"Yeah. Laurel says, find the light and draw a circle around it. Do you have a mantra or whatever?"

"Hm..." Will chuckled. "I guess I do." He cleared his throat. "We seek answers in the dark."

"Huh." Sage nodded. "I actually like it."

"You do?"

"I like anything that gives reverence to the dark." She grinned. "All right. Shuffle those slivers of paper made from dead trees and see what they tell you about tomorrow."

Will took a deep breath. "We seek answers in the dark," he muttered. He shuffled four times, cut the deck four times, and laid out four cards in front of Sage. He tucked the rest back in the bag and set it behind him.

"Four cards seems like a lot?"

"Four is my number. The four elements, the four cardinal directions, the four seasons. It's a strong number." Will flipped over the first card. "Five of Swords. That makes sense. You are about to go into a sort of fight, albeit a magical one." He flipped over the second and stifled a laugh. "The Chariot. You're definitely not nervous about this fight."

"If anything, Jonas Fortworth should be nervous about me," she said dryly.

Will flipped the next one. "Hm. Three of Wands." He scrunched up his brow and ran his hand over it a few times.

"You are being quiet. Am I losing?"

"I thought you didn't hold stock in the cards? What was going to happen was going to happen and all that," he pointed out.

"Yeah, but you believe them and your face got all worried."

"I'm not worried. But you might not succeed. It's not a Ten of Swords, so I'm not worried about you being defeated, but..." He paused and thought over his words carefully. "You might not have the outcome you were hoping for."

"Oh, great. The ghosts are going to come back if I fail. They're harmless, but you saw them. More than off-putting."

Will looked at the card again. It didn't feel like failure...only like the path was veering somewhere else.

"You going to flip that last card or make me wait in suspense?" Sage moved to kneel in front of him as she leaned forward. Her loose hair fell forward and brushed against his forearm.

"The Queen of Wands." He smiled. "I think I've found you in the deck."

"What do you mean?"

"Usually, as a card reader, important people in the deck have their own cards. You're my Queen of Wands."

"And what does the Queen of Wands represent?" She raised her eyebrows slightly.

"A woman who knows herself. Who walks into a room and does as she pleases. Powerful. A hard worker. A little on the nose, but a farmer."

Sage smirked. "It does not say that."

"It does! I can get my phone and show you if you don't believe me—"

Sage leaned over the cards and grabbed him behind the neck. "I don't care. I've been waiting for you to kiss me all night."

Will grinned. "Thank the gods."

Chapter Thirteen

Sage tried to play it cool. Hell, she had on a T-shirt. She sensually played with her hair. She wasn't about to cover her legs with sunscreen before going to bed though. She drew the line there.

But listening to Will describe her as the Queen of Wands pushed her over the edge. The way he had said, "powerful." Like it didn't scare him. Like he wanted her to be the powerful one. When he talked about her like that...

There was no way she was falling asleep without kissing this man.

He grinned and pulled her body until it was flush against his. "Thank the gods," he mumbled before devouring her mouth.

All the fire that she'd been trying to hold back came forward the moment his mouth was on hers. Sage moaned against his lips, dug her hands into his hair. She'd never ever thought long hair on a guy was hot but on Will—he might as well have been the sexiest man in the universe. Hell, everything about him was scorching. The slope of his shoulders, the line of his nose, the deep dimples in his cheeks—she couldn't get enough of him.

Will pulled her to the bed and fitted his hips between her thighs while guiding her legs to wrap around him. His mouth slid off hers as he kissed the line of her jaw, the column of her neck. He nuzzled against her collarbone.

Sage pressed against him in response as a wild feeling took root in her belly. Like she'd never be sated. Never want him to let go.

Was this soulmate stuff or was kissing a hot guy in a motel bed always this delicious?

"You are amazing," he breathed. Will dove back to her neck the second the words left his lips.

"I'm just me," she mumbled. Just Sage. But right now, just Sage felt more than enough. Emboldened, she pulled at his shirt until it slipped over his head.

Okay, she thought. They were in a bed and making out, and now he had his shirt off. Don't panic. She roamed down the planes of his chest, smoothing the sprinkling of dark hair. Goddess, his skin felt amazing. Soft and warm and so damn comforting. It felt so natural, being with Will. Like this was exactly where she was supposed to be. She flushed with desire, heat spreading to all the reaches of her limbs and settling in her low belly.

His hands went to her legs as he crashed back toward her, grasping at her thighs. She moaned and all that maybe panic floating in the forefront of her brain dissipated into the atmosphere. Will was hers. She was his. This was all perfect. Meant to be. Could they have sex now? That seemed like a good plan. This was all great, but she wanted more. She wanted to be naked and him to be naked and to finally know what it was like to have sex. She wanted the connection, the binding, and yes, the elusive orgasm she'd been wanting from Will since first laying eyes on him. Sage didn't want to leave this motel room with her stupid virginity.

She pushed on his chest until he rolled to his back, then straddled Will and pulled her shirt off, tossing it on the floor.

"Oh, fuck," Will mumbled. His hands traveled from her hips to her belly to her breasts. "You are beautiful."

Sage felt her cheeks go hot. She'd never thought of herself as beautiful before. She didn't mind the way she looked, but she was just herself. Not some seductress or gorgeous woman. She was Sage.

But she was beginning to see that being Sage was exactly what Will wanted.

Will flipped her to her back again and grinned. "You mind me being on top?"

Sage giggled and shook her head as Will slowed down. He kissed her softly and cradled her face. He grazed his nose over hers and brushed her cheek with his thumb. Sage mirrored him and explored him more slowly. She cupped his shoulder, tested her nails against his skin. She kissed him behind the ear and breathed in his scent.

Will shifted to lie beside her, freeing his hand to sweep up her entire body.

"I want...I want to get you off," he mumbled before kissing her again.

"Me too," she answered quickly. "You, I mean. I want to get you off."

"Can you go first?" he asked, his hand trailing over her belly slowly. Hell, Sage's nipples were hard even without his hand on them. Hooking up with someone was so fun.

"Sure, we could also go at the same time. We could have sex," she suggested. She wasn't innocent enough to think that they would magically come at the same time—though they were soulmates, so who knew what was possible?

"Oh, um, did you bring a condom?"

Shit. "I did not."

"Neither did I. Are you on birth control? Not that you have to be, or would even be cool with sex without a condom—"

"I'm not. And I don't want to get pregnant. And even though my sister has been hounding me to track my ovulation, I don't. So, for all I know, I could be super fertile right now." It would definitely help explain the insatiable lust she was feeling.

"Yeah." Will smiled. "Let's stick to things that won't get you pregnant."

"That's a good plan," Sage agreed.

He kissed her again and moved his hand over her breasts, down her belly, and to the waistband of her underwear. Fuck, she was glad she wore black underwear. It was plain cotton, but better than one of her weird plaid pairs that she got on sale last year.

"I'm so happy I met you," Will whispered against her cheek. His hand slid beneath her underwear until he touched her.

She only nodded in response, too lost in sensation to talk at all. Will was touching her, and he was doing a damn good job. She squirmed against him and shifted her hips toward him. He was gentle, achingly gentle, but it was perfect. She peeked down at the sight of his hand lost beneath the fabric of her underwear and moaned.

This was the first time anyone had touched her there. Sure, Sage had a pretty healthy self-satisfying sex life. She wasn't about to go her life without orgasms because she hadn't found a partner yet. She had no problem getting herself to great heights.

But this. This was different. When she touched herself, it was almost clinical. She wanted to come, she did exactly what needed happen to get that done. There was no buildup or mystery. She was also rarely alone so there was usually a time crunch. No time for lollygagging around or testing new theories.

But Will...oh, that man was taking his time. He explored every inch of her lazily. His fingers moved like he had all the time in the world to bring her to the brink.

He shifted his head away from her neck and pressed insistent kisses over her breast before using his mouth on her nipple.

"Keep doing that!" Sage nearly yelled. To Will's credit, her outburst didn't have him flying across the room. She ground her hips against his hand and grabbed his biceps. Hell, she was going to come—for the first time with another person. For a moment, her brain flooded with intrusive thoughts—*what if you make a weird noise or your face screws up funny, what if it isn't sexy*—but as soon as they came in, they were gone. Will thought she was hot. Hot enough to come when she was completely dressed. She doubted whatever crazy reaction she had to coming with him would scare him away.

So, she let go. She cried out, louder than she'd thought she would have, and her legs shook harder than they usually did, but Will didn't let go of her. He didn't stop or move away—he held onto her while she coasted down the best high of her life.

When her orgasm finally subsided, Sage rolled toward Will and pressed her face against his chest. She breathed him in—he smelled like paper and her facewash. Unbelievably familiar for someone she had just met. And perfect. Goddess, she never wanted to move. She never wanted to smell anything other than Will.

"That was—" She smothered a yawn against his chest.

"Exhausting?" he joked.

"Wonderful." She snuggled against him, and her thigh hit his hard on. "Oh! I was going to get you off," she started.

"Not now," he answered.

"But you're hard."

"I am. But I'm also really enjoying holding you while you feel like you have no bones in your body." He snaked his hand around her waist and pulled her closer.

"Won't you have a hard time falling asleep if you're horny?" Try as she might, Sage couldn't conceal another yawn.

"I'll be fine." He kissed her forehead. "Let's stay like this."

Sage nodded and snuck her leg between his thighs. She couldn't remember a time in her life when she'd been so relaxed. She'd just take a little rest. Then she'd get a second wind and finally get eyes on the bulge resting against her. Even through her exhaustion, she was really excited for more. She wanted to do everything with her soulmate now. It was like the floodgates had opened, and there was no stopping them.

But for now, Sage was content to fall asleep with her face burrowed against Will's chest.

Chapter Fourteen

The morning sun filtered through a slit between the windowpane and the curtain that was slightly too small. Will rolled away from it, away from the responsibilities of the day, and toward Sage. She was still sleeping, snoring softly as she did. She must have gotten up at some time during the night because she was wearing her T-shirt again and her hair was braided.

Will brushed his hand over her cheek. Beautiful. He couldn't believe he got to wake up next to her for the rest of their lives.

Last night had been amazing. Touching her, making her come...Will was in awe. Being with Sage was like nothing he'd ever experienced. Like it was a ritual, reverent and holy.

"Good morning," he whispered, pressing a quick kiss against her temple.

Sage mumbled for a moment, then her eyes popped open.

"What time is it?" she asked, flying into a seated position.

"I don't know, maybe eight?" Will reached to the bedside table and looked at his phone. "Whoa. Nine-thirty."

"Nine-thirty!" Sage repeated. She jumped out of bed and dashed into the bathroom. A minute later, she bounded out with her toothbrush in her mouth. "We have a big day! Get going!" she shouted at him.

Will jolted up and rushed into the bathroom to start brushing his teeth.

He really had to pee, but he didn't think he and Sage were quite at the stage of peeing in front of each other. One successful hookup, however phenomenal, didn't equate suddenly being completely open with each other.

Sage finished with her teeth and took a hint, closing the bathroom door.

While Will emptied his bladder, he realized his soulmate didn't seem to be one for snuggling in the morning. Or better yet, getting naked in the morning.

Oh well. Maybe she'd calm down in the winter. Will had heard of seasonal witches having different rhythms depending on where in the calendar they were. Maybe harvest witches were like that too. If it was the case, he looked forward to spending entire weekends in bed in January.

"You ready?" she asked, throwing the rest of the snacks into her bag.

"Yeah. I'll go drop our key off." Will picked up his bag and headed to the front desk while Sage scurried to the car.

So much for a sexy morning.

It didn't matter, not really. Well, Will did want to hold Sage again and kiss her and maybe touch her a bit. But it wasn't like they didn't have the rest of their lives for all that.

Will's plane ticket back to Cleveland was floating in his mind, an invisible deadline hovering over his every move. Should he move the date? Go home for a little while and then come back? Start his job search on the East Coast? There were so many variables right now.

Sage was a harvest witch. She had a farm on Star Island and worked at the farmers' market. And while she was seriously rooted there, it would be nearly impossible for him to find a job there. Maybe she would be cool with moving back to Ohio. There were lots of farms there. Not that he could afford a farm. He was living in his parents' basement. And she lived in an ancestral home. Witches weren't the type of people to abandon their ancestral homes.

But...he was a Zetic warlock. He didn't think he'd be content long term to work in a different field. It would be like asking Sage to get a job at a restaurant.

"Ready?" Sage asked, breaking him out of his spiral.

"Yup." He got into the passenger side and tried to shake off the dread of being completely unsettled in life at the moment of meeting his soulmate.

As Sage climbed into the driver's seat, something fluttered off her back and onto the ground.

"You dropped something," Will mentioned, pointing toward her feet. Sage crouched in her seat and revealed...

A tarot card.

"What the fuck? Not again," she moaned.

"Again?" Will asked.

Sage grimaced. "I had one stuck to my butt right after we met. Two of Cups. Seemed self-explanatory, what with the two people gazing in each other's eyes." She played with the new one between her forefinger and thumb.

"Which card is that one?"

Sage handed it over. "Five of Cups."

Will winced.

"Well, that face makes me think it's something bad." Sage snorted. She buckled her seat belt and looked over her directions before pulling out of the parking lot. "Give it to me straight, psychic."

"It's not bad. No cards are innately bad," Will started.

"Yeah, but I'm guessing it doesn't mean success. I mean, look at it. A bunch of knocked-over cups all over the ground."

"Disappointment," Will conceded.

"Well, shit. What the hell is going to happen today? Your cards are definitely trying to prepare us for some bad shit."

"At least it isn't a danger card. Disappointment is definitely better than, say walking into a trap."

"Are there cards that would say that? That's really specific."

"Eh, it would have to be more than a one-card draw." He tried to stay positive. Will was still completely in the dark as to what Sage was going to do when it came to the spell. Would there be blood? Maybe. A lot of spells had to do with blood, especially those of a sinister nature like binding a soul to their grave.

"No use focusing on these cards. It's about ten minutes to the field where Jonas Fortworth is buried. Let's get there, get his soul bound to the earth, and get on the road." She shook out her shoulders. "We have three angry ghosts to appease and a museum to visit."

By all accounts, the field where Jonas Fortworth was buried looked completely normal. There were a few bundles of trees growing on top of one another, some shrubs, and a footpath that disappeared into the denser woods. It didn't look like a place that contained the corpse of an evil warlock.

"Shit," Sage breathed the second she got out of the car.

"What?" Will asked, stepping out himself. The wind stirred through his hair, and the scent of the place—dry leaves and the slight sweetness of the warm air—surrounded him. Then realization washed over him, and he looked at Sage.

"I've been here before," she admitted.

"Me too."

"But not as Sage Bay," she added.

"When we were different people." Will could feel it too. A deep remembrance of a place he'd never been, in a time he didn't know. It felt nostalgic in a way that didn't make sense. It bombarded him all at once. He could smell open fires, fresh animal skins, the stink of fruit about to turn. His breath quickened, and his heart thumped against his chest. It was a wild feeling —like the edge of a panic attack—being somewhere that felt so out of time.

"We lived here, I think." He looked over the land and closed his eyes. His psychic abilities had never been tested in terms of the past, and there was nothing to latch on to. None of the trees here looked more than one hundred years old, and there were no structures to grab hold of. Maybe the soil was enough? If Sage had been a harvest witch before, their magic might be mingled within the earth still.

"Come here for a second," he said as he knelt on the ground.

She sat beside him, one eyebrow ticked up as he wove his fingers through hers and set his other palm on the earth.

Will breathed in and tried to find something in the earth or on the wind, something he could trace back...

A single thread of smoke out of a chimney. A warm fire with a strong woman. A full apple tree. Standing together as the sun set.

"We did live here," Will confirmed.

"Hm. We lived where Jonas Fortworth is buried. That feels..."

"Problematic?"

"I was going to say important. But probably disastrous." Sage sighed. "Let's see if we can find his grave."

"Do you think it's marked?"

"Nope. But if I had anything to do with his death, which is feeling likely, I think I'll be able to tell where it is."

Will nodded and stood next to her.

"Do you think you were a Bay before?" he asked as they walked through the field.

She shrugged. "Maybe? None of my sisters were. As far as I know, Jonas never found any of the Bays in North America. I thought we were all in Massachusetts and New York." Sage rubbed her hand over her forehead. "You know, this really sucks. I don't mind sealing a soul to this earth. Fine, whatever. But being embroiled in all of this...drama." She grimaced. "I cannot imagine any rendition of me getting involved in the cattiness level my sisters stooped to in past lives."

"Cattiness?"

"Laurel had this weird thing with Morana Stoch. They were both witches and Morana got Laurel executed so she cursed her over multiple lifetimes. Rosemary and Verbena both got in trouble because of their good looks and general sex appeal. Neither of those feel like my vibe."

Will shrugged. "Maybe it was a property dispute?"

Sage laughed. "Maybe. I do get pissed when people touch my plants without asking." She furrowed her brow. "He's over there." She pointed to a monstrous oak tree on the edge of the field. "It's like a string is pulling me to him."

Will followed Sage as she walked with purpose, though he felt no pull toward the final resting place of Jonas Fortworth. He had no bad feelings about this place either. Only a warm nostalgia. He breathed in the air and thought, *this is a good place.*

It was odd. If Jonas Fortworth, curser and murderer of witches, had been a part of his and Sage's past life, why wouldn't Will feel some of his animosity? He doubted the three of them were buddies in this past life.

"What if we lived here after or before he was here?" Will suddenly said. "What if our timeline didn't line up with his?"

"That sounds like an insane coincidence." Sage exhaled.

"Or fate? Maybe the land is what's important, or magical. And we don't have any connection with him other than a shared space hundreds of years apart."

"We'll see," Sage answered. She walked in front of the tree and stopped. "Fuck."

"What now?"

"He's not here."

"What do you mean?"

"His body—skeleton at this point—is here, under my feet, but his soul is gone. He's not in here anymore." Sage rubbed her temples. "The ghosts are going to be so pissed."

"Are you sure? How can you tell?"

"I don't know how to explain it. It feels empty. Like I'm standing next to an empty pool. The structure is there, but the important stuff is all gone. Fuck." Sage tapped her teeth together. "I'm connected to this asshole. Our souls are. Why else would I know this? It's as simple as knowing that it's a sunny day. The sun is shining, and Jonas Fortworth's soul has moved on." She grimaced. "I've been to graveyards before. Never felt like this. Damn it. I don't want to be connected to a curser of witches."

"Do you..." Will paused for a second. He didn't want to speak out something and make it true, but he had a feeling there would be no such luck. "Do you think he's alive right now?"

"I'm ninety-nine percent sure he's alive right now. And I think I know who he is."

Chapter Fifteen

Fucking Jonas Fortworth was fucking alive, and Sage couldn't help but seethe.

Of course that absolute asshole was walking the earth while the three witches he murdered were suspended in some sort of purgatory waiting for their souls to get another go at life.

Fate sucked.

At the moment, all Sage could think about was tracking down this version of Jonas Fortworth and punching him in the face.

Instead, she was standing next to her soulmate as he gesticulated wildly about Edgar Allan Poe.

She had to admit, while there was a lot on her mind, seeing how into this museum he was...it was pretty intriguing. There was something crazy attractive about how passionate he was talking about this dead writer, and Sage didn't hate it.

Will was dressed more relaxed than the first time she'd seen him, thank goddess. Not that there was anything wrong with tweed and suits, but there was no way Sage was going to match that kind of formality. Today, he wore a pair of dark jeans and a dark green button-up with the sleeves rolled up his forearms. Sage had on a pair of beat-to-hell jeans and a flannel, so they sort of looked like they went together.

But, in this moment, Sage started to feel something more for Will. He was surrounded by history, and his enthusiasm for it came off him like flames. Her heart thumped wildly as she watched him, not really understanding what he was talking about other than his love for the subject.

When Sage took a minute to think about it, it blew her mind. This man, standing next to her waxing poetically about *The Murders in the Rue Morgue* was her person for the rest of her life. He was it for her, the love of her life as decreed by fate. If she ever got knocked up accidentally, this would be the guy who did it. He would take care of her, and she would take care of him, and they'd live happily ever after this life or be fucked by the Stochs and try it again in another life. She was currently staring at her future.

It hit her like a wave of bricks. Sage felt like she was going to throw up.

"I need some air," she said quickly, then bolted out of the museum before Will could say anything.

She burst through the door onto the street and gulped down air.

Will was the guy she was going to be with for the rest of her life.

Fuck.

Sage was twenty-four. She didn't relish anything that started with "the rest of her life." She had done basically nothing with her life. No traveling, no college, no starter dating other than the disaster that was high school. She'd never smoked a cigarette or had a one-night stand. She had never even been fiscally irresponsible. With Will's appearance, she felt like her young adulthood was over and she was thrust into "ever after."

Sage's soulmate had arrived. It was time to settle down. But she had never been unsettled.

"Fuck," she breathed, this time audibly. If she had known her soulmate was coming so early...

She would have what? Not been a farmer? She was a harvest witch. That was like fighting fate. She couldn't have left her fields to travel even if it had been a dream. They were a part of her. And who the hell was she supposed to date on Star Island? None of the guys or girls she had met before had interested her to that point. Plus, Sage didn't really like talking to people for the hell of it. Dating sounded like torture. But still, meeting her soulmate at twenty-four...goddess. It was a lot to take in.

And she missed her plants. It was like an ache that she was so far away from them during the most important season. Ugh, she wanted to go home.

Will pushed through the door and jogged over to her side.

"Are you okay?"

"Yeah. Just...overwhelmed," she admitted.

"The master of horror too much for you?" He smiled.

She snorted. "If only he knew how haunted this country really was."

"You want to go?"

"We don't have to. You really wanted to go to a museum while we were here," Sage began.

"Yesterday. I really wanted to go to a museum yesterday when I thought at this point the soul-sealing or whatever would be complete. But you have to go disappoint three ghosts. And Jonas Fortworth might be running around reincarnated."

"I don't think there's any might about it. Fate has been pushing my sisters and I around for months. He's here, he's on his way to Star Island, and I've got a strong feeling he wants to finish what he started when he killed my ancestors."

"Want to hit the road?" Will asked. "We won't make the evening ferry, but at least we'll grab the morning one tomorrow."

Sage nodded. "Yeah. I can't help but feeling like...Jonas is coming for me. Just like Morana came for Laurel, and Ivan came for Rosemary, and Boris came for Verbena. We were connected in that life, I can feel it. And knowing me, I might have murdered him. Or at the very least did something that led to his death. I don't want my sisters getting hurt over something I did in the past. Plus, I really need to get home to the farm. There's so much to do."

Will nodded. "I'll get the car."

"Hey, Will?" Sage called. He stopped and turned around to face her. "Thanks for coming. This would have been a lot harder without you."

Sage was more relaxed around Will on this leg of the car trip, but her stomach was doing some annoying flips thinking about what was to come.

She was scared. Hell, Sage Bay did not get scared. She spit in the face of ghosts, evil warlocks, and generational curses.

But not knowing who Jonas Fortworth might be, what he looked like, if he was already on Star Island going after her sisters had her swimming in anxiety. Lavender had shown her a picture of Miloslav Stoch, but it didn't stir anything in her memory. A small part of her held out hope that they weren't the same soul. But she didn't know whether she would recognize a memory of a picture. Laurel didn't know who Morana was until after she'd seen her past life. Maybe Sage wouldn't have recognized Jonas Fortworth, even if she stared at his mug shot.

Sage: Are you okay?

Rosemary: Yes and HOW DARE YOU begin a text like that?! How was last night? TELL ME EVERYTHING.

Sage: It was good. Are Laurel/Verbena/Lavender okay? All Bays accounted for?

Rosemary: ...as far as I know. Lavender is working today, Laurel is probably still sleeping, and I think Verbena is fine. What's going on? Did something happen with the binding?

Sage tossed back in her mind whether or not to tell Rosemary everything that had happened this morning. It would make her worry. But she also didn't want to keep anything from her sister. So she settled for the truth followed by a whiplash distraction.

Sage: Just normal Stoch shit. Still being pains in the ass. Make sure everyone is vigilant. Fight isn't magically over. I hooked up with Will last night.

Rosemary: SAGE!!!! Lead with that!! How was it?

Sage: It was really nice. And I slept in today which seems insane.

Rosemary: HA! Finally, someone can orgasm Sage Bay into a late morning. I'm happy for you guys. Soulmate sex is so much fun! Go back to driving. Be safe. I'm not there to shower you with condoms so hit a up a pharmacy. Once you get home, the table next to the front door has a pack of fifty in it. They're all yours.

Sage chuckled.

"One of your sisters?" Will asked, reaching for a chip as he drove.

"Rosemary. She let me know there are fifty condoms at home, and we can have them."

Will coughed very hard, and covered his mouth so chewed-up chips didn't go flying.

"Sorry," he mumbled.

"No worries. Rosemary is really into sex magic so she's very open about all this stuff. Your family not like that?"

"I mean, not really. John and Cate did have a traditional witch-warlock wedding and went and had sex in the woods during the reception, which was a little weird as the best man, but it wasn't, like, in front of us. They were far enough away that we couldn't even hear them."

"I'm just going to lay it out there: I'm never going to want to have sex in front of anyone."

"Good." He laughed. "Me neither."

It wasn't like Sage wanted a traditional magical wedding. Hell, she wasn't sure she ever wanted any kind of wedding. What was the point of a piece of paper saying you were together forever or until divorce? Be together. That was the whole point. She didn't need the Commonwealth of Massachusetts to sign off on a relationship.

Ugh, were Rosemary and Asher going to have a traditional magical wedding? She could totally see Rosemary insisting they all wore nothing but plants and everyone went and fucked their soulmate in the woods somewhere.

That was fine. If it came to that, she and Will could take the house. And lock the door.

None of her sisters had gotten married yet, though three were currently shacking up with their soulmates. Was Will going to want to move in with her? She wasn't sure how Lavender would feel about that. But it would be hard for her not to live in the Bay cottage. Her entire farm was in the backyard. She worked out there twelve hours a day in the summer. Commuting even from Solaris would be a pain in the ass. Plus...eventually soulmates moved in together, right? Damn it, she did not feel prepared for this level of commitment at age twenty-four.

Oh, my goddess, what if Will wanted her to move to Ohio? She could not live in Ohio. At least, not again. She loved Star Island. It had her farm, her sisters, and everyone in the world she knew. Oh hell, what if he wanted to move to a city? All those damn old libraries and books and shit. He probably wanted to live in New York City. Sage could never. Not unless she got an ordinance from the city to turn Central Park into a working farm. A balcony garden would never work for her.

She shook out her hands. Did she even want to live with Will? Hell, she still felt like she barely knew him. Yes, she was attracted to him and sometimes he said things that made her legs feel like jelly and her heart get all warm and confusing. Did she want to feel like that all the time?

Maybe it would be okay...or maybe she wasn't actually ready for any of that. Why did he have to come this year? This all would have been much more convenient when she was...twenty-seven. Twenty-seven seemed like an age when most people had their shit together. Though Laurel was twenty-nine when Owen showed up last May and she most definitely did not have her shit together. Maybe Sage was like Laurel and would never actually feel like an adult ready to make adult-level decisions.

She checked the GPS; they still had three more hours until they got to Chatham where the closest motel to the ferry port was. She needed to get her spiraling under control. Right now, Sage had to be focused on Jonas Fortworth in this life. Not where she and Will would live if they managed to survive the next couple of months.

Break the curse. Get the Stochs off their backs. Only then could Sage allow herself to spiral about being soulmates with a city dweller.

But for now, they needed to get back to Massachusetts.

Chapter Sixteen

The drive back to Massachusetts was pleasantly quiet. As they traveled north, the trees put on a show, a mere taste of what was coming this autumn. Will loved that he and Sage were already comfortable enough to let periods of silence pass by without panicking and needing to fill the void.

They stayed in a dingy motel, so much so that neither of them wanted to get naked on the clearly well-used and unwashed bed and left the moment they woke up. After they returned to Star Island, Sage dropped him off with a quick kiss.

"You are allowed to text me now. I will answer," Sage said as she pulled back.

"Really?"

"Yes. Don't be weird. I have to catch my sisters up on everything. And check my plants. I'll come pick you up...in three hours? Is that enough time for you to hang out with your family on this family vacation?"

"No one in my family expects me to hang out with them now that you are here. But I could use a shower. And fresh clothes. Three hours is good."

He leaned in and gave her another quick peck. "I'll be counting the minutes."

Sage rolled her eyes. "It's three hours. I know I'm irresistible, but you'll be fine." She smothered a smile.

Will waved from the front step, then took a seat. He needed a plan before he was hounded with family questions.

How much should he tell his mother? Probably not that there was a generational curse on his soulmate's family. She'd only worry. Not about the ghosts either. That could lead to the curse. Or the Stochs. And he had never been one to share personal relationship stuff with anyone in his family. Not even John.

When it came to the future...Will wasn't sure. Could he really see himself living in Boston and doing long distance with his soulmate? That didn't seem feasible. But he needed a library or a museum for his skill set. As far as he could tell, the Star Island Public Library was a solitary storefront with two librarians. He doubted they also needed someone who concentrated on special collections.

But what was the alternative? Ask Sage to leave this island, her home, her farm, her sisters, and live in a city? She was a harvest witch. It was probably contrary to the fibers of her being.

He sighed. It would be nice if the fates considered jobs and such when putting soulmates together. He looked at his phone to see if he miraculously had an alert for a virtual special collections librarian position, but there was no such luck.

"Will?" his mom called from inside. "Is that you on the porch?"

"It's me," he called back and stood. He walked into the house, talking the entire time. "I'm only here to shower and change my clothes and maybe pack a bag to hang with Sage tonight."

His mom's mouth trembled. "Oh, my goddess. Are you staying here? On Star Island? What about Mabon? You were supposed to celebrate with the family."

"John and Cate aren't coming," he pointed out.

"Yes, which is why I thought you would be there. Oh, my baby is leaving me!" She pulled him into a tight hug. "I knew it would happen eventually, but I still don't feel ready."

"Mom, I already moved to Chicago once. And Michigan for many years."

"Yes, but that wasn't permanent! I always hoped you'd come back to Ohio and..."

"Kel, let him be," his dad interrupted. "Go take a shower. Pack a bag. Then sit and have lunch with us before you go."

Will nodded.

He disappeared into the bathroom and stared in the mirror.

Damn, he missed Sage.

Exactly two and a half hours later, Will heard his mom exclaim and start talking to someone. He wandered out of the kitchen and found...

Sage.

"What are you doing here?" he exclaimed. "Not that you can't be here, but you're early."

"I am." Sage was holding a large woven basket with a cloth napkin covering whatever was in there. She turned to his mom. "I am sorry for how I acted when I met you before. I was caught off guard. I thought you might enjoy some fresh produce while you are on the island." Sage handed his mom the basket.

"You are so sweet!" his mom gushed. She carried the basket to the kitchen. "Come in, come in! I can make us some tea before the two of you leave."

Will threw a smile to Sage as he fell beside her. "That was nice."

"When I'm wrong, I'm wrong. Plus, I have some of the best produce in the country. Why wouldn't I try to impress your mom with it?"

"Good point."

"Sage, would you like Earl Gray, chamomile, or lemon? Sorry it's bare bones. At home, I'd be able to offer you at least thirty different varieties of tea," his mom called from the kitchen.

"Lemon would be great, thank you." Will followed as Sage sat at the counter like having tea with his mom was something she did all the time.

"I'm just dying to see what's in here," his mom raved as she pulled the napkin off the basket. "Oh my word. Apples, eggplant, kale, tomatoes...are those figs? And what are these?"

"Sweet potato bars. Which technically, my sister made. But I grew the sweet potatoes, so I sort of helped."

"Everything looks amazing. Oh, I am so excited to cook tonight! I'm going to have one of these bars with my tea, would you both like one as well?"

"Yeah," Will answered quickly.

His mom got out teacups and small plates and set everything up for the three of them to sit together.

"I'm sorry Larry and Cate aren't here to meet you, but my husband took the grandkids to the park, and I told Cate to go get her haircut. I know once this third baby arrives she won't have any time to herself for months."

"It's okay, Mom. It's nice that it's just us."

"Yes," she reiterated. "It really is."

A half hour later with a freshly packed bag in his hand, Will climbed back into Sage's car.

"I really appreciate that," Will said the moment they were alone. "And I know my mom does too."

"Your mom is awesome. Doesn't seem to love that I live outside of Ohio, but I can't be perfect."

"Ha. She'll get over it. Especially after she eats all the food you brought her."

"It was a nice touch, wasn't it?" Sage smiled. "So, not to put a damper on this post successful meeting of a parent glow, but a lot happened when I went home," Sage began as she pulled away from the rental house, "and it's going to be one of those times I'm really thankful you're magical because I can just tell you and you'll understand."

"Okay..." Will answered slowly. "What do you need to tell me?"

"My sister Lavender thinks we should do a past life spell to see exactly how we're connected to Jonas Fortworth and also, so we know what he looks like. In case he shows up. When Ivan Stoch came, Rosemary and Asher hadn't done their past life spell yet, so Asher didn't recognize him right away. And the first time Laurel met Morana, Morana knew who she was, but she didn't know her. Verbena was a bit more complicated because it was the voice of a ghost rather than a person—"

"Please stop, you are making me more nervous." Will took a deep breath. "How does the past life spell work?"

"We eat some bread, we pass out for twenty-four hours, we wake up knowing exactly what happened in our most important past life. And apparently what it feels like to die in the exact matter we died in our past life."

Will grimaced. "Are your sisters all with warlocks?"

"Nope. Verbena is with a human. Rosemary is with a Guardian. Laurel is a with a sonofawitch."

"Rosemary is with a Guardian? I thought those were myths."

"I know! Asher is one. I didn't see it happen, but he blocked a bunch of metal shit from hitting Rosemary, and it totally should have killed them both but didn't. Crazy magic shit."

"Holy crap." Will had read about Guardians several times but assumed they had died out or never existed in the first place. They were far from loud in the magical community. "Must have sucked explaining all this to the human."

"Luke took it in stride." Sage turned onto the main drag to take them to the Vega peninsula. "So, everyone is at the Bay Cottage right now getting ready. And in some sort of male ritual, the men would like to meet you."

"The men?"

"My sister's soulmates. Well, not Lavender's because it looks like she's last in line. I'd say they want to welcome you to the family, but I assume there is a hint of fragile masculinity trying to 'protect' the youngest Bay." Sage pulled a face. "As if I couldn't protect myself. Either way. Today, you'll meet my family."

Will nodded. Not exactly what he had in mind. He'd thought maybe they'd let the ghosts down easy, have a nice dinner together, try out one of those fifty condoms in her house.

Not tonight.

"I realize this is probably not how you were hoping to spend your vacation."

Will huffed a laugh. "I thought we'd go back to your place, you'd show me your farm, maybe show me your bedroom."

"We can do both of those things. Especially the farm part. The bedroom part...my entire family is in the house."

"Let's shelve the bedroom part for when I don't have to think about your sisters hearing us."

"Thanks. The walls are paper thin in there."

"Give me the past life rundown," he said, changing the subject. "We're out for twenty-four hours? Are we going to piss ourselves?"

"So far, no one has pissed their pants but there is a first time for everything. I promise not to judge if you piss yourself if you extend the same courtesy."

"Done. And we know exactly how it feels to die? Yikes."

"Laurel was burned alive. Rosemary poisoned herself and Verbena died in childbirth."

"Shit."

"Yeah. Plus, Owen was beaten to death, Asher took an axe to the chest, and Luke was killed in battle. I think via sword."

Will's eyes went wide. He'd always been very thankful he hadn't lived in a time when battle was compulsory. He wasn't a fighter. Even as a child, roughhousing was beyond his scope of comfort. His brother, on the other hand, had excelled at roughhousing and rode that high right to a college football scholarship.

"I can't wait to see how I died. I hope it's gruesome."

"You *hope* you died terribly?" Who was this woman the fates had picked out for him?

"I hope I died for something. Protecting something. Or punishing someone. Doing something important for the greater good of the world."

Whoa. Will had never thought about it like that. How dying could really mean something and be more than just a tragedy.

"I better not be wailing in childbirth when I left this earth." She shook her head. "That would be disappointing."

"I'd like to preemptively apologize if I knocked you up in ancient times and delivering a baby killed you."

"Apology accepted. And I'd like to preemptively apologize if I got you involved in something that killed us both. Which seems likely."

Will cracked a smile.

Sage turned into the driveway of her cottage. Will hadn't been there since their fateful first meeting, and there was something calming knowing he wasn't going to embarrass himself tonight. Not unless he did something really shitty to her in a past life. He might not be walking in to spend the night between her thighs or even make out with her until they both fell asleep, but he was still getting to spend time with Sage. That's what he wanted. So, they were going to eat some bread that made them hallucinate. He could handle it. He was with a witch, after all. Date nights were probably going to be pretty weird from here on out.

She put the car in park and turned to him.

"Want to see the farm first?"

He grinned. "Let's go, Harvester." After less than a week of knowing Sage, seeing her farm felt akin to peeking inside her soul.

He was ready.

Chapter Seventeen

Will followed Sage around the side of the house, through Rosemary's gardens and the herb garden, and to the far reaches of the property. While it wasn't explicitly Sage's, when she took the white stone path to *her* fields, she felt like she was walking into her own little world.

Twelve apple trees, six pear trees, three cherry trees, a solitary peach tree, and one plum tree greeted anyone visiting her little farm. Right now, the apple trees were heavy, and she absentmindedly grabbed a discarded basket and plucked a few from the branches.

Most of her pears had been picked in August this year—it was an early year for pears—but there were three new ones she'd missed this morning and added to the basket.

"These are my fruit trees," she finally said. "All somewhat native to the island, but no one can get peaches like I can. For obvious reasons." She threw a look over at Will. His mouth was slightly agape as he looked over her orchard.

"These are gorgeous," he said quietly. "Can you really grow anything?"

She shrugged. "Honestly, I haven't tried citrus. Because if it was successful, I'd have a bunch of scientists banging down my door to figure out my secret. I have a small clementine tree in my bedroom, but that's it."

"It's so peaceful out here."

"It is. It's my favorite thing about being a harvest witch. I'm out here, every day, just me and my plants and the soil and the sun. It's almost like I become part of the process, you know? Like this apple tree needs soil, sunlight, water, and me. I'm just another ingredient."

Sage had never let herself speak so vulnerably with another person about her calling.

"You're amazing," Will said simply, almost as if it was an indisputable fact. "Show me more."

With a swelling heart, Sage walked him through the rows of zucchini, squash, and pumpkins. She showed him where she had pulled up the yellow summer squash, so the butternut had more room to spread out. He marveled at the varying sizes of pumpkins on the vine, each a little oranger than the one before. She picked a few more tomatoes and an eggplant that had been hidden when she'd come out earlier. That was the hard thing about September. An hour after going over the yard with a fine-tooth comb, there would be a new fruit or vegetable ready to go.

"Do you ever think about writing a book about being a harvest witch?" Will asked.

Sage felt her face go warm. "I'm...not a writer. I don't think I ever got higher than a C on a Lit paper in high school."

Will shrugged. "Might be worth thinking about. You clearly know a lot about your field. Maybe in fifty years, there will be a whole new batch of harvest witches who need your expertise."

"All right. Stop complimenting me. Let's go meet my family."

The welcoming committee was a bit much.

Sitting at the dining table, like a group of familial vultures ready to descend, Sage's sisters and their soulmates stared at her and Will. Like a ceremonial idol, the loaf of half-eaten past life bread was displayed on one of Lavender's favorite decorative plates with swirls of fall leaves adorning the edges.

"What's up?" Sage said dryly. "You all going to watch us delve into the past or something?"

"Of course not!" Rosemary answered quickly. She stood, causing Asher to stand, and then everyone followed like they were about to rush her and Will.

"We wanted to meet Will before it started," Lavender supplied. "Hi, Will."

"I've met Will," Laurel interrupted. "But Owen wanted to."

"Welcome to the family," Owen said and shook Will's hand.

"I heard you were beaten to death," Will said. Sage chuckled.

"True. Wasn't great." Owen grinned.

Everyone took their time introducing themselves to Will. Asher, Luke, and Verbena shook his hand, Rosemary and Laurel gave him a hug, and Lavender gave him a stern nod from her place at the head of the table.

He slipped into her life perfectly in that moment. It wasn't like he was suddenly best friends with everyone, but she could see him there, see him as part of the future. A new member of the family, a place at the table on Yule —Will was now a part of it all.

"I thought you'd like to use the attic," Lavender said. "There are pillows set up there." She handed them the plate with the bread. "You can have the rest."

"Don't you need some?" Sage prompted.

Lavender shook her head. "I did this spell in my sophomore dorm room. I'm good. I've seen all I need to see." She paused. "Also, I could always make more. It only takes me a couple hours."

"Okay then. We'll see you all later." Sage looked around the room. "Are you planning to sit around and wait for twenty-four hours?"

"I have a client tonight," Laurel said immediately.

"A shift at the florist," Rosemary added.

"A final walkthrough," Verbena laughed.

"A bar to run," Luke said.

"I'll be here," Lavender added firmly. "In case you need me."

"Thanks, Lav. Well, can't wait to tell all of you how we died." She looked at Will. "Let's go upstairs."

Will followed her up the main stairs, into her bedroom, through the closet, and into the attic. It was a bit stuffy up there—no central air in the late seventeen-hundreds when the house was built. There was a nice pile of oversized pillows, two blankets, and two water bottles set out on the floor.

Will wandered over toward the pillows. "Your sisters all have huge soulmates. What are they, all over six-three?"

"Maybe," Sage answered. "I've never been overly obsessed with height."

"Thank the gods," Will muttered.

Sage looked at her soulmate, his disheveled hair and wide smile. He was perfect. He wasn't much taller than her, maybe an inch, and wasn't much wider than her either. He looked like the ideal man to her. Match that with his passion about books and she was set.

"Let's get comfy." Sage collapsed on the pillows with Will close behind.

"Kiss for good luck?" he teased.

She smirked and gave him a quick peck, then broke off a corner of the bread for each of them. She lifted hers up toward him. "Cheers."

"Cheers."

"Here's to figuring out why the hell I feel connected to Jonas Fortworth."

Chapter Eighteen

The First Time

The wind changed.

Deep cold would come soon, on the backs of the wolves who loved the dark, bitter moons. The days grew shorter with every moment, like a warning in the night sky. The stars shouted at him *turn back!* But there was nowhere to return to. The dark times were coming, and they were alone in the world.

They walked away from Cneo, their old lives quickly buried under the failing light of the sun. And with that first darkness, they were truly tribeless.

She kept her face high, her determination unmatched. She would not apologize for what she did, and he placed no blame on her. That one had tried to hurt her, so she had killed him. He had tried to take something she didn't offer, and he deserved that fate. She was banished for her crime, and he would never leave her side.

They walked for hours, even past the sun's disappearance. They walked until the hills were no longer familiar, until the calls of the birds sounded foreign. Finally, she collapsed on the ground and pulled him beside her. He wrapped his arms over her, trying to eke out some warmth, but none would be had. When the sky was so dark it could have swallowed them whole, sleep finally settled over them.

She did not ask for him to come.

Her banishment she understood. She took a life, and hers was now left up to the gods. The sun and water and the one who whispered in the night—they would decide whether she lived or died on this new land.

But when he followed, that was her true punishment. She knew death would stalk them down their path, like a shadow they could not escape, with the cold nights closing in. Already there was frost on the earth this morning. Without the great fire to keep them warm and keep the beasts away, what chance did they have?

He didn't speak of this new life, didn't admonish her for her act. He only worked, day and night. Gathering dry wood and trying to start a fire. It was painstakingly hard, what with everything damp. It usually caught, but by morning the wicked wind would have put it out. They were too tired to stay awake all night and stoke the flames into surviving. Sleep was their only comfort. How could they give it up?

Death had already settled into their bones. They caught rodents and roasted their measly forms over the fire at night. They were too far from the lake—the constant food source they'd depended on all their lives was lost to the past. Plus, the fish were already diving deep for the cold moons. Even if they found a new lake, or the allusive sea, there'd be nothing to pry out of the water this late in the season.

It was part of the punishment, being sent toward the setting sun. There was nothing to the west.

Now, she could feel her ribs, one by one, poking against her skin. They threatened to puncture little holes along her sides with every day without food. She dreamed of eating every night. Of fish blackened over flames, of the berries she had saved all summer long. She fantasied of salted meat and hearty greens boiled with bones, of licking her bowl clean.

They should be going into the cold moons fat, not on the verge of starvation.

And now he would starve with her.

What a waste of a strong, good man. One who never took something that wasn't offered. Never took more food than his fair share.

Never grabbed her and forced her to the ground.

It wasn't fair for her to claim him as hers, yet she did. She looked into his eyes and thought, that man is for me. He is my spark of light on this miserable earth. A bit of warmth on the coldest nights.

Two moons after banishment, the snows came. There was no softness in their falling this season. They were like heavy blankets over the earth, wet and suffocating. They ate less and less now. Lucky to find a few tracks in the morning and come upon a skinny mouse to share beside a dying fire.

Though his belly twisted in hunger and his toes were blackened and his vision clouded whenever he stood, he would not have changed his decision for anything. He was with her, and if that meant they lived out their few days left in pain, at least they were together.

A wolf came that night, growling in the darkness. They were easy prey now, two bags of bones with little strength to fight. They each grabbed sticks from the fire, the tips flaming, and shouted at the wolf, thrusting the burning wood in its direction. They fought it through the night until the sun rose, and the wolf padded into the distance, then collapsed still in eyesight.

It meant to wait them out.

He looked at her.

They needed to move while the wolf slept.

They carried their sticks with smoking embers and walked as quickly as their legs could manage away from the wolf. They stumbled over the icy landscape. The blackened skin that had begun on her toes now traveled toward her ankles. She hadn't felt anything on her feet for days now. She knew they would soon be too damaged to move, no matter what her legs commanded. When night finally came again, they slumped to the earth. There was no strength left to make a fire. There would be no strength left to fight the wolf if it returned.

She rolled to her side and pressed her face against his chest. He patted her hair, matted with dirt and dusted with frost.

They had done all they could.

The sky was clear that night. Stars blinking in the far distance, and he thought to himself, I will see her again. There will be another chance for us.

She breathed in his scent one last time. *Find me again.*

Chapter Nineteen

The Second Time

Once flesh is rotted and bones are turned to ash and all of a life is swept away from the rocky earth, the goddesses knit us back together into small, wrinkly babes to be delivered into the world once again.

Callistrate wrapped her hand around the straw broom in the corner and set to her work for the morning. The sun still slept, though the moon had already disappeared from the sky. She made her way from her sleeping quarters to the temple as silently as possible. If the elder priestesses were woken before sunrise, namely Artemesia, Callistrate would have foul moods to endure all day.

She crept into the temple, slipping her shoes off at the entrance, and bowed her head quickly toward the statue of Nemesis, her divine patron. Then, she got to work.

As the youngest priestess at Rhamnous, most of the tedious tasks were allotted to Callistrate. She swept every morning, clearing away anything visitors from the previous day might have discarded. She sat with grieving families calling out for vengeance. She attended prayers but did not lead them. Her life was quiet one.

Ten years earlier, her mother had brought her to the temples of Nemesis and Themis under the guise that they were there to pray for vengeance after her father's murder. It was a messy thing in her memory, mostly filled with screams in the darkness, men in their home who shouldn't have been there. Callistrate had been forced into a cupboard while they ransacked the house. She'd stuck her fingers in her ears to block out the screaming.

When she was finally pulled out of the darkness by her mother, so much time had passed, she'd pissed herself twice. Their house was destroyed, her father was dead, and they left that day for Rhamnous.

When they reached the temple, the priestesses were kind, listening to her mother as she wept, while another kept Callistrate occupied in prayers to The Daughter of Night. They spent the day in the glorious temple, with its cool floors and flood of worshippers.

She remembered when Artemesia had taken her by the hand and led her out of the temple, away from her mother and the crowds. There had been food then. Bowls of olive oil so golden and crispy bread. A plate of figs she did not have to share. Roasted lamb with fat slices of tomato. Callistrate had never eaten so well. She gorged herself on the feast, until her eyelids became heavy and Artemesia led her to a bed that was not her own.

When she woke, her mother was gone and Callistrate belonged to Nemesis.

After Callistrate called out for her own vengeance and screamed at the sky over her abandonment, Artemesia had taken her in with a gruff kindness. Her role was clear: Callistrate would work for the priestesses until she was old enough to become one. She scrubbed floors. She swept ash. She cleaned the dishes the priestesses ate off. When women traveled miles to the temple, sometimes barefoot, Callistrate washed their hands and feet, braided their hair, fed those weary travelers. Until one day when it came time to light the sacred fires for prayers, and Artemesia handed her the smoking stick and allowed her to complete the ritual.

In that moment, Callistrate became a true priestess of Nemesis, The Inescapable.

The promotion from servant to priestess had been a welcome one. She no longer scrubbed out pots or plucked feathers from chickens for meals or cleaned up the vomit that always seemed to land precisely at the entrance of the temple. Now, Callistrate was a dignified priestess of Nemesis. Even if it still required a lot of sweeping.

She finished her morning chores, then headed back to their quarters for breakfast. The other women—Artemesia, Zosime, Tyche, and Nicaea—had already begun the morning meal, a hearty barley bread with olives and wine. Callistrate's stomach groaned loudly, but she took her time. After years of having her hand slapped for grabbing, she'd been conditioned into proper meal etiquette.

"Join us, Pais." Callistrate flinched at the pet name. Artemesia still referred to her as child, even though she had sixteen years behind her. In her village, she would have married and even had her own child by now. But there was no one here to recommend her for marriage, nor did she particularly care for the contract.

Enough women had stolen away at night, begging the goddess of revenge to punish their unfaithful husbands, often with children in tow, to keep Callistrate from ever wishing for a man in her life. She was content to serve her patron. She met new people, helped those in need, and had developed a sort of familial relationship with the other priestesses. While Artemesia set a clear boundary that she would not mother Callistrate, she still believed the old goat cared for her. And in turn, Callistrate wanted to learn everything she could teach her.

"Tyche will lead the prayers this morning," Artemesia announced between bites. "Callistrate, you will assist her. Are the floors swept?"

"Yes, Hiereiai." Callistrate fought the urge to continue on and remind Artemesia that the floors were always swept well before she woke. That even though Callistrate was now a full priestess, she was the last asleep and first awake every day. But she held her tongue. If she wanted to lead this temple one day, as Artemesia did now, she needed to appear amiable, even if internally she wanted to spit fire.

"Good." Artemesia clapped her hands once. "Let us begin our day."

If Ariston could have plucked out his ears as one did their eyes, he would have.

His mother had been wailing for nine days. Nine straight days.

Occasionally she collapsed into a fevered sleep, crying out still but in more hushed tones than when she woke. Her voice was raw with overuse, the skin around her eyes swollen and red, her knuckles bloody from pounding against the floor.

His father was dead. Murdered by a moneylender who grew weary of waiting. A man called Lysander who informed Ariston that he now owed his father's debt and had precisely three moons to pay it.

The sum was far greater than Ariston could ever make as a scribe. So now, Ariston found himself with a dead father, a hysterical mother, and an unpayable debt. He had no idea how he was meant to survive this. Finding another moneylender to pay off this one only bought him time, and not any real time at that. Before long, he'd have a different violent man threatening him. He had mentioned going to the leaders of the community, but that had only driven his mother deeper into despair, sobbing that their family name would be tarnished beyond repair.

Ariston saw little point to having a family name when one was dead.

He had never been a fighter. Violence sickened him and the sight of blood made his head light. When he was young and the boys in the neighborhood wrestled each other to the ground in play, Ariston stood back. He preferred his studies. Working as a scribe for the wealthy families to earn some coin had allowed him to provide for his parents. But it hadn't been enough.

His father had fallen from his position of scribe half a decade earlier when Ariston was starting out. After the death of his youngest son, his father became a man Ariston didn't recognize. Gambling, whoring—he pissed through the family's coin in no time, and when Ariston began refusing him funds, he went to moneylenders. If only…

If only his father hadn't lost his wits with the death of his child. If only his mother hadn't done the same with the death of his father.

Ariston couldn't resign himself to his own death, or the beatings that would precede it. He needed to construct a plan. There was no family to borrow money from, no great treasures to sell. Even the house he and his mother lived in was worth less than the debt.

On the tenth day after his father's death, Ariston went to the oracle, Menodora. She was not a particularly powerful oracle. No one came to her in pilgrimage or threw coins at her feet after her prophecies came true. But

Ariston trusted her. She had warned him about his father's fall, so he sought her counsel again.

Menodora lived outside town, sleeping between four carob trees. She was older than Ariston, close to his mother's age, but she kept no family. Her hair hung in knots to her knees, her tunic never looked clean, and she spoke constantly, whether or not a person was near. She claimed the gods never stopped speaking to her, and it was unwise to ignore a god.

Today, she paced. She walked a square, over and over, touching each of her carob trees as she did. Her voice was low and uneven, as if she was being interrupted over and over again.

"You!" she called once Ariston caught her attention. "Go to Rhamnous."

Ariston paused and checked to make sure no one stood behind him.

"I am speaking to you, scribe. Your father is dead?"

He flinched. He wasn't sure why; a year earlier she had told him his father's feet had touched the path to death, and there was nothing he could do to change it. "Yes."

"Killed by the moneylender? With the smile like a snake?"

He nodded.

"Then it is time for you to go to Rhamnous." She turned back to the trees and whispered something sharply. "Go on now."

"What is in Rhamnous?" Ariston trusted her, but going on a days' long journey with no guidance seemed at best stupid and at worst dangerous.

"Nemesis."

Ariston shuddered. He had no dealings with The Daughter of Night, nor would he ever. Those who sought her out had great evil come down on them and wanted to spread her deeds through the land.

"I seek no vengeance. My father was killed for his own stupidity. It would do no good to ask the goddess to go after the moneylender."

"Well," she huffed, "Vengeance seeks you. She has her eye on you, and you cannot hide. Go on. Leave tomorrow. Make an offering to the One from Whom There Is No Escape." The oracle laughed. "She is watching you."

Ariston shifted his weight between his feet. Go to Rhamnous? It wasn't far, only a few days on the road. Ariston had been hoping for a chance to appease Plutus and find a small fortune underneath a tree in the forest. He was a much less terrifying god to do business with than The Inescapable.

"Do not think you can outrun her," Menodora called. "She has her claws in you, deep in your soul, and you must go now." She hobbled over to him and grabbed his wrist. "Nemesis is not to be trifled with. She gives gifts, she takes them away. She punishes those who deserve it."

"Are you insinuating I deserve punishment?" Ariston had a fool for a father, but that had cost him his life. Surely, he was not to be further punished for his father's sins?

"I am saying the goddess beckons you to her, so you must go." She released his arm and backed away. "Leave me, the gods are loud, and I have no time for the voices of men."

Ariston ran then, out of the woods and away from the oracle who had set him on a path he didn't understand.

Sweep, serve, attend the mourning, pray at the feet of the goddess, light the candles, extinguish the candles, clear the food, prepare the food, wash the day off her hands and face, fall into bed at the end of the night only to rise again the next morning and continue.

Callistrate didn't dream of much. She would serve Nemesis until she died. She would be a lowly novice until she was not. And when she was old and gray with wrinkled hands and sightless eyes, she would be the bane of some young slip of a girl's existence, forcing her to do all the meaningless minutiae that kept the temple running smoothly. For now, Callistrate would fill her days with tasks that felt like nothing and appeared to mean nothing.

That night, the temple was quiet. The older women had all gone to supper, which would quickly be followed by bed. Only Callistrate remained. The floors had managed to keep relatively clean today, so there wasn't much work to do, and Callistrate took the opportunity to enjoy the solitude. She took a seat on the edge of the room, hidden by shadows, and relaxed a moment. Soon, she would blow out the candles and scavenge something to eat, but for now she crossed her arms and settled into her spot, focusing on the likeness of Nemesis.

She had always thought the statue was too pretty. Vengeance was an ugly thing after all. The people who came here, they asked for ugly things from their goddess. They wanted blood or ruin for their enemies. They begged horrible wrongs to be weighed and measured and returned to those who carried them out. They were the beaten, the raped, the survivors. They had lived through terrible evils and wanted retribution for their pain. Nemesis took them in her hands and said, yes, I will help you when all else is failed. I will blight their crops, kill their children, rip the comfort from their lives. I will make them feel the pain you live with. A pale, serene face hardly seemed appropriate. Nemesis was like a monster on the edge of darkness.

"Hello?" A voice calling out from the door jolted Callistrate from her musings. "I am here."

She looked toward the doorway but only saw the outline of a figure against the black night. The candlelight danced too wildly over him for her to see his face.

"Daughter of the Night, you have bid me to come and so I have. My father was killed by Lysander, the moneylender. He has transferred his debt to me. I seek nothing but your will. I make no demands on you, Nemesis the Inescapable. Do with me what you will." The man walked farther into the temple, then got to his knees in front of the likeness of the goddess. "I am here to find my fate." He kissed the feet of the statue, then sat back on his heels.

Callistrate's cheeks reddened. She felt like she was intruding on something personal. She heard prayers all day long, but never one giving himself to Nemesis such as this. Those who came begged for their own wills to be done, not to be used as an instrument of the goddess. Yet, here was a man putting all his faith into the Daughter of Night.

He bowed his head low in reverence and suddenly, he was familiar to her. Her hands and feet buzzed first, then it spread down her arms and up her legs. She flushed with excitement.

"It's you," she breathed, scrambling to her feet and causing him to jump. "You've returned to me." Callistrate couldn't contain herself. It was him—the other side of her soul.

She stepped into the light as he stood, and they finally stared at each other.

"You." He smiled. "You." He opened his arms, and she rushed to him nearly tripping over her tunic. She folded into his embrace as it all came back to her—every time they'd loved each other. It always came back. She only had to look at his face and knew. All the pain and the love and every inch of life they'd lived together before.

"You look different." He pulled away from her and cupped her face with his hands. His thumb traced her cheek down to her chin. "You've never had such curls in your hair," he teased.

"And you!" She couldn't smother her grin. "What happened here?" She ran her finger over his nose where a crooked bump lived.

"An elbow when I was a child." He buried his hands in her hair. "An oracle said I had to come here. I thought Nemesis had some grand plans for me, but it wasn't the goddess calling me to Rhamnous, it was you. You've always been my fate." He pressed his forehead against hers.

It was true. No matter what life she lived, he was there. Their souls were intertwined, calling to one another until they landed side by side once again.

"I'm Ariston," he whispered against her ear.

"I'm Callistrate. I'm a priestess of Nemesis."

"We are reunited." He kissed her forehead softly, then pulled her against his chest. "Nothing can separate us."

A month passed in bliss. Ariston and Callistrate slowly reacquainted themselves with each other. Ariston found a room to rent nearby and work as a scribe to save some coin. Callistrate had given Nemesis her vow to live in service to her at the temple, so if he ever wanted to have a home with her, it needed to be in Rhamnous. He wanted to build his life here, to provide for Callistrate. They could live together, as husband and wife. He could work as a scribe, she as a priestess. They would live a quiet, perfect life, just the two of them, surrounded by their happiness.

He thanked Menodora for her guidance. Here in Rhamnous, Ariston didn't worry about the moneylender. There was no threat of violence hanging over his head. He could enjoy his days, enjoy his work, enjoy his love. Occasionally his thoughts turned to his mother, how she might be handling his absence, but mostly he thought of Callistrate. His mother was of this life—a solitary thread holding them together in one lifetime.

Callistrate was woven in his soul. He could live a thousand lives, and she would be present in all of them.

She was as strong as he remembered, a spirit like a wildfire and the tongue to match. The more time he spent with her now, the more he felt the memories of before fading into darkness...he lived in the moment with her. It did no good to focus on the pasts they had experienced. He wanted to make the most of this life with her. One where neither of them starved in the cold darkness. They lived in joy beneath the warmth of the Grecian sun.

He passed into the temple, bowing to the likeness of Nemesis, then searched for his love among the droves of people come to pray to the Daughter of Night. Were so many seeking vengeance? He wondered if it wasn't only retribution they sought, but a community. The temple gave those who were hurting a place to feel less alone. Every pair of feet that walked across the threshold had lost something. Here, they could sit in companionship with others.

"Ariston. I see you have returned." He glanced up to find Artemesia walking toward him. Callistrate spoke often of her mentor during their stolen moments. How the priestess had taken her in when her mother abandoned her, how she worked her hard, but Callistrate still believed in some corner of her heart, there was love between them.

"I have."

"My patroness has not answered your prayers for vengeance yet?" She raised an eyebrow. "Or have you found something else while here?"

"I..." What could he say? He no longer believed the oracle sent him here for vengeance. He was sent here to find Callistrate and leave the horrors of his father's murder behind. He loved Callistrate. He was here for her, nothing else.

"I see the way you look at my Pais. She is sworn to the goddess and this temple, you know that?"

"She took no vows of virginity," he countered.

"And we are thankful for that. I would hate to punish her for such an offence, as I am sure she no longer holds that virtue." She sighed. "She has no family, which I assume she has told you." He nodded. "She is enamored with you. Do not take advantage of that." She bit the words out and left.

Take advantage? Ariston wanted nothing but to treat her well and adore her all the rest of his days. Yes, there was a chance he would get her with child, and then life would become much more complicated, but it didn't matter. He had work as a scribe and nothing forbade Callistrate from continuing her work as a priestess if she had a child.

"There you are!" Callistrate appeared and slipped her hand into his for a brief moment before standing across from him. "My duties will be finished just after nightfall. Should I come to you?"

"I'll wait for you outside the temple," Ariston answered. He glanced at the goddess, her gaze penetrating even in stone. Perhaps he needed to give her more adoration. "I have some things to take care of before then." He ran his fingers over her elbow before leaving her. His skin ached for hers, every moment of every day, and skimming the surface of her would have to do for now. He needed to think of a way to give Nemesis thanks that had nothing to do with vengeance. He wanted to rain praise on the great goddess for taking his love in, giving her a home and a purpose, before he could watch over her.

Ariston ducked out of the temple and into the bright summer sun. The sand kicked up as he walked. It had been weeks without rain. Soon, everyone would begin their panicking until the gods gave way and allowed the skies to open and drown them in salvation. Ariston did not feel panicked, though. He had Callistrate, and that was all that mattered. But now, he needed to plan for the rest of their lives.

He was not so young of a man that he could not have a wife. With twenty-two years behind him, Ariston should be able to provide enough to keep Callistrate. He would get a few more scribe jobs, then buy an animal to sacrifice to Nemesis, and when he could, he would find a house to bring Callistrate home to. She would no longer live with the priestesses. No more sneaking through the streets in the early morning to return to her tasks. They could walk hand in hand in the daylight for all to see.

They were together again, and life was just beginning.

"Hello, Ariston."

He looked up, and his gaze met the man in front of him. Golden hair, eyes that shone like wet stones, a smile that held all the evil in the world.

In that moment, Ariston knew that he hadn't outrun his fate. Nemesis didn't protect him here. Callistrate didn't save him. That wasn't her purpose. His was to love her as long as this body let him. As long as the gods deemed him worthy enough to walk this earth. Time wasn't on their side this life.

"Lysander." The name felt like ashes and dashed hope against his tongue. The moneylender had found him.

"You left. Do not do that. Leaving town when you owe a great sum of money is never a good idea." His eyes narrowed into slits. "I am unhappy."

"I do not owe you money. My father owed you money." Ariston cleared his throat. "Perhaps you should have considered that before you killed him. It's difficult to extract money from a corpse. They have little means to earn it."

Lysander smirked. "There was no getting money out of that man. If you'd had a sister, I'm sure he would have sold her to me as payment. As it was, I am uninterested in your mother, and you aren't to my taste."

Ariston felt his cheeks redden in anger. He wished—oh, how he wished —that he were the type of man to raise a weapon and crash it against another's skull. To beat this man out of existence. To take his life in retribution for the life of her father. But while the woman he loved served Nemesis, Ariston had never been one of her children. He didn't have a violent streak.

"Now, I realize your father owes too great a debt for me to demand payment say, tomorrow. But," he said as he leaned in and lowered his voice, "that sweet young priestess with the black curls. I am interested in her. A handful of nights with her would clear your debt."

"Stay away from her," he growled. Ariston may have not been a violent man, but he wouldn't let any harm come to Callistrate. He'd rather rot in a shallow grave than let that filthy soul touch her.

"There we are!" Lysander exclaimed. "We have a perfect payment." He licked his lips. "I don't want to hurt her. But she is so small. It would be no trouble to wring her little neck."

Ariston took a step toward Lysander, but he put his hand against his chest. The man stank of sweat, which pooled against his tunic under his arms. "I'd much rather fuck her than kill her. But I don't like when they put up a fight. It's no fun to have a girl cry beneath you the entire time. Talk to her. If she comes to me of her own accord, takes her time with me, moans a little for me at all the right times...stays for a few nights..."

Black spots decorated Ariston's vision. "She is not a prostitute," he growled.

Lysander put his hand up to stop him. "I'll consider your debt paid. If not, you can either come up with the sum, or I start hurting the people you love. I've killed your father. It's no matter to me. Your mother, that priestess —you have so many people you love left to lose." Lysander stepped away from him and looked up at the temple behind him. "I should pay my respects to the Daughter of the Night. Perhaps that sweet priestess can assist me with my prayers." He pushed past Ariston and disappeared into the darkness of the building.

Hell. Ariston was no soldier or mercenary, but he should slit Lysander's throat for speaking about Callistrate that way. He should be his own hand of vengeance and cut down the man who took his father's life.

But he wouldn't. He still feared death, especially now that he was with Callistrate. How could he give her up so quickly? He'd never have his fill of her. He wanted one hundred years. One hundred different times.

Callistrate knew something was bothering Ariston, but she was not sure what it was. The joy and playfulness that had surrounded them the last moon dissipated in the air and was replaced with an uneasy tension. He was distant now, still loving and adoring, but she caught him looking past her when they spoke in the temple and jumping whenever a stray noise disturbed the night. They still shared a bed, with Callistrate stealing from the temple after dinner and waking early to return before any of the other priestesses woke. It wasn't sustainable—she'd nearly fallen asleep on her feet more than once. But for now, she was determined to spend every waking moment with Ariston.

There was a new man visiting the temple every day, one who watched her with eyes like a hungry wolf circling his prey. She kept her mind sharp whenever he drew near, which he did nearly daily, asking for assistance when praying and the like.

"Priestess, I wish to make an offering to the goddess, one of blood." The temple was busy this afternoon. A large group had arrived, needing food and rest and a priestess to listen to their woes. Callistrate had barely had a moment to herself when this man interrupted her again.

"Priestess?"

Callistrate fought the urge to snap back at him. After days of loitering around her, he'd yet to speak of that which he sought vengeance for.

"You are welcome to sacrifice an animal for our great goddess, Nemesis. Though one of the older priestesses must attend you. I am not allowed to take part in animal sacrifice. It is a task for those more experienced than I." If it was another patron come to pay their respects, Callistrate would have asked Artemesia for permission to attend the ritual. But the idea of spending more time than required with this man turned her stomach.

"But you are the one I want for this offering. Not another priestess. I must have one as beautiful as you." He reached his hand up to stroke her cheek, but she dodged out of his reach. He chuckled. "Has he not spoken to you yet?"

Callistrate furrowed her brow but remained silent.

"Ah, he has not. Ariston should tell you. It would be better coming from him." He leaned close to her face—so close she could feel his hot breath against her ear. "I believe you and I could come to a very nice arrangement that would see both Ariston and yourself better off than you are now. You are very beautiful."

Callistrate didn't know what this man spoke of, but she did know that Ariston would never betray her. A love over several lifetimes was nothing to trifle with.

"I know your skin would taste as sweet as a ripe apple."

She darkened her gaze at the man, grinding her teeth together. "If you seek a prostitute, Demona is always welcoming new customers. You can find her near the markets. You will know her by her red hair. I am a priestess of the goddess of vengeance. Do not insult me again."

"Or what? Your little goddess will come down and torture me?" He laughed, then made a show of looking for something to come falling out of the ceiling of the temple. "I don't see her."

"You are very brave, insulting a goddess in her own temple." Callistrate watched Artemesia enter the temple from the corner of her eye and turned to face her mentor. "Hiereiai, this young man would like to sacrifice an animal to our great goddess." She called loudly so that every soul in the temple could hear her. His mouth went to a hard line. "Maybe more than one," she added. Served him right. Animals were expensive. If he were going to insult her and her goddess, the least she could do was cost him coin.

"Ah yes! Good man, come here. I will make plans with you." Artemesia's face broke into a welcoming smile. "We must decide which type of animal, or should I say animals, you are interested in. I will take you to Kostos; he has the best lot in town. Sheep with pure white coats..." With any luck, Artemesia would have him paying for goats and sheep, then donating even more money to feed the priestesses. She wanted that man to suffer for what he said to her. What he insinuated Ariston was a part of.

Callistrate looked around the temple. Tyche sat with a family, and Nicaea rearranged candles. It was a perfect time for her to duck out and find Ariston.

Ariston counted the coins he'd earned that morning. It might be enough to appease Lysander for a few days, but not permanently. The amount of debt his father had incurred was unpayable. He'd spend his lifetime giving these small amounts, without ever making a dent in the debt.

His father had well and truly fucked him.

He crossed the threshold of the room he rented and collapsed on the straw bed in the corner.

He was trapped. He couldn't leave Rhamnous, not without Callistrate. She served Nemesis, it was her life's true calling. To ask her to relinquish her vow to the goddess was unfair. And now that Lysander knew he was here, there was no escaping him. Not unless he died.

Ariston knew he did not have it in him to murder the man.

"There is something heavy on your mind." Callistrate interrupted his thoughts as she slid beside him in the bed. "And you should share it with me."

"Won't the priestesses note your absence from the night meal?"

She shrugged. "You are here now. Yes, I am a devotee to Nemesis, but I will not let my devotion to the priestesses injure us. You are more important." She pressed a kiss against his jaw. "The man who has been watching me propositioned me today," she began slowly.

"He did what?" Ariston moved to jump out of the bed, but Callistrate held him in his spot.

"I am fine. He is currently spending quite a bit of coin to appease both Nemesis and Artemesia." She paused and turned her face so she looked him in the eye. "Who is he?"

"A moneylender."

"You've incurred a debt?"

He shook his head. "My father." And with that, the whole story tumbled out of him. His father's terrible living, his mother's grief, even his brother's death which began it all. Callistrate held his hand and listened to all his woes, her eyes clear and understanding.

"I am sorry I kept it from you. I wanted...I wanted to live in this sweetness a little longer."

"You do not owe me an apology." She sighed. "It is difficult for me to remember the times we were together before. I know it was more than once, but now, I can see only snatches of memories, nothing concrete."

"It is the same for me."

"But I do feel that every time, we are met with great hardship. Perhaps that is why we meet each other over and over again. We've been ripped apart so many times, it's only fair we find each other again. The gods give us another chance to make it right. To live long together."

"Do you think this is the chance in which we are able to survive the hardships?" Ariston pulled her tightly against his chest. He didn't want to lose her. They'd just found each other. He wanted years and years with her. The dark cloud of Lysander was inescapable.

"I think we have no choice other than to try. Is the debt truly unpayable?"

"It would take a lifetime."

"And I regret that I could never willingly give myself to that man."

"I would die before I allow him the privilege of lying with you."

Callistrate smirked. "I could never get through the act with him. I'd strangle him before he'd finish."

Ariston slid his hand up her back to cup the nape of her neck. "I don't know how to fix this."

"Neither do I. But neither of us is alone any longer." She wove her fingers through his. "We are together now. As we have been before. We will figure out what to do. Somehow."

Callistrate did not return to the temple that night. She couldn't. A familiar sense of dread from another lifetime had sunk its claws into her once again.

You will lose him.

She knew that fighting fate was a useless battle, but she could not give up so easily. Yes, she would lose him, all people in the end were lost. Either she would go to the underworld first, or he would. The chances of them departing together were slim. She'd be damned though if she allowed a moneylender to take her love over a debt that was not his own. It was not fair, and she lived in a world of equaling wrongs.

When the sun rose that morning, Callistrate knew she had missed breakfast. She would be missing it from now on. She would not shirk her duties but sitting beside the women who had cared for her when she was young...they would understand. Her vows were to the goddess, not the dining table.

"You must be awake," Ariston murmured against her neck. "You are squirming like a fish."

"I am."

"Are you in a hurry to leave?"

She turned to face him and pressed her forehead against his. "Never again. I will only hurry to see you from now on."

Ariston ran his hands over her body, finding places he'd been the only one to touch, grasping at her skin like it was his only nourishment in the world. In these moments, Callistrate felt that every version of her and every version of him was present. They were made up of all their pasts woven together like fabric. She was a woman on the cold plains, a witch in the dense forests, a priestess, a wife, a secret lover hidden away from the world. She was her soul, and he was his. And when they moved together, their bond was unbreakable.

His hands were roughened from his work with parchment, and she loved the insistence with which he pushed her tunic away, parted her thighs, trapped her wrists. She trusted him completely, the way he touched her, tasted her, took her. She was safe and loved with him.

"I am yours," he panted against her neck as he plunged into her.

"You are mine," she whispered back. "No one else can have you."

"Never." He moved her hands to his shoulders as his mouth traveled the length of her neck. "I'll be yours until the stars rain down from the sky."

Eventually, Callistrate did tear herself from Ariston's arms, both sated and still wishing for more. She wanted...she wanted to lie in bed with him all day, all night. She wanted to whisper against his jaw and breathe in his scent.

But she had given her vows to Nemesis before she knew he existed. So, while she could spend her nights and free time in his arms, the goddess required her devotion, and she would give it, even if she was slightly less enthusiastic than before.

Her life felt divided into halves, much like it had when she was a child. For years, she thought of herself as two halves—the girl before Rhamnous and the girl after her mother left. Now, it all felt like one big jumble, marked as complete with Ariston's arrival. There was only time without him and time with him. Nothing else held as much significance. Not her mother's abandonment, nor her admission into the service of Nemesis.

She entered the temple while the sun still kissed the horizon in the distance. A few stragglers from the night before slept in the courtyard, but they knew not to enter before a priestess welcomed them in. Nicaea was already lighting the candles and speaking in low tones to herself when Callistrate picked up the broom in the corner and dutifully began her sweeping. The stone floor was cleared in no time, and ready for the patrons of the day. The air was still and hot before the sun even crossed the sky, and Callistrate knew the heat would bring even more worshippers. The temple stayed cool even on the hottest of days, and heat in the air brought out emotions of all kinds, including revenge.

As people filed in, some grasping Callistrate's hands as they walked past, the day became a flurry of activity. She busied herself helping new travelers, relighting candles that were snuffed out by sobs, and keeping the doorway clear so more could enter. By noon, the temple held at least fifty visitors.

Every priestess came now, dividing the masses into smaller groups, attempting to move some on. The temple could hold the crowds, but anytime too many people were in too small a space, they risked a catastrophe. One person pushed another, and they could have a stampede on their hands.

Callistrate moved from one group to another, trying to get a few to step outside to speak in private when a pair of hands grabbed her from behind.

"Let go," she said insistently but couldn't shake free. Her arms were pinned behind her, and she was pushed through the crowd by the body at her back. They burst through the side door of the temple into the bright sun, but she wasn't released.

"Stop fighting," he grumbled behind her.

"Get off of me." There was no mistaking her tone. She would not forgive this offence. He loosened his grip on her wrists enough that she slipped one arm free while he held fast to the other.

"Didn't he tell you not to fight?" Lysander complained. "I will not consider the debt paid if you aren't sweet to me."

"I am not going with you to pay a debt incurred by a dead man. You chose to murder the man who owed you money. Your money is now forfeit."

Lysander smirked. "I can take whatever I want. If I want to kill Ariston for his father's offence, I will. If I want to fuck you, I will. You may be a priestess of Nemesis, but you have no power over me. I am a man. A man with money. There is no greater power than that here, little girl."

Callistrate wrenched her arm free, but before she could run, Lysander caged her against the temple wall. He pinned his body against hers and dug one hand into her hair and pulled.

"Now, I said I didn't want you to fight, but I'll make do if you do. Understand?" He fisted her tunic with his other hand as she fought against him. She could feel her hair tearing from the roots where he held, but she wouldn't go still. Callistrate was not timid. She would fight him all the way to Tartarus. She opened her mouth and bit his upper arm as hard as she could.

"Fuck!" he yelled but didn't let go of her. "Bitch!" He rammed his shoulder against her face, slamming her head against the wall of the temple, dazing her enough for her jaw to open.

He was moving, but her vision wasn't clear anymore. The blur of him moved away, but immediately she was hit in the face so hard she fell to her knees. She slid to the ground.

This was it. It was too crowded in the temple for anyone to hear her.

Nemesis. She called to her goddess with a mouth that didn't work. If she was to be violated by this man, let her goddess rain vengeance upon him. *Nemesis, please.*

"Callistrate! Get away from her! Help! Someone, help! Help! A man has attacked one of the priestesses!" Artemesia's voice rang high and clear over the muddle of her mind.

"I'll return," Lysander spat as he pushed off her. "Know that," he mumbled as the quick crunch of dirt and rocks let her know he was leaving.

Artemesia kept yelling and soon Callistrate was surrounded by people.

"We're here," Nicaea's calm voice broke through the din of the crowd. "You are safe now. He is gone."

"Wicked man," Tyche hissed. "Attacking a priestess under the eyes of our goddess? She will surely strike him down as he runs. Coward. Will beat a woman but will not stand up to a man." Callistrate heard her spit on the ground. "I call down vengeance for you, Pais."

Her fellow priestess pulled her to sit, looked at her injuries, carried her to their sleeping quarters. A few of the men at the temple offered to chase the assailant, but she only wanted one thing.

"Someone please find Ariston," Callistrate begged as she was covered with a blanket and a cold cloth pressed against her face. "Please."

He was walking home from a job when Nicaea came, running so fast dust kicked up with every step. The priestess he barely knew recounted what had happened to Callistrate while he was working.

He should have been there.

By the time he reached the temple, Callistrate was tucked into a bed that had been hers before he arrived. Her face had been cleaned. The dirt he imagined dug into her wounds had been washed away. Artemesia rinsed a cloth in a basin, then patted the sides of her face while she winced with every moment.

"Ariston is here," the elder priestess announced after he stood in shocked silence for much longer than was appropriate.

Callistrate reached her hand up, which he immediately took in his own as he fell to his knees beside her.

"I am so sorry," he breathed against her knuckles. "I brought this evil with me to Rhamnous. If I had stayed away..."

"No," she choked. "No, I want you here. Lysander is not your doing. You are my fate."

"If your fate is to be beaten by a man chasing me"—he shook his head—"better I never came."

"Stop it." She shooed Artemesia away and pushed herself to sit up. Her face, her beautiful face. Lysander's violence had marked every inch of it. Bruises under her eyes, abrasions all over her forehead. Her jaw was swollen and purple.

"You and I are meant to be together. I do not care what Lysander thinks he can do to keep us apart. We are bound over lifetimes. No one can break that." She gestured to her face. "I will heal. And he will be punished."

"Who will punish him? The courts will take his side."

"Nemesis will. It might not happen immediately, but my patroness will see my vengeance realized."

"You think we should wait for a goddess to help us?" Ariston believed in the gods, but they didn't live in the human world. Time had no meaning to immortal beings. Ariston didn't care if Lysander's line was cursed—he wanted retribution on the man now, not one hundred years from now when Nemesis finally heard this prayer.

"I believe she will come when we need her." Callistrate reached for his hand again. "He is strong. He hit me with well-practiced skill. And we have no money for a sword for hire. Let us put our faith into Nemesis. I have served her well. And we have many lives to live. I have many more lives of service to give her."

Ariston pressed his mouth to her knuckles and nodded. But he did not agree. Lysander had stepped too far. Callistrate was innocent. In attacking her, he had provoked Ariston beyond ignoring.

He was not a fighter, but he would not allow someone to hurt his woman.

He stayed with her until she finally slept. He wanted to stay—he wanted forever. But Ariston could not live with himself and not seek out retribution for her injuries. With kisses against her cheeks, he stole away from her bedside.

"You are leaving her, then?" Artemesia asked in a low voice.

"I will return. I...I can't let him get away with it."

The older priestess nodded. "You would die in defending her, and then leave her defenseless?"

"If I die, I would be no defense."

"You would leave her, alone in the world again?" Artemesia pressed.

Ariston hung his head. "If I am gone, Lysander will leave."

"And if he does not? If he comes back for what he tried to steal?"

Ariston furrowed his brow.

"She did not tell you? He didn't simply beat her. When I found her, he was trying to have her. He beat her because she fought him."

Anger flooded his body. His arms and legs were heavy with it, his vision clouded by it.

"I will kill him." He ground his teeth together. He would drag Lysander to Tartarus with him if needed. He would never touch Callistrate again.

Artemesia grabbed his arm, but he shook it off.

"Do not abandon her!" she called. "Callistrate needs you!"

She did need him. She needed him to destroy the man who had hurt her so grievously. He would not fail her.

She dreamed of him. Of lives past and future. Of days spent in his arms, nights in which they never released one another.

She saw icy plains, thick forests, and rough seas. He wore many faces, and she did as well. They were happy together, or sorrowful. Every moment worth living was spent with him. She saw his face as she died a dozen times, she watched as he slipped away from her. She watched as the fabric of their souls knit together over thousands of years and lifetimes.

Consciousness flitted in and out, and at some point, Ariston's face was replaced with Artemesia. She tried to open her eyes. Tried to reach out for him. She wanted Ariston, now and forever. He was hers to have.

Finding Lysander was not as easy as Ariston hoped. He wanted to walk into the low sun of the evening and happen upon him immediately. Tackle him from behind. Squeeze the life out of that worthless man.

But he was nowhere to be found. Ariston wandered the streets of Rhamnous all night asking after the moneylender. He went to his room, stole a cooking knife from the woman who owned the place, and stuck it into his belt. He should have tried to sleep, but he couldn't. He was mad with vengeance.

He became like a wild animal, stalking the shadows, his eyes trained on every man who passed by. But Lysander eluded him. Had he fled? It didn't matter. Ariston would find him.

After spending the entire night on his feet, he returned to the temple. He needed to see Callistrate. He still felt a wildness inside his soul. She was his love, and she needed to be protected. He approached her sleeping quarters like a lion come to look after his pride.

"Where have you been?" Callistrate yelled the moment he walked into her room.

"I was looking for Lysander," he muttered, his voice not his own.

"Don't. Don't go after him."

"I have to."

She huffed. "You could listen to me. You could stay with me. Life is fleeting. I want you here with me."

"I cannot wait by your side while he walks free. Someone needs to punish him."

"Nemesis will punish him," she bit back. "Ariston—"

"He has returned!" Tyche called. "He is in the temple!"

Ariston stood up like a shot. "He is in the temple now?"

"Yes, I saw him—"

"Do not go!" Callistrate shouted, but he was already leaving. His mind was made up. He would face Lysander, right then, and the gods would decide who would live and who would die. Because he would not leave that man alive while he still breathed. He would have to cut him down to escape.

"Please!" Callistrate called after him, her voice echoing down the hall.

He could not be stopped. Lysander was in the temple. Before the day was over, one of them would be dead.

She screamed, yelled, begged, but he didn't stop. He ran toward Lysander as if that man would not kill him in cold blood. As if the moneylender wouldn't wrench him out of her arms permanently.

Callistrate shifted off the bed, kicking her blanket. Her body screamed as she did, but she ignored it.

"Pais, get back into bed this instant," Artemesia commanded. "Your man may be determined to die within our temple walls, but you will not." She grabbed her shoulders. "You are still in my care. I promised your mother and our goddess that I would care for you. I do not release you from my watch."

"Hiereiai. Please. I have to go to him." Her voice wavered. "If he is running toward death, I have to stop him."

"You are more than your love for him," her guardian said. "You are a servant of the Daughter of Night. You are dear to every priestess in Rhamnous."

"He is my fate. Life after life. I am bound to him and he to me. I cannot abandon him." She pulled the elder woman into a hug. "If I do not return, know that I appreciate everything you've done for me," she whispered. "Goodbye, Artemesia."

She pushed away and ran toward the temple before she could change her mind. Her head pounded with every step, her wounds ached, and her heart seized with fear. She never wanted to see Lysander again in her life, and now, less than a full day after he beat her so mercilessly, she was running to him.

I call down your vengeance. Do not let him steal anything more. Please, Inescapable. Do your worst on this soul.

She could hear them before she could see them. The temple had emptied, confused people standing outside wondering why such violence would be happening in a sacred place. Callistrate pushed past them, yearning to reach Ariston before it was too late.

They were entangled, both faces bloody, with Ariston clearly losing.

"Stop!" she screamed, hoping if Ariston wouldn't listen, perhaps she would distract Lysander long enough to end it.

They didn't stop, though. Ariston pulled away for a moment, long enough to take a hit to the face that sent his blood spattering across the temple floor. He didn't cower though—he charged Lysander and took him to the ground.

"Ariston, leave him! Please! Listen to me!" Callistrate watched as he ignored her, pulled a knife from his belt, and stuck it into Lysander's shoulder.

The moneylender bellowed in pain, gripping Ariston's forearm. Lysander threw Ariston off him, the knife still stuck in his body. They fell apart and Callistrate saw Lysander pull the knife from his wound, and in a moment, plunge it into Ariston's belly.

"No!" she howled. She rushed to Ariston—she had to get to him. He was dying, he was leaving.

She wanted longer this time. She wanted more time. It was never enough time. Each life...it was never enough time. He was there, steps away, she needed to hold—

Her body was not her own any longer.

"You dare spill blood on my holy ground!" A voice that was not Callistrate's filled every inch of the temple. Her arm raised and pointed at Lysander. *"You attempt to rape my servant, then you kill this man in my temple."*

"Callistrate?" Lysander said slowly.

"You dare to speak to The Inescapable? You will never outrun my punishment." In three steps, she was upon him, taking him to the ground. Her hands were around his neck, stronger than they'd ever been. She watched as her goddess used her body to squeeze the life out of Lysander. She tried to let go—she needed to get to Ariston. Callistrate didn't care about vengeance anymore. Her man was dying alone.

Lysander tried to fight her body off, but he was no match for the strength of a goddess. Was she? Would she survive this? Perhaps Nemesis sought to use her up and cast her aside. At least she would go with Ariston this time. She liked it better when they left together. Life without him had a heaviness she didn't relish to repeat.

The body beneath her lost all life, like a creek fading to a drip and then into nothingness, and with it her body was her own once again. She crawled off the corpse and rushed to Ariston, pulling his hand into hers.

No life stirred in him.

"Please, please, come back for a moment," she begged. "You didn't let me say goodbye. You should always let me say goodbye." She bunched her tunic and pressed it against his wound. There was so much blood, far too much for him to be anything but gone.

She gasped through her tears. She didn't want him to leave her yet. She wanted him for longer.

"I won't be long," she promised. "Wait for me wherever it is we go between. I will see you again."

Without Ariston, life was long. Callistrate served her goddess. She loved her priestesses. She held the mourners and sacrificed animals and lit candles. She passed sweeping off to the younger ones.

New girls always came, with wide eyes and hearts devoted to The Daughter of Night. They came with vengeances of their own. They learned the rhythms of the temple.

Years passed like eons. Artemesia left first, her eyes glassed over in blindness. Then Tyche and Nicaea, until Callistrate was the elder priestess who used a walking stick and barely stayed awake for the evening meal. But she never gave up her quiet mornings in the temple. That was when she could hear her goddess and talk to Ariston.

The stone was cold on her bare feet this morning. Her hips ached worse and worse each winter now, and her hands were too gnarled to handle lighting the candles. A slip of a girl called Nasa did it for her, then had the decency to disappear and allow her the temple alone.

"Inescapable. I give you my devotion, and my thanks," she began. It was different, this morning, though. Callistrate got to her knees in front of the statue, knowing well she could not get back up on her own. This was where Ariston had revealed himself to her: on his knees in front of her goddess.

She bent forward and pressed her forehead to the feet of the statue. "I am tired. I have given you more than eighty years. I have said goodbye to everyone I ever loved. I have been without him for far, far too long. It is time. Have mercy on an old woman."

The temple was silent in response. Callistrate laughed a bit to herself, wondering which of the young priestesses would find her and have to get her to her feet while they used their soothing tone and walked her back to bed.

"I'll always come back to you."

Callistrate whipped her head up faster than she had in years.

"Ariston?" He stood there, just there, as he had seventy years earlier. He'd lost none of his youth, none of the kindness in his eyes.

He held his hands out to her. "It is time. Finally."

"Finally," she repeated. Callistrate pushed herself to stand, something she hadn't done in over a decade. The age of her bones melted away. The aches were gone, and she felt as she had when she held him last. Young and strong. Before life took its many tolls.

She took his hands and relief washed over her.

"I am yours," he whispered.

"And I am yours." She smiled and melted into him.

Somewhere, she could hear a commotion—people yelling her name. But none of that mattered anymore.

She was returned to him.

Chapter Twenty

The Third Time

Winter was the cruelest of the seasons, but there was a certain sort of evil found in late spring. To walk out to a vegetable garden tilled and see fresh snows that had frozen away the small sprouts. To find a sheet of ice down the front path. To feel that chill in her lungs reminding her that she was alone now. No one was coming to help. The winter stores were gone, though they had lasted longer than she ever could have dreamed. A year earlier it had been three of them. Thomas, Sarah, and herself. Her sister and her husband had taken her on their journey across the ocean. A chance at a new life, they believed. A chance to outrun the ill will of their neighbors.

They began in the spring, with wide eyes and dreams. By May, Sarah's belly was showing all the signs of a baby. They cheered—it was a sign of hope. A new life born in this new place. A solid piece of land they could work without paying a lord. That summer, they feasted on rabbits and deer, berries and greens. Their bellies were full to match the hope in their hearts.

By the first frost of September, Sarah was dead. The babe had tried to come but couldn't and took both of them to the grave. She and Thomas buried them under a sturdy elm and marked the resting place by moving a patch of black-eyed Susans to rest over their remains.

Thomas was heartbroken and grief-stricken. He'd lost everything in that moment. His wife, his child, his future. He and Sarah were a love match, sweethearts for longer than Martha could remember.

There were neighbors, a few miles away, who she visited sometimes. The old woman there said to her, three days after the death of Sarah, "Martha, you must marry Thomas. It's unseemly to live with a man you are not married to, and the Good Lord knows neither of you will survive without the other." When she tried to explain that Thomas was like a brother to her since childhood, the woman simply lifted her hand to stop her speech.

At that moment, Martha decided she didn't much like the neighbors and would have little to do with them from then on.

Thomas spent the days cutting wood and hunting animals. He spent the evenings processing the kills, stretching their skin taut over the fire, salting and drying the meat. Martha kept house for them both, cooking all the meals, plucking feathers from the geese he managed to kill, doing all the cleaning. She'd found a stray cat in the summer and fed it a bit, so it came by and killed the mice. The vegetable garden had been small this past summer, with little time to plan, so in the evening, after the kitchen was cleaned and the floor swept, Martha made plans.

She wanted a large garden with room for flowers once they didn't have to worry about starving. She wanted more fruit too. There were apple trees at one end of the property and if she could get a few closer to the house, they'd be full all autumn. She'd saved seeds from blackberries and would make a patch. Martha never thought she'd be making this home without Sarah, but in her honor, she had to try.

It was mid-January when Thomas went out to fish. She insisted it was a stupid plan. The fish were hibernating, just as the bears and skunks and bugs were. But he wouldn't be dissuaded. He walked out over the pond, axe in hand, to chop a hole and fish within it. He'd been told that on this new continent, ice fishing was possible.

The ice broke, Thomas fell through, and by the time Martha crawled out to the hole, he was gone. No thrashing, no movement at all in the water.

He gave her one gift, going that way. Martha didn't have to bury him. The fish would take care of that.

And now she sat, a woman alone, at the end of spring with a handful of wilted greens and sour berries, and wondered how long it would be until she joined them.

Henry hated the sea with every fiber of his being. He hated the smell of the salty air, and he hated the stink of below deck even more. He despised the taste of food gone off, the sounds of every person crammed into the space. He yearned for open spaces, green pastures, air that didn't hang with the odor of fish guts.

In the belly of the ship, he watched. The living, the dying, the newly born. There were days of mourning and days of celebration. Through it all, a deep hunger and longing.

Sixty-four days into his first and hopefully last sea voyage, Henry spied land. It took another three days until he stood upon it, but when he did, he finally felt like he'd found his home.

Henry Braddock was the twelfth child and seventh son of George and Margaret Braddock. They lived a simple life, farming the land their family had sat upon for hundreds of years. By the time Henry was fifteen, his parents had passed on and his eldest brother, James, had two children of his own. Henry stayed on, helped work the farm, lived with the family, but once he was twenty and his brother had five children, he knew it was time. He could have found another nearby farm that needed help, or gone for work in Birmingham, but Henry didn't want to live in a city. He wanted his own piece of land. He wanted something to hand down to his sons.

With wanderlust in his heart, he said goodbye to all of his siblings and booked passage to the colonies.

Now, Henry was here. His feet touched land no one in his family before him ever had. Even the air tasted different on this side of the ocean. Fresh and new and full of promise.

You won't survive another winter.

"Yes, but it isn't winter. It is summer. And in summer, I can grow food. I can gather berries. Hell, I can beg the neighbors for food if I must."

And what if they want something in return? A piece of your soul traded away for a full belly?

Martha gritted her teeth and chased the thought away. She'd rather starve than give anymore of herself. She scrubbed out the pot and hung it over the fire, then swept the entire cabin. She straightened her bedroll, checked her water, and walked outside.

She didn't relish the idea of starving, so she got to work. Martha filled her basket with wild berries, planted onions, pulled a few late radishes out of the earth. She checked the sprouts where she had planted the blackberry seeds and pulled grubs away from them. Her cat wandered nearby, rubbing against her leg as she worked.

"There is a mouse in my house. I can hear him at night. Go on, make a meal of him," she commanded. The cat padded away to do her bidding.

Martha walked on, away from the house, and searched. This land was still unfamiliar, but the plant life was not entirely unknown to her. She collected fragrant herbs with blue-green leaves by the handful, pink flowers that smelled like the oranges on the ship. It was a whole new world, but she still needed a way to worship her Lady.

She brought her wares back to the house and set them aside. She went back out, the cat happily chomping on a mouse as she did, to check her traps. She was not an insufficient woman. Martha could catch a fish and clean it, skin a rabbit and roast it, and butcher a pig, chicken, and goat. But, to eat any of those, first she needed a fish or a rabbit or a pig, chicken, or goat. She currently had none.

Her traps were empty, though one had a tuft of gray fur clinging to the side. Lucky rabbit. She reset the tripped mechanism, and headed home, her stomach rumbling as she did. Tomorrow, she would fish. Tonight, she would make a soup of the last onion, one radish, and a duck egg she'd found the day before. It would be smart to let that egg hatch and keep it for herself and hope eggs became plentiful, but a starving woman didn't need food in a year, she needed it now.

One week after landing in the colonies, Henry found work at the docks. He wanted to get as far away from the sea as possible, but to do that he needed supplies and money, both of which he had none. Mrs. Franklin, a widow with an empty attic, offered Henry the room on the condition that he kept her woodpile full, her front walk clear of ruffians in the evening, and her house protected. Her children were thrown across this new land, and none visited.

Henry was more than happy to oblige, especially since that meant he could save all his earnings. He wanted to stake out a piece of land in the wilderness. Something with a river or a lake, with good land for farming and a view of the sunrise over a field.

He spent his days at the docks, washing vomit away, lifting goods off ships in port, putting goods on other ships. By the time he came home and sat beside Mrs. Franklin for an evening meal, he was bone tired.

"Anything exciting happen today?" she asked, as she did every night.

"A ship came down from Philadelphia. Mostly textiles. Should be out at the shops tomorrow or the day after."

"Oh! That is exciting. I don't think I've had a new dress in five years." She smiled big, her dimples dotting her cheeks under ringlets of white hair. She passed him the plate of bread and he took a large slice.

"Thank you," he muttered before taking a bite.

"Any women at the dock?" she asked, taking a sip of her tea.

Henry smirked. "I should hope not. The women who frequent the dock...they are not for me." He could feel his cheeks pinken. How could he tell his lovely landlady the only women at the dock were either fresh off the boats and terribly seasick or prostitutes?

"Well. If you find a nice woman one of these days, one you mean to marry, I hope the two of you will stay in town. So many young people flit off to the unsettled lands, and it just isn't safe. Anyone could come upon you there, cut your throat, and steal your life away. Better to stay in the city, where there's a bit of civilization and dignity."

Henry nodded and hid a smile. It was funny how settled Mrs. Franklin had become in her old age. He knew for a fact she crossed the Atlantic fifty years earlier, when boats were scarce, and Baltimore was little more than the dock the boats sat upon. Her wandering spirit had found its place though and settled deep.

Henry was not quite ready to settle.

Martha worked day and night that summer. She sowed seeds, caught fish and rabbits. She dried meat, cleaned furs to trade, sewed blankets. Her nails were broken and bloody, the skin on her nose turned so red that it peeled away, leaving dark freckles behind. She was strong, though. Stronger than she ever thought she could be.

By August, the fruits of her labor began to show. Her vegetables ripened, she had a rabbit nearly every night in her stew, and she traded some furs for ground wheat. She listened to this new land and the way it moved through the air. It was a different beat than England. The gods felt softer and lower. They weren't pressed up against every movement she made like they had been. Here, they were gentler spirits, skipping through the water and leaves. She left them bundles of herbs and cups of flower wine she had brewed herself. When the moon was full in the sky, Martha would sit in the darkness, her nakedness bared to the world, and thank them for her good fortune these months.

On warm summer days, she felt as though she would live forever.

When October came, Martha was ready. Her garden was empty—fruits turned into jams, squashes, carrots, onions, and turnips squirreled away to the dark root cellar that Thomas had thankfully dug as soon as they arrived. Now, she spent her days trapping. Mostly rabbits, though occasionally other small furry creatures were caught, and Martha would never waste a life by deigning not to eat. She made stew out of nearly everything. On quieter days, with still winds and good cloud cover, she fished. She pulled as many as she could out of the pond, and somedays she would walk to the river to see what could be gained. The shiny-scaled creatures were more difficult to find now that the air had turned cold, but that didn't stop her from trying. It would be a long, cold winter and Martha didn't mean to waste any time before the first snowfall.

On a dark November night, when the moon was fat and omens filled the air, she felt him in the wind.

The new world was as cruel as the last. Henry had never relied much on the kindness of neighbors, but here, everyone felt like an enemy. When a new boat came into port, full of men with long beards and wild eyes, he'd known trouble was on its way.

They were from England, his homeland, and their voyage had been blown off course by angry autumn winds. The occupants tumbled off the ship shoving one another, each more frantic than the next to put their feet on sturdy land. Henry tried to calm the masses, but they were beyond that. Hysterics broke out, mothers lifted their children into their arms, and everyone ran. Young and old were knocked down and stepped on. Henry grabbed the ankles of a young boy and pulled him out of the fray before his head was trampled. He kept him away from the thundering masses until finally, the crowd dissipated, and the evening was calm again.

"I'll lift you up," Henry began, "And you point out your mother or father." He went to scoop the child up under the arms.

"Mama died on the ship. Father died before that."

"Was there anyone else on the boat that you knew?" The boy's eyes shifted around, glancing at the passengers who were regrouping with their families.

"Not really."

Henry furrowed his brow. "What's your name?"

"Marcus."

"How old are you, Marcus?"

"Nine."

Henry shrugged. He'd worked his family's fields much younger than that. Dock work was very heavy, but Mrs. Franklin could use the boy around the house. Her hips were bad, and it didn't do any good to have her feeding the fire along all day while Henry worked. Henry didn't want to live in town forever too. If Marcus was a good little worker, he wouldn't feel so guilty leaving Mrs. Franklin when the time came.

"I think I have a place for you to stay, if you like." Marcus smiled a wide toothy grin. "You'll have to work, and Mrs. Franklin is in charge. What she says goes. Even to me."

Marcus nodded.

"When was the last time you ate?"

The boy shrugged.

"All right then." Henry turned to his boss and yelled that he'd be right back, just needed to settle this boy, and the two of them walked off to see Mrs. Franklin.

Martha knew he'd come. By the hang of the moon in the sky, the way the wind moved through the trees that night—change was on the back of the hours.

She didn't know who he was, or what he'd want, only that he was almost there. A traveler in the night, his feet pounding down a path through the woods.

He was magic, she was sure of it. Not as powerful as her though. Men rarely were. Her brother had been privy to a bit of magic before he passed but not like her or Sarah. They could read the seasons in the stars and feel life in a plant. Sarah could whisper in the ear of a cow, and it would make more milk than ever before. Martha had premonitions of important things to come.

It didn't mean they were any easier once they passed, though.

She sat by her low fire, cat by her side, and peeled an onion. She chopped it, added it to a bit of water, and threw in some rabbit bones. She would reserve her opinion on whether or not this man was worthy of meat once he showed himself. But it wasn't long ago that she was a traveler in this new world, and she'd never deny a newcomer a warm meal on a cold and windy night.

The cat hissed.

Martha uncovered the pot and let the savory scent of soup fill the cabin before she opened the door. A starving man will take a bowl of soup over violence.

She opened the door to the wilderness and watched the rustling of overgrowth as he trundled through the darkness.

"Do you have a spot by your fire for a weary traveler?" he called.

"I do if the traveler will swear on his soul that no harm will come to me or my animals while he is a guest in my house," she answered.

She heard his breath catch. A swear on one's soul was a far more powerful promise than swearing on any god or inanimate object. An oath on one's soul had to be kept, otherwise damnation of the worst kind waited.

"I swear it," he hissed into the night.

"Then welcome." Martha stepped aside and held the door open. He emerged into the light, and she finally got to look upon his face.

He was clean shaven with chestnut brown hair peeking out from his tricorne hat. His clothes were dirty from the road, but in good condition. No worn patches or stains.

"Who might I thank for the hospitality?" he asked, his voice low.

"Martha."

He hummed. "You'll have me call you by your Christian name so soon? That doesn't seem very proper."

She raised her eyebrow. "And what is your *Christian* name, sir?"

"Jonas."

She nodded and walked into the house. "Close the door behind you, Jonas, and take a seat by the fire. I'll serve you some soup to warm your bones. You may sleep in my brother's bed tonight. It's far too late for you to travel any longer."

"Your brother is not returning to his bed tonight?"

"He lies at the bottom of the pond just outside." Martha turned toward her room. "Your oath is not the only thing that lies within this house. The ghosts of my family are here. The ghosts of many, many who have lived this land and gone before us."

"Ah." His lips curved into a sly smile, and he paused spooning broth into his mouth. "Are we to be that open? So be it, *witch*. Do your neighbors know what you are?"

"No. And harm will come to me if they do. I wouldn't bet your soul on that."

"Witches are such fascinating creatures. Much more interesting than warlocks. You were clever to get that vow out of me."

"I haven't survived this long by being stupid." Her cat rubbed against her leg. "If you plan to stay more than the one night, you'll have to work for your keep. The fish have all but disappeared, and the garden is dormant. Trapping or hunting, and if you have no skill in catching animals, you may chop wood for the winter. The axe is around back beside the woodpile."

"I've never chopped wood a day in my life," he mused and went back to slurping his soup.

"You are in the new world now. And alone. I would have no qualms turning you out and setting the neighbors upon you. You've gotten no vows out of me." Martha turned into her room and closed the door behind her.

She had half a mind to throw him into the darkness with a curse of ill will on his heels, but she couldn't help thinking there was a reason she'd known he was coming. They were connected, but Martha didn't yet know why.

Winter came like a bear that year. Henry knew no different of winters in the new world, but Mrs. Franklin swore it was the worst she'd seen in the fifty years since she arrived. There were days Henry couldn't get out of the house and down to the docks, the snows had fallen so high. By January, the bay was frozen over, and no ships came to port until late February.

Marcus proved a good child. He kept Mrs. Franklin doting over him, did his chores without complaint, said sweet things to her about her cooking, and stayed in high spirits. By the time they'd been housebound for over a week in January, even Henry began to feel like he was trapped in the bottom of that boat again, but Marcus stayed positive. He told jokes, sang little songs, and kept a smile on his face.

Henry had to admit that the boy was growing on him. The little family of Mrs. Franklin was getting him through the darker days.

In February, the bay thawed and ships that had been stuck at sea came with such a ferocity that Henry felt like he only came home to shove food into his mouth and fall into his bed for a precious few hours. The goods that had been trapped in the water poured into the port now. His back ached from unloading. A few passenger ships arrived also, full of poor souls who'd been trapped in the winter weather and lost more than any of them had bargained for.

Once March came, Henry knew town life was not for him. He began his planning.

Jonas didn't leave. He slept night after night in Thomas's bed. He chopped wood in the morning and attempted to trap in the afternoons, though he had nothing to show for it. While Martha kept them in meat with her caught rabbits, Jonas returned every evening empty-handed, with nothing but blisters to show for his days' work.

But he was always watching. His eyes were trained to follow Martha's every movement when they were together. He perked up his ears when she gave thanks to the land, watched with squinting eyes at the herbs she burned.

"Have you ever dabbled in curses?" he asked one night over a steaming bowl of root vegetable stew.

"Of course not," Martha answered quickly. "The rule of threes makes anyone who attempts such a thing a fool."

Jonas smirked and spooned some more of his dinner into his mouth. "My sister was a powerful curse maker."

"And is she dead?" Martha asked.

"Yes. Two years now." He turned back to his meal as if he'd only commented on something as simple as the weather.

Martha stayed silent. She didn't relish the death of any witch, but a curse maker? Fate came for them all.

"I hope her curses died with her then," she finally said when her bowl was clean. Her cat jumped onto her lap and hissed at Jonas.

"They did not." He chuckled. "They most certainly did not."

The heavy snows this year made certain that neighbors were not visiting Martha. But spring would come soon, and if she were to have a man living in her home, a man who was not her husband nor her sister's widower, no one would believe she hadn't had him in her bed. The general public knew nothing of witch vows and their potency.

She needed Jonas to leave.

The first week of March, he caught his first rabbit and acted as if he'd taken down a deer that would feed them for months. She begrudgingly skinned and butchered the animal, then roasted it for dinner. After the long winter months eating out of the stores and small mammals and birds they could trap, Martha wanted nothing more than a bowl of greens and an oily fish. She dreamed of the sweetness of berries, the crisp bite into an apple. Her body had gone so long without anything fresh. It would be another month before the fish were easy to catch. In a few weeks, Martha might be able to pull some early greens from the earth, depending on what the weather held. A late freeze could kill off anything for another month or so.

Martha and Jonas sat across from each other, the fire between them, enjoying their rabbit. She had to admit it was a good catch. The rabbit was fat compared to most at this time of year. The last three she had caught were little more than skin on bones.

"We should marry soon," Jonas said as if he'd asked her to pass the water.

She wrinkled her brow. "Why would I ever marry you?"

"We've been living as man and wife for nearly half a year. At this point, it would be a formality. I already do half the work of the house you boldly call your own. As if a woman can own a piece of property. You need me to marry you to keep this house. Otherwise, the neighbors will run you out and you'll be forced to return to town."

She snorted. "You do not do half the work. You would have starved in November if I wasn't here. And I think your parents forgot to tell you how man and wife actually live. I have been living with you like I lived with my brother."

Jonas sneered. "I know what a man does with his wife. I know more than you could ever imagine. In London...in London I had many women in my bed. If you hadn't weaseled that vow out of me, I—"

"You'd what? Have already forced yourself on me? Listen to me, Jonas Fortworth. I may not dabble in curses, but I would not hesitate. Remember that."

"You witches are all the same. Tormentors to warlocks."

"Tormentor? I could have left you to die in the autumn. Thrown you out of my house, put wards up around the property. Turned the neighbors against you as well," Martha spat. "And you say I torment you?"

"You think I don't want you? You think I don't wrap my hand around my cock at night thinking of you?"

"Shut your mouth," Martha shouted. "Do not speak to me like that or I will throw you out of my house this very night."

"You would have already." He shook his head. "No. You are keeping me here for some reason I haven't garnered yet. But as long as I play by your rules, don't bring ruination down on myself, you'll let me stay." He smirked. "I should be getting to bed. I'll be thinking of you." He brushed past her before she could dodge out of the way.

Martha gritted her teeth and held her spoon so tightly it bruised her palm. There was a reason he was here. Their souls were connected in some way. He wasn't her soulmate—thank every immortal being—but there was something. She couldn't find it, no matter how many circles she had drawn in the snow, no matter how many dried herbs she crushed and left to be carried away by the wind. It was a mystery. One Martha intended to solve.

She added a neatly cut log to the fire, something she had enjoyed about Jonas's presence. Living in the new world alone was not an option. If he hadn't come, she surely would have starved to death for all the time chopping wood would have taken.

The fire shimmered and popped, sending a hum through the room. Her cat hissed and darted to her side.

"You feel it to?" she whispered, running her hand over the back of her cat. "What is it?"

Until she could figure it out, he had to stay.

Damp spring arrived and with the heavy rains, Henry's resolution to leave town grew. If he wanted to be settled before the freeze of winter, he needed to build his small cabin this summer. Next year, he could work on something larger, something that would take many months to complete and be a house to live out the rest of his days.

Once the snow melted and the land turned to muck, Henry spent his Sunday afternoons walking. He walked for miles, until the sun dipped so close to the horizon he had to run back to avoid being lost. He explored all the lands around Baltimore. Much of it was already claimed, but he wanted a good piece, not a convenient plot. There needed to be a pond or a lake for fishing. Room to grow food as well as keep animals. He'd want a house and a barn. This was where he would live for the rest of his life. It needed to be the right piece of land.

"Why on earth would you leave us? Town is where you should be. The church is here, Marcus and I are here. What could the wilderness offer you? This was such a wild land when I arrived, and now it's very nice here. Rarely does anything terrible happen. You wouldn't have liked the early days. No one did. But now, it's settled."

"I didn't come to the new world to be settled," Henry explained. "I came to make something for myself. I'll never do that at the docks. I'm not a shipping man. I'm a farmer. I can trap, I can build things. That's the life that is meant for me."

"How are we to survive winter without you?" she pressed.

"You survived many before me. And you have Marcus now." He clapped the boy on the shoulder. "He'll take care of you in the cold months."

That seemed to placate Mrs. Franklin for the moment, but Henry wouldn't leave it like that with the boy.

"If Mrs. Franklin dies while you are still a boy, you'll come live with me," he promised.

"Truly?"

"Of course. But stay with her for now. Setting up a homestead is back-breaking work. It'll be cold and miserable most nights. Lots of hungry evenings too. Stay with Mrs. Franklin for a few more years. But if something happens, you'll have a place with me."

Marcus embraced Henry and skittered off, a smile on his face. Good. Henry finally felt like there was a brightness to the future.

Within the week, all three of them were so ill they couldn't lift their heads.

Martha sat on the shore of the pond, her eyes on the water. It was still spring. The deep green algae hadn't bloomed yet and she could see the clouds floating by in the surface.

She whispered to the land, water, and sky. She didn't know the names of the spirits here yet. There was no use calling out to Sulis or Modron. They were a world away. This new place had different powers at play. They flitted in the corners of her eyes, sticking to shadows and rippling water.

She needed them. And she could not wait years while she courted them slowly.

Martha began leaving offerings. Bits of jam or saucers filled with sweeten teas. She wove flower crowns from the first wildflowers and left a trail of them around the pond.

After a near moon of offerings, She came.

Martha didn't see Her at first. She was just another flicker on the edge of her sight as the sun kissed the horizon and threw golden light across the land. Jonas was already inside, washed and ready for his meal. He would sit by the fire until she served him like the wife he wanted.

But that flicker grew like a candle coming closer in the night, until She sat beside Martha, Her smallest finger linked over her own. She didn't turn to face the creature. There were stories of otherworldly beings disappearing the moment human eyes gazed upon them.

"You have given many gifts. Were they in trade?"

"Not in trade but in good faith. I worry about the man living here." Martha chose her words carefully. Asking a favor of a being such as this came with heavy consequences if one wasn't careful.

"The warlock," the creature hissed. "We do not like him."

"I have thought of sending him away," she continued slowly. "But I am unsure whether that is the right course of action."

"No, no. You must not send him away. The two of you are woven together, tight as a blanket."

"He is not my soulmate," she spat.

"Ha! No, he is not. But you are not done with him. Nor he with you." The being chuckled. "You've known him before, and you'll know him again. You'll not be rid of that soiled soul for a very long time."

"I'm meant to live with him the rest of my life?"

"I did not say that." The being shifted a bit, turning less solid and more into light. "I like the jam. My people all like the jam," She said and then shimmered away.

"Martha? Are you putting dinner on?" Jonas called from inside. She stood and brushed her hands against her skirt. Couldn't be rid of him yet. Maybe not rid of him ever.

The being had not given her the answer she'd hoped for.

Henry had never burned with a fever like this.

When he was a boy, the entire family had the measles. It was a dreadful disease, and he still remembered the headache that had accompanied his illness, but nothing was like this fever. He was in a constant state of freezing chills and burning up. No matter how many blankets he tried to pull over him, he couldn't stop his body from shaking.

Marcus had fallen ill first. He took to bed one night and didn't come down for breakfast. When Mrs. Franklin went to wake him, she had yelled her prayers that they'd all survive it. Henry was ill second. He tried to stay on his feet, keep the fire fed, pour water down Marcus's throat, but eventually there was nothing he could do. He collapsed into his own bed, hoping sleep might overtake him and find him healed.

He wasn't sure how many days had passed in this stupor. He still dragged himself out of bed every morning to fetch water for everyone. By now, Mrs. Franklin was in her bed, her breathing labored and awful. Marcus seemed a little better. His cheeks had some color in them, and he was able to take all the water Henry offered. Mrs. Franklin didn't wake when Henry tried to stir her, so he left a cup beside her bed and prayed she would wake and drink on her own.

In his fever, he dreamed of a piece of land with a wide pond surrounded by flower crowns. A woman was there, sitting on the edge, fishing. Her hair was tucked beneath a bonnet but a few wisps at the nape of her neck flew free and shone gold in the sunshine.

She is waiting for you, a voice whispered in his head. *She needs you strong and able. Needs your heart and your hands.*

He tried to reach out and brush his fingers against her shoulder, but she slipped away, and the dream was gone.

He slept on, for days, weeks—sometimes it felt like years. He would wake for moments, drink water, check on Marcus, who seemed better all the time, make sure Mrs. Franklin still lived. But he always collapsed back into his bed and fell into that sweet oblivion.

Until one day, Henry awoke—drenched in sweat—his fever finally abated. He groped for his cup of water, downed it, then carefully stood. He was thirsty and hungry. And for the first time in what felt like eons, he was fully awake.

He made his way to the kitchen and devoured some dried meat. Then he filled a pot with water and put it to boil. There were some onions and a bit of rabbit from before they were ill. Once the food was going, he filled cups of water and brought them to Marcus—who was sitting in bed reading and looking much better—and Mrs. Franklin, who barely stirred. She looked so tiny in her bed, as if she were wasting away.

"Damn," he breathed. Henry wasn't an innocent man. He'd seen fever take young and old. Mrs. Franklin didn't look likely to survive this.

There was no use mourning at her bedside when the house was in shambles from the lot of them being bedridden for so long. He cleaned the kitchen, collected the half-finished cups of water that had been discarded throughout the home, and went to the market. He bought food for the first time in weeks and was privy to gossip. Apparently, what had stricken the entire town was called influenza. At least five people had died so far. Henry was glad he and Marcus seemed to be in the clear, but Mrs. Franklin clearly was not.

With a few spring vegetables, two chickens, and a new tin of tea, Henry returned with clear eyes. He and Marcus ate most of the first chicken, and with the remains he made another soup. He tried to coax Mrs. Franklin to eat some, and she rewarded him with a couple mouthfuls. Then, he made her a fresh cup of tea and left it steaming beside her bed. He hoped that at the very least, the scent might stir her awake.

He chopped wood, fed the fire, and at the end of the day, collapsed in front of the hearth with a cup of tea in his hand.

"I thought you both were going to die," Marcus interrupted his thoughts, "and I was going to be alone again."

"I'm young and strong," Henry said quickly, hoping to settle his fears. "And I'll not leave you. Mrs. Franklin..." He didn't want to scare the boy, but he also didn't want to give him false hope. "She could use as many prayers as you can spare."

"I'll be sure to ask for her to live as many times a day as I remember," Marcus answered solemnly.

"Thank you. Now off to bed. We have another day ahead of us. And I'll have to go back to the docks soon to earn more coin. I'll need you to take care of the house while I'm gone. Feed the fire. Clean the kitchens. Try to get Mrs. Franklin to eat something." He wasn't sure how long this would last, but life always marched on.

Martha turned her knife over in her hand, mesmerized by the glint of the sun on the blade. There was a vengeance in her heart that she didn't quite understand.

Yes, Jonas had been terrible. Awful really, with the way he spoke to her. Lazy and spiteful and a waste of a human body. But there wasn't anything outwardly violent he had done toward her, thanks to the vow he'd made. But now...suddenly her blood boiled for the man.

He was all sly smiles and leering glares as the weather turned from early spring to midspring. The earth was awakening and with it, Jonas's true self. He brushed past her time and time again, let his hand linger on her shoulder.

She knew him from before.

Martha knew well enough she was not once-born. She was one of those who came back life after life, had magic running through their veins and their souls. Jonas was too. They must have known each other before. That was why she had such a terrible connection to him. Why she couldn't throw him out to the elements. There was something else bothering her. Something from the past she couldn't see yet.

It was like her memories from before were locked away in a part of her mind she couldn't access, an itch she couldn't scratch. She needed to get to them, to have a clearer picture of who Jonas was, but she didn't know how.

Martha sat by the fireside darning a pair of stockings. She'd worn holes through both pairs she owned, and while working with needle and thread was her least favorite chore, she'd let it go long enough.

"Have you considered our marriage?" Jonas asked, slumping beside her. He pulled his shoes off, then his socks, and stuck his bare feet next to the fire.

"I have not," she answered quickly. "I've barely had a moment to turn my head to anything other than the vegetable garden and fishing."

Jonas nodded his head a few times. "I have thought on it much while I hunt."

Martha fought the urge to roll her eyes. His hunting had turned up a total of three rabbits in the last six months. Before he'd died, Thomas had taken down a dozen deer in their time in the colonies.

"I thought you might need a bit of persuasion."

Martha set down her work and looked at him. What could the fates possibly want her to do with him? Was she to keep him here and away from his poor soulmate?

"In England, my family is quite powerful," he began as if he were to regale her with tales of greatness. "My sister was a great witch and I one of the few practicing warlocks."

Martha couldn't help but peek over her shoulder. Speaking those words aloud were never smart. Their kind had been hunted for hundreds of years. When she'd first come to the colonies, she had hoped she could practice more openly, with the talk of religious freedom. But several women and men had been killed in the north for witchcraft not twenty years earlier. Martha would keep her craft to herself.

"I wanted to make an advantageous marriage. You see, I will have powerful heirs. There was a woman in England, a witch, who I thought would make a good bride, good mother to my children. Sadly, she refused my hand." He paused and leaned toward her. "My sister and I cursed her entire line. I killed her entire family and came to the colonies to finish the job. Once they are all dead, the power of all the Bay witches will transfer to me. I'll be more powerful than any living witch or warlock. I will be powerful enough to bring about an age of warlocks in this country. No one could withstand my rage."

Martha stared at him.

So, this was her purpose. She didn't need to unlock her pasts to learn what to do next. Jonas offered it freely.

She smoothed her skirt and met his eyes.

"Why didn't you tell me?" she answered, her voice as sickly sweet as she could manage.

Mrs. Franklin recovered, much to Henry's surprise. By mid-April, that woman was up and about, no one the wiser that she'd basically shook hands with death and told him to come back later. She also had plans for their little unit.

"You will settle a piece of land this summer. Get a house of some sort built, start thinking about where the animals will live and where you'll grow the food." She paused to have a spoonful of soup. "In a few years, you'll fetch Marcus. I don't want that boy going through the first few winters. You'll find all the cracks in the house and fix them up and then come to town to pick up the boy and he will live with you."

Henry tried to smother a smile. "Is that what will happen?"

"Yes," Mrs. Franklin reiterated and set her spoon down. "If anything, that fever showed me I won't live forever. And Marcus is not going to be alone again. He'll be a good worker for you. Plus, he needs a family. You have the option to give him one." She slammed her mouth shut.

"What do you think, Marcus? You interested in working a farm?"

Marcus nodded with a big smile. "At home, I took care of the chickens by myself. I'm really good with birds. Chickens, ducks, even geese, the squawking bastards."

"Marcus!" Mrs. Franklin exclaimed. "Language!"

"Oops. Sorry, Mrs. F., but geese can be a handful. Truly."

Henry rolled his lips between his teeth to keep from laughing. "I'd love to have you as my poultryman, Marcus." He let himself smile now. "It's time I found a bit of land, then!"

That evening, Martha sat by the fire. She had brushed out her hair slowly, until there weren't any knots and it shone gold in the firelight. Jonas wasn't back yet from his trappings, but she knew what the evening would hold. She had cleaned her nails and her teeth, stripped down to nothing but her shift. She'd even bathed in the nearby river at noon, when the sun was the warmest it would be all day.

Now, she sat and waited. He would be expecting dinner. He would not get it.

Martha understood why she and Jonas were connected. A warlock able to kill witches was no small feat. A warlock in position to inherit the power of an entire family of witches...it was almost unthinkable.

Jonas stomped loudly up the path. She hoped he had at least a pair of rabbits in his hand for all the noise he made. He would surely frighten all the fish to the bottom of the pond with his clamoring.

"What an awful day," he complained the moment the door opened. "No rabbits, no fish, not even a—" he stopped abruptly when his eyes swept over her.

"Good evening," Martha said quietly. She rose from her spot by the fire and stood in front of it, knowing it illuminated every curve as she did.

Jonas set his empty trap down and shrugged out of his light coat. His brow furrowed as he stared at her.

"I've thought a lot about what you told me," she began. Martha slowly closed the distance between them. "You are a powerful warlock. I am a simple witch, but if you think I would be well-suited to stand beside you in this life"—she raised her hand to his shoulder and set it against him—"I would be honored to be your wife and give you children."

Jonas's mouth fell agape. "Do…do you want to get, um, married?" he asked as he tripped over his words.

"I would prefer a simple handfasting," she continued. She took his hand in hers and placed it at her waist. "And that is something we can do tomorrow. In the morning." Martha took a deep breath. There was no going back from this. "I have never been with a man," she said slowly. "I do not want to disappoint you, but I beg that you be gentle with me."

Jonas nodded and dipped his head toward hers. "I am so pleased you will be mine."

After their first coupling, Jonas fell into an almost immediate sound sleep. Martha shifted until he rolled off her and she stared at the ceiling.

It was done. The blood of her maidenhead stained the sheets, and she would worry until her next bleeding came whether or not he had gotten her with child. But it would all be worth it.

It had to be.

Martha didn't sleep that night. She watched the sky until the first smudge of morning light began to kiss the horizon. Then she rolled to Jonas and ran her hand down his chest and nestled it between his legs. He jumped awake, then smirked when he saw her.

"You want another go?" he asked, pawing her body. She was still a bit sore and forced herself to quell her revulsion as he touched her.

"I do. I'd like...I'd like to ride you, if you would like that," she said demurely.

"Ride me?" he repeated.

Martha nodded. "My sister was a married woman...before she died, she told me how she pleased her husband, that I might do the same one day." Martha swung her leg over Jonas's hips and positioned herself above him. She pulled her shift off and shook her hair out.

His lips curled, and he grabbed at her breasts and hips. Martha leaned forward to seat herself upon him, then started moving slowly.

"Oh, Martha. Who knew you were such a little whore?" he sneered. "Ride me like I paid you," he commanded, slapping her bottom.

She nodded and leaned forward, planting her hands on either side of him. He groaned and grabbed her hips, slamming her against him over and over. He was lost to the pleasure he found in her body.

So lost he didn't feel her reach beneath the pillow.

So lost he didn't notice her bracing her weight on her left hand.

So lost, that when she drew her knife across his neck, there was no look of shock in his death mask. Only the screwed-up face of a man about to spill his seed.

Martha climbed off his body and fished her shift off the floor. She pulled it over her head and looked over the bed. What a waste. It would all have to be burned. But not him. She would bury Jonas.

Henry set off to find land. It would take him days, sleeping under trees and catching what he ate. There were no open parcels close enough to Baltimore that they could be reached on foot in the span of a day. So, he slept in the late spring air, ate fish from rivers fat with rushing water, and enjoyed the solitude this land had to offer. He basked in the silence he'd missed in town, when any time of day or night someone could be bumbling down the streets.

On his eighth day of searching, he came around a bend just as the sun came out from the clouds. Rays of sunlight danced across the land, giving him an unending feeling of confidence in this place. This was the place. He was meant to live here. The heavens had actually parted as he walked down—

There was a house. And a woman outside. She worked tirelessly with a shovel, filling in a hole.

"Hello, there!" Henry called. "Do you need help?"

She set the shovel down, wiped her forehead, and locked eyes with him.

Her. He'd found her. An eon later, he'd found her.

A million memories rushed him. It was always like this, every time he saw her. He couldn't remember her until the very moment he saw her face, and then suddenly, her face was all he could remember.

"You!" she called, a giggle on her mouth. "Where have you been?" she laughed.

"Baltimore! Before that, Devon. Where have you been?"

"Here. Before that, Suffolk."

"You mean I didn't have to cross the ocean to find you?" He jogged to her now, a smile about to split his face.

"I suppose not, but I am glad you did." He skidded to a stop in front of her.

Aye, she was beautiful again. Her golden hair and sparkling eyes; those eyes had seen him a hundred times before.

"What are you called?" she asked.

"Henry. You?"

"Martha." He took her hand in his and kissed it. "What are you burying?"

"A man," she answered. "He tried to force me into marriage by claiming he was a more powerful warlock than I was a witch."

"My girl? No one could be more powerful than her." Henry kissed her forehead. "I'll finish the work."

"Thank you, love." Martha sat on a stump beside him. "Should we be married?"

"If you like. Neighbors might talk if we aren't."

"True." Martha sighed. "I'm so happy you are here. That piece of shite has been trying to convince me my soulmate wasn't coming." She shook her head. "As if I could abandon you."

"Who was he?"

"Jonas Fortworth."

Henry nodded and looked back at his work. He needed to finish burying the prick so he could take Martha inside and show her just how much he'd missed her since their last time together.

He'd called her so many different names over their lives, but he always called her love. His love, his soulmate, the one he walked beside. They'd had children sometimes, and sometimes none. They'd spent sixty years together or one. Every time, it was a new and grand adventure. This life would be no different. He would cherish every moment with Martha, no matter what faced them.

"Finished," he announced, brushing his hands off on his trousers. "Would you happen to have a ladle of water for a traveler?"

Martha raised her eyebrow. "I think I can muster a bit more than a ladle of water. You're going to marry me, after all."

Henry grinned. He set the shovel against the wall and followed Martha into the house as he reached for her waist.

Finally.

Chapter Twenty-One

"Sage. Will. Sage. Will. Sage. Will."

"What?" Sage snapped. Fuck, her head was pounding. Lavender's voice was like a bee buzzing in her ear that wouldn't go away.

"Are you awake? Oh, finally. Will? Will? Will?"

Will grumbled beside her.

Sage slowly opened her eyes and peered at Lavender. "Why are you less than a foot away from my face?"

"I've been having a minor heart attack for the last six hours and that's what you say to me?" Lavender shot back.

"You are very close to me."

Lavender backed up and Sage slowly sat, rubbing her forehead.

Will pawed around until he wove his hand through hers. "Hello, Harvester."

Sage smiled and looked back at him. His eyes were still closed but he was slowly waking up.

The flood of it all hit her—Henry, Ariston, the man on the plains. Will had always been there with her. Life after life, love after love.

"Hello again," she answered quietly. It would take a little bit of time to feel like she did just moments ago, fully immersed in her life as Martha. But now she knew she would get there with Will. She always did.

"Hello!" Lavender shouted. "You guys were out for thirty-six hours! Way longer than anyone else."

Sage shrugged. "Probably because we saw more than one life." She lay back down next to Will and stretched her arms above her head. "One life probably takes twenty-fourish hours. We had a lot more to see."

"What do you mean you saw more than one life? The spell is only supposed to show you the most important life." Lavender jumped to her feet and ran to the bookcase, pulling a homebound book off the shelf. "No one has ever seen more than one life."

"Guess we're too important for that." Sage let the last day and a half wash over her. "Fuck, yeah." She smiled.

"What?" Lavender asked as she scribbled notes into the book.

"I killed Jonas Fortworth." She settled into her smug satisfaction. "I killed that asshole. Cut his throat while he thought I was falling in love with him."

"Yeah, you did," Will mumbled against her neck. "My queen of vengeance."

"Well..." Lavender paused. "That's a new development. Have you looked at a picture of Miloslav Stoch?"

"Why?" Sage asked, burrowing against Will. She was so sleepy still, she didn't even mind her big sister was watching her cuddle Will. Pre-past life viewing, she never would have done anything like that.

"Because he's the only known Stoch we haven't met. And you've seen Morana and Ivan."

"Not in a few weeks. Blond, right?" All those damn Stochs were blonde.

"Okay." Lavender's eyes were moving quickly like she was figuring out a million ways to solve every problem. "I have to go to work. I lied and said you were really sick so if you see anyone, act sick. But you should look up a picture of Miloslav. His mugshot is easily available online."

"I will," Sage said as she stifled a yawn.

"Do it. Please. Sooner rather than later." She looked between Sage and Will. "There's a lot of food out on the dining table. Probably more than you need." Lavender checked her watch. "I'm going to leave. Sage, front hall table." Lavender nodded once, then exited the attic.

Will slid his hands around her waist and squeezed a little tighter. "You smell so good." He settled against her body and spread his hand wide over her ribs.

"I haven't showered in ages. Neither have you." She rolled onto her side to face him. "Shower time. Me first, then you." Sage slowly sat up. "I changed my mind. Eat first, shower second."

After a huge meal that was comprised of cinnamon donuts, apple muffins, a tomato and spinach quiche, and chicken salad with sliced grapes and almonds, Sage was showered and sitting on her bed waiting for Will.

She nervously smoothed a condom package between her fingers. She felt electric, like a live fuse that was jumping around and spitting sparks. It was like every inch of her was awake for the first time.

Hell, she remembered being with Will. Not Will. Henry and Ariston and...she didn't really speak in that first life. But she remembered him. It was always good. And not in a like orgasmic way—though it was good in that way too. With every other incarnation of Will's soul, it was good because it was with him. And they would laugh, and he was gentle.

"Hey," he mumbled from the doorway. His hair was wet, but not dripping, and he had thrown on a T-shirt and shorts similar to what he had slept in when they were at the motel.

"Oh. Hi." Will's gaze immediately went to the condom in her hand. She slowly set it beside her.

"We don't have to do anything today," Will started. "We can go for a walk or go down to the beach or you can show me your fields. We've been so busy, what with Baltimore and then the spell—"

"Will Markham," she interrupted, "if you do not have sex with me today, I will cry. And I never cry."

Will grinned. "Hm. I don't want to make you cry," he teased. Sage left the condom on the bed and walked over to stand in front of him. She slipped her arms about his waist and hugged him. Will wrapped his arms around her and tucked his chin against her shoulder. It was such a simple movement, a simple display of affection, but needed. After everything they'd seen...the horrors they had faced together, it was imperative Sage feel him with her.

"Now that I've seen our past...I didn't realize how much I missed you," he said, his words muffled against her skin. "Goddess, I missed you."

Sage didn't answer, but she felt the same sentiment swelling in her chest. Instead, she found his mouth with her own, and like water breaking through a dam, she kissed him.

Their mouths moved in a way that felt like perfect rhythm. They tangled together, hands, bodies, tongues. Sage felt like a vine wrapping around a tree. They were turning into one, solitary being.

He was here, and she wasn't afraid or annoyed. She didn't wish she had more time on her own, to grow up a little more or become more set in her life. It was the right time, no matter how she had felt when she saw him at the farmers' market, and it had felt like all too much. Now, she was ready for him.

She intertwined their fingers and led him to the bed. They stood at the foot, staring down at her twin-size bed, still holding hands.

"The queen at the motel probably would have been a little easier," she said slowly. Her bed suddenly looked impossibly small. How did two people ever sleep in a bed this size? Sage knew it was done, but never by her.

She glanced at Rosemary's twin on the other side of the room. She should have planned ahead and pushed the beds together, but they might have suddenly separated, which would definitely kill the mood—

"I have every confidence we can make it work," Will said, bumping his shoulder against hers.

Sage laughed softly and looked down.

"Hey," Will said, turning toward her. "I can't wait to be with you for the rest of my life." He brushed his thumb over her cheek. "And we have the rest of our lives. Nothing big has to happen today. We could just...see where today takes us."

"See where it takes us?"

"You know. Let's see what feels good and right for us." Will wrapped his hand around her braid and tugged it playfully. "Look, I may have loved you since Paleolithic times, but we—Will and Sage—have known each other less than a week. We don't have to rush anything. Not to say we won't figure out how to have a lot of fun right now."

Sage couldn't suppress a grin. "We can definitely have some fun." She found the hem of his shirt and pulled it over his head. She balled it up before tossing it to the floor and ran her hands over his chest.

It was...perfect. He was perfect. He was different than Henry and Ariston but...he was like a house built with the same plans over and over again. Each iteration of this soul was new. But his skin always felt magical under her fingertips. He still felt unapologetically hers. She could have been blind and deaf, but the feel of his heartbeat beneath her hand was enough to tell her it was Will.

"Beautiful," he mumbled, smoothing his hands over her hair, over her braid and down her back. They moved lazily, like they had all the time in the world. Today would be a day of exploration, getting accustomed to each other again. They didn't need to rush into a physical relationship.

Sage had been so concerned something was off with her. She didn't really date, and there hadn't ever been anyone she felt the overwhelming need to be with. She had never seen another person and thought, I want to sleep with them. It wasn't that she didn't find men or women attractive, but before Will, they'd all been missing something.

It was as if the past had opened the floodgates. She knew Will, had known him over lifetimes. Their past intermingled with the present and gave her a blanketing sense of calm.

Will didn't mind that she was brash. Or sarcastic. Most of all, he didn't mind that she had murdered Jonas Fortworth in a past life to keep the other Bay witches safe. Hell, he had relished it. What had he called her? His queen of vengeance. She was one of the chosen of Nemesis.

Will's hand slid under the hem of her shirt and danced along the skin of her belly. She grinned and pulled her shirt off, then whipped her sports bra over her head.

"Mm," he hummed, running his hands up her belly and settling them on her breasts. "Remember that night in the temple?"

Sage giggled. "You were afraid Nemesis was going to curse us."

"Not so afraid that I turned away, though." Will found the waistband of her pants and slowly slid them down her body. "I'm brave when it comes to a chance to be with you."

"You're brave a lot." Sage mirrored his action and pulled his shorts down until he stepped out of them. "Facing Lysander? Leaving the tribe in early winter? You always did a lot for me."

Will pressed his forehead against hers. "You've always been worth it." He kissed her quickly. "I feel so lucky I found you so early. I couldn't imagine being one of those people who met their soulmate at forty."

"Too impatient?"

"Definitely." With a wicked grin, Will manipulated her until she was sitting on the edge of the bed, then dropped to his knees and ran his tongue around Sage's nipple before sucking it into his mouth. She grabbed his shoulders and steadied herself. Her head was swimming with every single sensation. He eased her onto the bed, covering her body with his. Her thighs split over his hips, and he rocked against her a few times.

"Goddess, I missed you," he breathed against her neck. "I had no idea how much. Life isn't the same as before. I feel...I feel so fucking alive when I am with you."

"Will," Sage panted. "Lie on your back and let me go on top."

He kissed her softly, then did as she said, his hands never leaving her body while he moved.

Sage kissed his mouth, his neck, his collarbone. The space over his heart. Between two of his ribs on his right side. His hipbone. She glanced up at him. His eyes were wide, and his lips parted.

She grinned.

She took him then, in her hand, in her mouth, and moved over him intent on making it too good for him to last. She wanted to capture that first time when he'd been so excited to touch her, kissing set him off.

She looked back at him but this time, his head was thrown back, the cords of his neck protruding while he panted and groaned. He fisted the blankets on either side and pulled the covers toward his body.

Sage loved it. She felt completely in control of both him and his desire—she was holding the keys to his very being at this moment.

"Sage, Sage, Sage," he mumbled. She felt power growing within her with every muttering of her name. Like he was speaking an incantation, and the power of the sun was glowing within her soul, getting brighter with every moment.

His hand moved from grasping the blanket and wove with hers. He was so warm and strong. She never wanted to let go.

He dragged their clasped hands to his belly. It raced wildly now, sucking in deep breaths. Sage felt warmth spreading throughout her entire body, from the tips of her fingers and toes, to the crown of her head. It wasn't like she was about to come. It was a different warmth.

It felt like magic running through her.

Will came with a grunt and with every contraction of his body, every jerk and groan and uncontrollable movement, Sage felt more cemented in them.

"That was amazing." Will finally breathed as she eased off him and crawled up the bed to lie beside him. He tipped her chin to his mouth and quickly devoured her. He flipped her underneath him and kissed his way to her breasts before taking his time teasing both nipples, back and forth, until Sage wrapped her legs around his back as she writhed.

"Goddess, I want to make you come," he murmured against her skin. He trailed further down, nuzzling against her belly as he did.

"I've never," Sage began as she shifted her legs open, "you know, received oral. So, I don't want you to feel bad if…I don't finish."

Will smiled. "You tell me what feels good. If you'd rather I use my fingers like before, I can do that instead."

"Uh, I didn't say that," Sage stammered as he ran his finger over her. "I'm very…interested in oral. Definitely give it a go. I'll reserve judgment until after we try."

He nodded, still playing with her clit. "Give me directions. I'm very good at following them." He stuck his middle and ring finger in his mouth, then in a fluid motion, slid his fingers inside her while also leaning down to tease her clit with his tongue.

"Holy fuck!" Sage shouted. Will stilled for a moment. "Don't stop," she added. "Never stop. Who's the goddess of orgasms? Hedone? Hedone," she babbled. "We should praise her more often."

She felt Will hum against her as he teased her with slow, long, languid licks. His fingers gently moved in her, pressing up as he did.

Hell, Sage had been worried about coming. It had been less than two minutes, and she already felt that delicious, warm building in her entire body. Her knees shook, her hips ground against Will. She reached above her head and grasped the headboard. Just as she felt she couldn't take anymore, Will reached his free hand up and pinched her nipple hard.

She threw her head back and watched as stars danced through her vision, holding onto the ascension of her orgasm before it broke her into a million, little stars beneath the mouth of her soulmate.

Sage had no idea what she'd been missing.

Chapter Twenty-Two

"Will?" Sage asked.

"Mmm?" was the best reply he could manage. He was still basking in the post-hookup haze and could barely open his eyes let alone his mouth.

Sage wiggled her body next to his and wrapped a leg around his waist.

He was up now.

Sage slowly pulled her body over his and then stepped off the bed.

"Where are you going?" he exclaimed, not even attempting to hide the desperation in his voice.

"I promised Lavender I would look at a picture of Miloslav Stoch." She fished her phone out of her bag from the corner of the room. "Let me just do a quick search..." Her fingers danced over her phone. She clicked a few times and then burst out laughing.

"Is Miloslav Stoch...hilarious?"

"Nope," Sage said between belly laughs. She crossed the room and climbed back into bed next to Will, sidling her naked body against his. "What do you think, did I murder Miloslav Stoch in another life?" She handed Will the phone.

"Shit. That's definitely Lysander. And that paleo asshole. Is he also Jonas Fortworth?"

"Yup. No wonder he's hellbent on carrying through this curse, sending his little minions to test us out." Sage blew out a breath. "Hell, he probably knows we're here and together. It's not hard to search my name and find my picture from my high school softball team."

"Fate's really kicking you and your sisters around. Your soulmates show up but also with a Stoch who wants to murder you?" Will snuggled against her neck.

"Miloslav can do his fucking worst. I don't know how many times that man needs me to kill him to understand he should stay away from me, but if the answer is four..."

"Sage. It's not the 1700s. Or Ancient Greece. Or...the Paleolithic period. If you murder Miloslav Stoch, you'll go to prison. Please don't go to prison. I just met you. I don't want to switch to conjugal visits."

Sage laughed and rolled on her side to face him. "I promise I won't straight up murder him like I did before. Self-defense is on the table though. Morana and Ivan both came pretty close to killing my sisters. And Boris nearly killed Verbena, but he was already dead, so that was complicated. If Miloslav so much as raises a fist to either of us." Sage drew her finger across her neck. "Again."

Will hummed. "Is it bad that I find you irresistible when you are discussing your vengeful soul?" He buried his face against her neck and inhaled. Goddess, she smelled good. Some warlocks could smell their soulmates as well as other magicals, but Will had never taken the time to hone the skill. Sage...she smelled like crisp, dry leaves and spiced apples.

And sex. Sage smelled like the best sex Will could imagine. He ran his hand over her skin, finding new places he must have missed before. The space behind her knee. The round edge of her shoulder. There was a freckle at the base of her neck he couldn't believe he hadn't noticed.

He remedied his omission with a lingering kiss on the spot.

"You're very touchy," Sage sighed.

"Are you not into it?"

"Not at all. Touch away." Sage spread her arms overhead and her legs wide and pursed her lips. "I am yours to explore."

Will melted into her. Every inch of her skin became a balm to his soul. The worry of the Stochs, the curse, the overbearing grief of seeing their past lives, especially when they were Ariston and Callistrate, faded now that he was with her.

They were each other's perfect complement.

He kissed her jaw, her neck, the space between her shoulder and collarbone. Will allowed himself to be greedy with her skin. He scraped his teeth between the valley of her breasts, palming one as he did. He moved his cheek roughened with stubble over the soft skin of her belly until she squirmed beneath him.

"Will," she moaned. She wrapped her legs around his back and pinned him in place. "I want..." She stifled a cry as he ran his mouth over her pebbled nipple. "I want you."

"You have me, Sage Bay. For now and forever. I'm never leaving you."

"That's all wonderful, but I meant I want your dick. In me. As soon as possible."

"Oh," Will answered, a bit startled. "Do you want...I mean, should I get you off first? Mouth or fingers?"

"I'm good to go from the amazing oral you gave me less than thirty minutes ago," she teased. "I think I'd rather fuck first."

Will grinned. "I'd love to fuck first." He might not have had a lot of experience with women, but he didn't live in a hole. If he couldn't get Sage off with his dick, well, he knew he could do it with his tongue or his fingers. And there was no end to the absolute delight he received making her come. Nothing was better than listening to her shatter apart because of something he did.

Sage wiggled out from under him and walked toward the door.

"Are we...fucking in the shower?" he asked.

"No. My first time will be in a bed. But the condoms are downstairs."

"I thought you had a condom in here?"

"I do. I have one. I think I'd like to grab more than one. Just in case."

"You are going to walk downstairs completely naked?" Will pushed himself to sit on the bed.

"No one will walk by. We're far enough off the road, our only true neighbors are Verbena and Luke, and they know not to wander around our property unannounced, especially now that you are here. Would you rather I throw a shirt on?"

"Absolutely not."

"Thought so."

Sage disappeared out of the room, and Will rolled onto his back.

He was so damn happy. Sure, he was still processing the myriads of past lives he and Sage had witnessed, but in this moment, none of it mattered. And hell, ending on a high note of getting to live a long and happy life with Martha was a treat.

"Let's do this," Sage interrupted his thoughts. She crawled over him like a wild animal, her thighs split over his hips, and she ripped open the condom.

"I paid really good attention in health class," she continued, rolling it over him. "Seemed like one thing they teach you in high school that actually matters in the real world. But if it feels wrong, tell me."

"Doesn't feel wrong," he choked out. "Feels perfect."

"Good." She took him in her hand, hovered over him for a minute, then sank down on him in the most delicious relief.

"Holy hell," Will groaned.

"Finally," she breathed. "Finally." She slid over him achingly slow, moving her body at a languid pace that drove him mad.

"You feel so good," he blurted out. Fuck, did that sound corny? He wanted Sage's first time—their first time—to be perfect.

"So do you," she answered on a moan, and all his anxiety melted away. This was Sage. His soulmate. His Callistrate, his Martha, his forever and always. Their first time would be great because it was them. They were destined to be great.

"Could you...could you touch me also?" she asked.

"'Course. Where?"

She took his hand and guided it between them until his knuckles hit her most sensitive spot, and he was immediately rewarded with a shudder. Sage moved more quickly now, slipping her body over his hand and his dick in a hurried frenzy. She was loud, moaning, panting, his name interrupted by quick mentions of different gods and goddesses.

"Keep saying my name," he begged. "I love it..."

"Will, Will, Will," she moaned as she moved with purpose, harder and insistent, until she cried out and collapsed against his chest in a flurry of spasms.

"I've got you," he whispered against her hair and flipped her to her back.

He was still buried deep, trying to keep still for a moment. Which was nearly impossible with her still clenching around him.

"You can move," she panted. She grabbed at his shoulders, his arms, his waist. "Keep moving."

He didn't have to be told twice. Will drove into her again, relishing in this absolute joy. Goddess, he'd never felt as alive as in this moment, inside of his soulmate. He plunged into her hard as he finally came, grabbing onto every inch of Sage he could. She squeezed him with her arms, her thighs, her core. She buried her hands in his hair and pressed kisses across his head.

"Goddess, I can't wait to marry you," he breathed against her neck, then pumped one last time. "I can't wait."

Sage stiffened beneath him.

Chapter Twenty-Three

"What did you just say?" Her legs were still wrapped around his body, his face pressed against her neck. He was still inside her, for goddess's sake, but she could feel herself instinctively shrinking away.

"I said I can't wait to marry you," Will answered slowly.

Sage wiggled out from beneath him. He gave her room to move, rolling to his side.

"What a fucked-up thing to say," she mumbled. She pawed around the ground for her clothes. Where were her fucking clothes? They had to be here somewhere. She stood up and surveyed the floor. Shirt was by the door, shorts near there too. Her underwear seemed to have teleported into another dimension, so for now, she'd forego them.

She pulled her shirt on, then stepped into her shorts. She undid her braid and combed through her hair a few times, then started to re-braid it.

"Is something wrong?"

"You brought up marriage and we've known each other for six days. We literally just slept together for the first time." Sage laughed a little. "Moving a bit fast for me, Will. Might want to know you for a month before we make a lifelong commitment."

"A bit fast?" Will sat up and leaned against her headboard. His eyebrows raised halfway up his forehead. "We're soulmates, remember? There isn't really a timeline, seeing as we've had multiple together."

"You're the one who literally just said that we could take things as slow as we wanted. And now you are talking about getting married?"

"I didn't want you to feel like we had to rush the physical."

"But rushing the emotional is okay?"

Will screwed his face up. "This morning we woke up from seeing three whole lives in which we were in love. I think we already rushed the emotional," he pointed out.

"Yeah, but that doesn't mean marriage. Shit, Will. We're basically still children. If we were sixteen you wouldn't be saying things like that."

"We're not teenagers. We're in our mid-twenties. Lots of people get married in their mid-twenties. My parents got engaged after three days and were married two months later, and they were twenty-six."

"And my parents dated for over a year, had a six-month engagement, and got married at thirty," she shot back.

"You don't want to get married until you are thirty? You want to date for six years?" Will's voice sounded panicked now.

"I don't know! Do we ever need to get married? Hell, it's been a big couple of days. We went to Baltimore, saw our past lives, and I lost my fucking virginity five minutes ago. And now you are talking about marrying you? Come on, man. Give me a minute."

Will shook his head. "I'm confused. Where do you see this going? In every other life—"

"You mean in the Paleolithic period? Or Ancient Greece? Or the colonies? We're in the twenty-first century this time around. Our lives are going to be wildly different. We didn't even get married in Greece. I don't think we should rush into anything." She wound her hands together trying to stop the freight train of words coming out of her mouth, but she couldn't. She couldn't ignore what he'd said. He wanted marriage.

She did not.

"Rush into it? There's a family of witches and warlocks trying to kill you and your sisters and steal your blood. And you straight up murdered one of them in a past life. I wouldn't say wanting to be with you as much as I can is rushing into anything. I just watched a past-life movie where I lost you after two months in a spectacularly horrific way. Lysander had no qualms about killing me and trying to assault you, I don't think we should treat his soul coming so flippantly."

"I can handle Miloslav Stoch alone," she began.

"Um, screw you," Will interrupted. "I don't care if you think you can handle him alone, I'm pretty certain the soul of Jonas Fortworth has a strong vendetta against you, and he'll have no qualms going to prison for murder if he gets to kill you. I'm not abandoning you to face him alone."

Sage rolled her eyes. "I'm blessed by a goddamn vengeance goddess. Excuse me if I'm not aching for a librarian to help me."

The moment the words escaped her mouth, she regretted them. Will's face crumbled. "Shit, I didn't mean it," she started. "I'm so sorry. That was bitchy. You are an unending resource of knowledge and—"

He put his hand up to stop her. "Be honest with me. Do you want to get married?"

Sage felt her heart twist.

Honest. She would be honest.

"No." Sage had never, ever pictured a wedding. Hell, when they were Martha and Henry, they'd gotten married so people wouldn't shun them for living together out of wedlock. But now? Did it even matter? She didn't like dresses, she disliked parties even more. Even the whole ritual part of it had never been her cup of tea. If you loved someone, you should just love them. You didn't need a legal ceremony to prove it. "I never really saw the point of it."

Will nodded, his jaw working as he did. "Do you want to have children? Not today, not tomorrow, not this year. Do you ever want to have children?"

Shit. They were really going for it now. He had asked for honesty, so she would give it to him.

"I don't know. We didn't have children in Greece or Baltimore," she pointed out. She knew there were more lives, other ones Callistrate and Martha sort of remembered on the periphery but she didn't for some reason. She'd been a mother at points, she could feel that, but not in the important lives.

"We had Marcus," Will interjected. It was true. While Martha had never been able to keep a pregnancy in the colonies—they'd all ended before they were little more than a heavy period—they had raised Marcus into a fine young man together. They had doted over his wife when he'd met her, had loved their grandchildren with the fiercest of hearts, but Marcus had not been of their blood. He wasn't magical, he didn't marry a witch, but he was their chosen son, and undeniably one of the best things in all their lifetimes.

"Yeah," she answered softly. "We had Marcus."

"So, you don't think you want kids? Ever?"

"I'm being honest when I say I don't know. I'm twenty-four-years-old. Right now, it's a no. But I don't know if my answer will change."

Will nodded and pulled the covers back. He walked past her to the bathroom, and she assumed threw away the condom, then came back and got dressed.

"I need to pee," she said suddenly. She knew you were supposed to pee after sex for health reasons, but she also didn't feel like she could stand being in the same room as Will at the moment.

Why had she been so mean to him? She hadn't even meant it. She didn't care that he was a Zetic warlock and not something more battle ready like fire. Or chaos. She didn't even want someone like that! Oh, why did she say that? She was upset and unbalanced in the moment and let the cruelest thing she could think of out. Sage sat on the toilet and buried her face in her hands.

Marriage? Why the hell had he brought up marriage? She was a high school graduate with no higher education who was basically a farmer. Getting married and popping out kids in her twenties was what everyone would expect. She'd just be another Bay witch who didn't go to college and married the first guy who came along.

She peed and washed her hands, then walked back into her bedroom.

"Your phone is going off. It rang and you've gotten a bunch of texts." Will was making the bed, keeping his back to her.

Sage sighed and picked up her phone. She wasn't one to be glued to the thing, but at the moment, doing anything other than talking to Will sounded preferable.

"What the fuck..." she mumbled. She had six missed calls and twelve texts. She'd only been in the bathroom for about seven minutes.

Lavender: Sage! Answer your phone!

Verbena: I'm only two blocks away, I'll be there ASAP.

Rosemary: I'm here. She's doing okay. See you soon.

Lavender: Sage, call me the minute you see this.

Sage closed her texts and called Lavender.

"Where were you?" Lavender answered, her voice hard.

"Peeing, what the fuck is going on?"

"Laurel was attacked. I think by a Stoch. She hasn't been able to say but...he got her blood, Sage. Owen took her to the hospital for stitches. We're all meeting there. I have to go, I can't talk while I'm driving."

"I'll be there," Sage answered quickly. She hung up and tossed her phone on the bed.

"What's going on?" Will asked.

"Laurel was attacked. I need to get to the hospital."

"Oh, shit." Will took a few steps toward her and grabbed her hand. "Is she okay?"

"I don't know. But Lavender thinks the Stochs were involved, and if Miloslav is behind this..." Anger swirled in her chest. "No one hurts my family."

A familiar rage began building inside her, not unlike when Lysander killed Ariston.

If Miloslav hurt Laurel, he'd have a lot to account for.

She'd killed him three times before. He knew what happened when he crossed her soul.

Chapter Twenty-Four

Will had to run to keep up with Sage as she tore through the house. She grabbed her keys, somehow slid her shoes on faster than he could have imagined possible, and was out the door. He snatched his shoes and ran after her in his socks.

"Wait up!" he called, hopping toward the parked car.

Sage stopped at the car door and threw him a dagger look, which had Will forgetting about putting his shoes on until he was in the passenger seat beside her.

Once they were both seated, Sage whipped out of the driveway and onto the main drag.

"How far is the hospital?"

"About ten minutes if I go forty. It's not a major hospital, though. Lavender didn't say how bad her injuries were. But Laurel...she's a hedge witch. She's been working on her healing abilities. I watched her heal a huge wound in her neck. If she couldn't heal it herself..."

"Hey." Will reached for Sage's hand. "She's going to be okay. Modern medicine is amazing. Is there a helicopter pad here?"

"One of the wineries has one."

"That's good. If her injuries are bad enough, she'll be taken to a hospital in Boston. They'll take care of her."

Sage nodded but kept her jaw firm. "If Miloslav... I should have known he was here. I should have sensed it! Clearly, our souls are intertwined. Oh, that fucking asshole! His problems are with me, not my sisters. And now Laurel is hurt..."

"Don't think like that. We don't even know it was him yet. Doesn't she have a history with Morana?"

"She's in Guardian prison. And she already got Laurel's blood, she'd be going after a different Bay sister. Fuck, it has to be Miloslav."

Will exhaled. He and Sage still had a million things to talk about. If she never wanted to get married, if she never wanted kids...those were both things he always thought he would have in his life. But now wasn't the time. First, they needed to check on Laurel. Next, they had to survive a warlock who had killed him at least once before. They could save the big relationship fights for later. "Have you talked to your other sisters?"

"Rosemary is with her. Lavender and Verbena were on their way."

"No one else has been attacked?"

"Not yet. But I'm sure that bastard has his eye on all of us. Four to go and he'll have the power of the Bay Witches, which is more power than a solitary warlock has ever managed."

"You knew him as Jonas. Can you remember if he was powerful?"

Sage shook her head. "No. But none of us were then, remember? No practicing. They had just stopped burning witches. We took so many risks leaving offerings for the spirits of the land. Hell, I definitely wasn't a harvest witch then. I barely survived the winters before you. I wasn't doing real spell work, just sensing shit and putting out flowers and jam for gods and goddesses. But the ghost Bays said his sister was the real power."

"What kind of warlock is Miloslav?"

"Chaos. I have no idea what that means."

Will's stomach sank. "I do. It's not good."

"Tell me what it means. I want to be prepared."

Will took a deep breath. When he was in high school, he'd gone to a summer camp that pretended to be "exclusive" but was really just for warlock kids. All different warlocks from around the country hanging out in cabins in northern Wisconsin for three weeks in July gave a lot of parents of teen warlocks a much-needed break. But it also taught Will a lot about different types of warlocks.

He didn't care for many of them.

"Basically, he'll be able to take any situation and turn it chaotic. He could make the sky look like a storm when it's clear. Or touch your head and make you think you're in mortal danger. Chaos warlocks can cause mass panic in groups. Make a house look like it's on fire, make a normal group of people look like a mob. They suck. There were two brothers I knew, in high school, who were chaos warlocks. Assholes with stronger powers than every other warlock because they could make you believe anything."

Sage huffed. "Great. Makes you wonder if a good chaos warlock even exists."

"Probably not." Will looked over at Sage, her knuckles white from gripping the steering wheel so tightly. "He isn't going to win. I promise."

"Damn right. Not if me or Nemesis have anything to say about it." Sage blinked and for a moment her eyes looked like solid darkness.

He recognized that gaze, and it wasn't Sage.

"You okay?" Will asked. He rubbed his hand over her thigh, trying to bring her back to him. "Want me to drive?"

"What? No. I'm fine. You don't know the way."

"You looked a little...Ancient Greek for a moment there."

Sage whipped her head to face him, then turned back to watch the road. "What do you mean? My hair was suddenly dark and curly?"

"No. Your eyes looked like you were possessed by Nemesis. Which is fine, it would be a good time for her to decide to show up again, but I don't think it's a good idea for you to be in control of a vehicle if an ancient goddess is about to inhabit your being. She might not know how to drive a car."

Sage chewed on her lip, then pulled to the side.

"You drive," she barked, jumping out of the car. "I'll tell you how to get there. And don't drive slowly. I know all the cops. They'll understand that I'm going to see Laurel."

Will nodded and slid into the driver's seat. He reached his hand out to Sage, and she took it. He was still mad at her, still had a hundred things they needed to discuss, but right now, he needed to deliver his soulmate to her sister's side.

After parking in a small lot, rushing into the ER, and then barreling down a hallway, Will and Sage stood at the foot of Laurel's bed. Owen was in bed with her, holding her while she slept against his chest. Lavender had claimed the chair beside the bed and was furiously typing on her phone. Rosemary stood on the other side of the bed, weaving a bracelet of flowers around Laurel's wrist.

Her upper arm was bandaged, from just below her shoulder to her elbow.

"What happened?" Sage demanded, her voice loud considering her injured sister appeared asleep.

"She was in town," Owen answered, his voice much more hushed. "Just walking. We had made plans to meet at The Muse for lunch." He paused and brushed a kiss over her forehead.

"She burst into the florist," Rosemary continued. "Grabbing her arm, yelling that she'd been bitten."

"He bit her? In broad daylight in public?"

Rosemary nodded. "She was pretty panicked, but knew it was a man, and it wasn't Ivan."

"Even so, isn't he in magical prison somewhere?" Sage interrupted.

"Hopefully." Rosemary tied off the bracelet.

"Why is she unconscious?"

"The nurse gave her a sedative," Lavender answered and looked up from her phone. "A man attacked her on the street, bit her arm hard enough to need stitches. It's a normal reason to need a sedative. She was visibly shaken. And scared."

Will stood back, watching the Bay family interact.

"Who are you texting?" Sage asked.

"Asher. I want him to contact the Guardians and make sure Ivan and Morana are still with them."

"Why isn't her magic working? I watched her heal herself before," Sage pointed out.

"I don't know," Owen answered. "But please stop yelling. I would really like Laurel to get some rest before we inevitably have to leave."

Sage's eyes flitted around the room. "I have to go," she spat abruptly and pushed out into the hallway.

"Sage?" Will called. He turned back to her family. "Sorry, I'm going to—"

"Go," Rosemary answered.

Will ducked out of the hospital room to see Sage disappearing down the hallway.

"Sage!" he half-whispered, half-yelled. He jogged in her direction and whipped around the corner just as she pushed out of the building.

"Sage, wait!" he called again once he was outside. "I have your keys." He ran to stand beside her. "She's going to be okay."

"That asshole!" Sage seethed. "I'm going to kill him."

"You're not," he lowered his voice. "You can't kill him, and you are talking really loudly. If you are going to kill him, be quiet about it, and let's get in the car at least." Will wrapped his hand around her wrist and guided her back to where they'd parked before they climbed in.

"How do I find him?"

"Lysander? Jonas? Miloslav? I don't know. He probably isn't sitting around waiting for you to surprise him. And walking around with a vial of Laurel's blood might cause a scene." Will slipped his hand over her thigh. "I doubt he's staying under his own name in the hotel."

Sage shook his head. "He could have killed Laurel. He is not a good person."

"I remember." As much as Will wanted to forget, the exact feeling of that knife in his gut still hung in the forefront of his mind.

Sure, he'd stabbed Lysander first but...it was an awfully painful way to go.

"What a beautifully, fucked up, twist of fate that I end up being a Bay? I stopped him from stealing the Bay magic three hundred years ago after his witchy murder spree, and now he has a chance to kill me and my entire family."

"That's not going to happen," Will said quickly.

"Damn right, it's not. Miloslav Stoch isn't leaving Star Island alive. Not if he comes near another person I love. I don't care if I have to go to prison for the rest of my life. I will end him."

Chapter Twenty-Five

The only thing on Sage Bay's mind this Saturday morning was finding Miloslav Stoch and ridding him of his life.

But it was farmers' market day, and it was September. There was no way she could trust anyone to run her stall other than herself. Leaving Laurel in charge for a long period of time last Saturday had been extremely uncharacteristic of her, and doing it two weeks in a row might have her losing customers.

Laurel had been released the night before with a clean set of labs, a precautionary round of antibiotics, and some good old-fashioned anti-anxiety meds to help her sleep. For now, she and Owen were staying at the Bay cottage, as well as Rosemary and Asher, to keep everyone safer with numbers. Luke and Verbena were a few stalls down running the bar tent, and Lavender had insisted on coming with Sage and Will to run her stall today.

Sage busied herself setting up her produce, but her mind was running a million miles a minute. How was she supposed to concentrate on her harvest magic when a chaos warlock was coming after her family? It was September. She was supposed to be at the height of her magic and mood for the year. She wanted the burst of joy she usually had now, not an overwhelming sense of dread when thinking about Miloslav.

"Maybe we should wear baseball hats?" Lavender suggested. "So, he doesn't recognize us?"

Sage shrugged. "I don't think a baseball hat is going to hide our connection." She eyed Lavender, who jumped when a baby cried out nearby. "Are you okay?"

"My little sister was attacked last night. This guy is probably going to at least try to attack the rest of us. I've been better."

"If he attacks me, I will do my best to rip off one of his appendages. Whichever is the closest to my hand. Ear. Finger. Dick." She pulled another basket of green beans to the table.

Will inhaled and organized the tomatoes. "Sage, come on."

"What? Modern times are ridiculous." She lowered her voice. "This is a magical issue. If I want to rip his dick off before he tries to murder me, I think I should be able to."

"Haven't you murdered him three times?" Lavender prompted.

"Technically, Nemesis was in charge one time. But the first and third times were all me."

"So, track record wise, you are the more dangerous magical person."

"No. I murdered one person two times. He murdered Will and all the Bay witches in England. For no reason other than one of them wouldn't sleep with him. He also tried to rape me more than once. Bad guy energy all around. Shouldn't be allowed in society." Sage turned to Will. "You aren't going to tell me not to murder him?"

"I defer to your judgement, but I would like to spend time with you that isn't through bulletproof glass. So. Try not to kill or maim him?"

"No promises."

The farmers' market began, with swaths of locals and tourists pouring into the park with their canvas totes and fat wallets. Sage made a killing these days. She also supplied veggies to Convito's, the Italian place in town, but her big money makers were these farmers' markets. Everyone loved a farmers' market in fall.

Now, every tree in the park had little hints of color. Orange-tipped maple leaves and yellowing hickories shone against the bright blue sky. Sage rolled up the sleeves of her flannel and tied on her apron, ready to begin. Will hung back in his jeans and sweater. He looked a little less out of place compared to his first trip, what with the tweed jacket. But he still didn't look like a farmer.

Didn't matter. Will was hot in his frazzled professor way. Sage was dying to lean over and kiss him, but the day she showed any sort of public affection at her job would be the day the Stochs got all the Bay blood. Never.

Plus, things were still weird after yesterday. He wanted to get married? Now? They were way too young. Sure, they were in their mid-twenties, but Sage hardly felt like an adult. She'd never lived away from Lavender, and until these soulmates started showing up, it had been all Bay sisters all the time. Couldn't they just have great sex and hang out? Why did there need to be some sort of commitment ceremony? Laurel and Owen weren't married, Rosemary and Asher weren't married, and Verbena and Luke weren't married. They were all content to live in perceived sin with their soulmates, couldn't she and Will do the same?

And kids? Fuck, Sage had never thought about having kids. She'd been parented by four older sisters for the past thirteen years. She didn't know how to take care of anything other than a plant. Creating life was not high on her to-do list. What if that was a deal breaker for Will? She thought the universe took care of these things.

She was twenty-four-years-old, and a warlock she'd murdered in three separate past lives was attacking her family. How the hell was she supposed to think about marriage and kids?

She risked a glance at Will. He seemed extremely interested in fiddling with the veggie display.

He was probably still mad about her saying he was just a librarian. She hadn't meant it in a mean way. Only that she had watched Lysander kill Ariston. She didn't want Will to get hurt in this life. He wasn't a fighter—she didn't care! She liked him how he was. She was the vengeance-hungry witch. He didn't have to get mixed up in it and possibly killed. It would be easier for her if she faced Miloslav alone this time.

Hell, she wanted a day with just her plants. If she could spend all of tomorrow watering, picking, giving her crops the TLC they deserved, she knew it would do wonders for her mood. And then she could spend some serious time thinking about all the changes coming now that Will was here. It was like she'd been sneak attacked into adulthood in the last week, and she didn't care for it.

"You have staff now?" Theo interrupted as he walked up to her table, hands on his hips.

She did not have time for him today.

"Theo. Yes. I do have staff today. I run the busiest table at the farmers' market, and it's Saturday. You know Lavender, my sister. And this is Will. I'm twenty-four. I'm allowed to have a man hang out near me without you getting your panties in a twist. So, go back to your table, and leave me alone. Or else I'm going to ask the chamber of commerce to move you to a shittier location."

Theo huffed and shook his head. "Well, you didn't have to be rude," he mumbled as he walked away.

"I sort of did!"

"Sage," Lavender hissed. "He's here." Her sister grabbed her wrist and tugged her until they stood beside each other.

Sage looked up, and there walking through the crowd, he was. Lysander, Jonas, Miloslav fucking Stoch. Bane of her lives. Sickeningly bleached hair, purplish circles beneath his eyes, and a ratty T-shirt. He looked like he hadn't showered since their last life.

Suddenly, the crowd seemed to dissipate. Everyone walked away from Sage's tent, even the neighboring vendors. Theo picked up his cash box and walked straight to the parking lot, like he was leaving for the day. It was probably chaos magic. Damn. This was going to be interesting.

"Well. If it isn't my two favorite Bay sisters. And Ariston? Huh. Shouldn't be surprised, I guess." He leered at Will. "Didn't see you in Baltimore. I was too busy absolutely railing Martha."

"Railing? I slept with you two times and slit your throat the second. The only reason there were two times is because I needed you comfortable so I could kill you. Again." Sage wove her fingers through Will's. "What do you want?"

"How's Laurel?"

"Fuck off," Sage bit out.

Miloslav grinned. "And then there were four." He chuckled and looked over at Verbena and Luke, two tents down but frozen in their spots. "So, Luke is fucking a Bay. Bastard. But then again, he was from the shitty line." He shook his head. "Morana and Ivan are out by the way. Wasn't too hard." He pointed at his chest. "Chaos warlock. Causing pandemonium is kind of our thing. Nice try though, the whole Guardian angle." He leaned in closer. "If you think I'm not connected to my siblings, you have no idea what I'm capable of."

Sage seethed. "True. But I think you know exactly what I'm capable of, Jonas. Lysander." She felt her eyes shift, the power of Nemesis settling over her. "Stay away from my family, Miloslav," she growled.

"Sage," Will said slowly, squeezing her hand.

She blinked. The crowd had come back, and a line was forming at her stall.

Miloslav grinned again. "See you around, Sage. You too, Ruby. You look good." He gave them one last nod, then disappeared into the crowd.

Chapter Twenty-Six

"Fuck that chaos warlock," Sage mumbled. The market was quickly shutting down now that noon had come and gone. The other sellers pulled down their tents and packed up their wares, then headed to trucks and cars. Sage's only vegetables left were wilted and uninteresting to the few stragglers. "And what the hell was that with Lavender? He was talking to her like he knew her, calling her Ruby," Sage added.

"He was talking to you like he knew you because he did. Sort of." Will had noticed it also.

"Oh, shit. Do you think he was in one of her past lives too? Why the hell do these people follow us from life to life? In our next life, are we going to deal with this crap again?"

"Probably," Will answered half-heartedly. He spun his phone around in his hand. "Hey. Can I tell my family to leave? I'm not going to leave obviously, but my sister-in-law is pregnant and my niece and nephew...if a bunch of magical shit starts happening, I don't want them to be a part of it. They're all supposed to stay until Monday morning."

"Oh. Yeah. You should tell them to get off the island. Your parents should leave also." Sage's eyes flitted around. "Maybe you should go too."

"Nope. Not leaving you. You had to face that soul alone in Maryland, you're not doing it again." Will stood firm.

"I handled it pretty damn well by myself." Sage raised an eyebrow.

"You did. You don't have to again." Will took two steps toward her and wove his fingers through hers. "Don't send me away. Even if you tried, I'd come back."

Sage wrinkled her nose and leaned against him for a moment. "You're good with your words, warlock," she teased. "Call your mom while I finish cleaning up. We'll come up with a plan."

"If you think I am abandoning my child and my child's soulmate in the face of a chaos warlock hellbent on destroying my child's life, having already taken my child's life in ancient Greece, you don't know me very well. Your father, Cate, and the kids will be on the evening ferry and on a red eye tonight on their way home to Portland. Dad will go home with them and then come back for me. I will be staying here to show this chaos warlock exactly what a storm witch can do when her family is threatened."

Will smiled. It was pretty cool having a storm witch for a mom. She definitely wouldn't back down from a magical fight.

"Thanks, Mom. Sage and I are going to try to find some spells that might help. Maybe there's something in their attic that can slow him down at least."

"Send me a picture of him," she went on. "If I see him, I'll make sure a torrential downpour follows him around the island and makes any sort of nefarious actions much harder. It's difficult to be menacing in wet underwear."

"Good plan. I'll call you if anything changes."

They said goodbye and Will tucked his phone back into his pants pocket. It wasn't that he *needed* his mom to stay, but hell. If Miloslav had already attacked Laurel in broad daylight, they were going to need as many magicals on their side as they could muster. And while his dad was a warlock and Cate was a forest witch, it was much more important that John's family make it back to Portland unharmed.

He followed Sage up the stairs to the Bay cottage. She opened the door and locked it behind them as soon as they crossed the threshold. The hum of protection magic swirled around them the moment the bolt clicked.

A heaviness settled in his chest as it had before. When they'd walked the frozen lands together stalked by wolves, when he'd wandered the streets looking for Lysander after he'd attacked Callistrate. Will started to feel that maybe this life wasn't destined to be a happy one. They'd had their happy life in Maryland with Marcus. That had been a lifetime of joy and normal sorrows. A life of a couple who'd lived quietly, at least once they had met each other. Despair was beginning to inch its way into his soul. Miloslav was a formidable warlock.

"Come on," Sage said, "all the books are in the attic. Can you work your absorption magic?"

"Of course," Will answered. He followed her through the house, up to her bedroom, and into the attic. He still cringed seeing their absolute disaster of a library, but he pushed past it and got to work.

"What do you want me to find?"

"Anything to do with chaos warlocks. Their weaknesses, if they have a sort of kryptonite that negates their powers. Basically, something to give us a leg up on him." Sage handed him a book. "How long does it take you to... consume a book?"

"Couple minutes." He looked over the piles of books. "Can you organize them? Take out stuff that most likely won't have anything to do with chaos warlocks. Even with my abilities, it would take over a day to go through all these books. And I can get...fatigued." Will had learned that the hard way his freshman year of college. He'd waited until the morning of a huge biology midterm to try to absorb the contents of the textbook and ended up giving himself such a bad migraine he threw up on the way to the test and ended up with a C because reading hurt his head.

"Got it. I'll make piles, you learn everything you can." Sage smirked. "This is a power I could have used in high school. I sucked at school."

"Most people feel that way." Will set his hand on a book and closed his eyes.

It was difficult to explain how it felt to suddenly know a book. It wasn't like he'd read it in the past and it appeared in his memory in a normal way. It was like watching a slideshow of every page, but the page flashed for an instant and somehow, he understood everything that page had to offer. He'd come to learn that it was only to be used in dire circumstances. He'd never read a novel like this and had attended many a book club with a half-finished book because it didn't give him any of the joy of reading or learning when he did it this way. It was like downloading a file.

But a few moments later, Will knew that *General Spells for the Modern Witch and Warlock* had nothing to offer them in the way of chaos warlocks. They continued like this until Will had gone through close to thirty books, and their hope began to dwindle.

"What?!" Sage yelled.

Will dropped the book he was going through and blinked his eyes. Sage gripped her cell phone against her face. "Where are you?" Her eyes shot over to Will, and she put the call on speakerphone.

"I am okay. I'm at home now. He didn't get my blood."

"Miloslav attacked Rosemary. Will is on too now," Sage added.

"Tried to attack me. He didn't notice the tree of a man next to me, and apparently for all of him springing Ivan, his brother forgot to mention that I have a Guardian. Asher jumped in front of me and...I don't know. It was something weird and magical and Miloslav ended up bouncing down the street like he'd run into a wall of rubber." Rosemary sighed. "Before it started, though, I felt really weird. Dizzy and almost like I was having an aura migraine. The sky looked all prism-y. That was probably the chaos magic. We need to be careful. He is literally altering our perception of the world."

Sage didn't answer, but her face was set like stone.

"Sage? Don't go after him," Rosemary warned.

"I think I have to." She looked at Will. "I set all of this in motion three hundred years ago."

"Not you. Him. You never antagonized him. He was always the problem, the one who caused every issue between the two of you. The three of us." Will reached for her hand and wove his fingers through hers.

Sage ended the call and set her phone on the table. "He's going to try to take you from me."

"And he'll try to take you from me." Will didn't continue. Didn't tell her that his biggest fear was that he would succeed this time. That this was another life in which they would be ripped apart too soon.

Instead, he pulled her against him and wrapped his arms around her. He spread his hands wide against her back, wishing the rest of the world would melt away and let them have some time.

"We should get back to work," he breathed against her neck.

"We can take a fifteen-minute break," she soothed, her hands already pulling his sweater over his head. They hadn't been together since he'd mentioned marriage, and Will wasn't sure how she would feel about it now. But their mouths found each other in a frenzy. It hadn't been like this before. Now, Will had an overwhelming ache of time running out. If Will and Sage would be separated in this life, so soon, barely having any time together, he wanted that time to count.

Maybe she didn't want to get married or have children because there wouldn't be time for either of those things in this life. Maybe they were not destined to spend more than a week or a month together. The thought twisted his heart sickeningly tight.

If that was the case, he wouldn't waste any of their time together feeling hurt by her reaction. He'd only bask in the time they had.

He worked on her buttons, which felt like three times the amount on a normal shirt. He ached to touch her skin, run his hands over her.

"Hurry," she breathed, as if Sage also felt the sword hanging over them. A thousand years wouldn't be enough time. Clearly, all the lives they'd spent together weren't enough.

It would never be enough.

They fell together, a mess of clothes pulled off, mouths on skin, and breaths drawn and exhaled in measure. He wanted every part of her today; her body, her soul, her undying love. He wanted Sage and Martha and Callistrate and his woman. Everything they'd ever been and would be.

"Will?" Sage moaned.

"I'm here," he answered, sliding between her legs and up her body.

"I need you to look at me." She took his face in her hands. "I am going to protect you."

"Sage—"

"I mean it. Miloslav isn't going to hurt you this time. I won't let him. I can't...I can't do it again. When I was Callistrate...it was so many years. I lived to be a very old woman, each day knowing what I'd lost. I did nothing but wish I could join you. I had Nemesis and the other priestesses, but my life without you—it was dark and lonely." She pressed their foreheads together. “We were happy last time, remember? When you were Henry and I was Martha. We got a long time together. I want that again.”

“I want it too,” he gasped. She rolled them over until she was on top, slowly moving over him. “I want everything with you.”

She nodded and placed a hand against his heart, which he quickly covered with his own.

“You and me, Sage. I’ll never leave you,” he promised, knowing there was no way he could keep it. Even if Miloslav failed, even if Sage’s vengeful spirit chased him away, he could get hit by a car tomorrow and leave her again. “I love you.”

It was such a beautiful burden knowing of their past lives. All the joy, and all the hurt. All the happiness, and such sharp pain. He knew exactly what could happen. What it would feel like to love her for years. To leave her tomorrow. Either way, he wouldn’t squander a moment they had together.

Sage cried out as she came, then crashed against him, their bodies entwined until he followed suit.

“Forever,” she breathed against him.

“Forever.”

Chapter Twenty-Seven

Sage dropped Will off to see his mom with a pile of books from the Bay library. She hadn't asked if she could take them out of the house, but right now she didn't care. Will needed to get as much knowledge as he could and check in with his family at the same time. Their place wasn't warded, but Verbena was on her way to place the spells later today. They'd be safe in their house.

Sage needed to find Miloslav.

Will didn't know she was doing that. He thought she was going to check on Laurel and Rosemary. She did check on them, via text, and both were okay. Laurel and Owen were back behind wards at their rental house, and Rosemary and Asher were at their apartment mostly unworried after Asher had managed to throw Miloslav down the street without even trying.

Sage, on the other hand, was actively looking for the chaos warlock from hell. She combed the streets of town, went to the hotel and campsite, even checked out the mostly empty beaches. Star Island wasn't huge, but it wasn't like she could see every corner of it in an afternoon. Parts were densely wooded, a lot was private property, and Miloslav wasn't standing out in the open.

She closed her eyes and tried to think about him. About Martha and Jonas. About Lysander and Callistrate. She thought about her exile after killing him in a time when none of them spoke anything like modern language. She thought about delivering his execution time and time again.

"Come on, Miloslav. I know you want to find me." Sage didn't have a lot of inherent magic other than harvesting. But she was connected to two souls, life after life. Will and Miloslav. If fate could send Will to Star Island, she could coax Miloslav to her. "You must hate me with every corner of your soul. Every time I've managed to thwart your plans. If only you hadn't come to my cottage in Baltimore. You would have gotten all the Bay blood hundreds of years ago. Reshaped the world into something new. Something built for a chaos warlock."

She focused on his face, the sound of his voice. The sneer that followed him life after life. The hooded lust that visited the eyes of all three versions she'd met before. He'd always wanted her, and he'd never gotten her. Not really. Not the way he wanted.

Her phone rang.

She pulled it out of her pocket and saw an unknown number, knowing full well who it was.

"I thought you'd never call," she answered.

"Yeah, right. Like I couldn't feel the shit you were just doing. Calling to me. I could basically pinpoint you on the island," he snarled.

She hummed. "Seems like you finally got the power you wanted so badly. But...not quite enough?"

"Look, bitch. I could kill you twice over and it wouldn't make up for everything you've done to me. The plains. Greece. Raetia. Baltimore."

"Hell, I didn't get to see Raetia! I hope it hurt like hell," she teased him maliciously.

"It did."

"Same old, same old, I presume? You do something insanely fucked up, I kill you over it?"

"You deserve everything you have coming to you, Martha."

"Stop murdering my soulmate. Stop trying to rape me. Stop killing witches. I don't know what you did in Raetia, but your track record is abysmal. I have no doubt whatever I did was justified. You're stuck in a loop of your own madness, man. Chill out and maybe you'll have a normal life."

Miloslav laughed on the other end. "I get to win this time, Sage. I've waited thousands of years. This is the time I win. I didn't recognize you before. Now I know you. I know all of you. The fates put my siblings and me together to finally destroy the Bay line. And you made it so easy. Five magical sisters living on an island. No far-flung cousins, no children I would feel a smidge of guilt as I bled out. You set us up perfectly. The fates even gave me a brother and a sister who hate you all as much as I do."

"Skip the villain monologue, Miloslav. What do you want?"

"You. More than anything. Even more than Lavender."

Apparently, Miloslav did know her sister. Sage tucked the information away and turned her mind back to him.

"What like, you want me to fuck you? Because no. I've been pretty clear on that life after life."

"I don't want to have sex with you, Sage. Learned my lesson last time. You come, alone, and we see where it takes us."

Sage chewed on her lip. She could beat him. She had every lifetime before. Sure, he was never a chaos warlock, but she had Nemesis on her side.

"You'll stay away from my family?"

"For now."

"Fuck you."

"Well, obviously I'm not going to stay away forever," he said over a low chuckle. "I learned my lesson giving you vows that are...antagonistic to my ends. What do you say?"

"Where do you want to meet? I've got a nice little field that would be perfect." She knew it was stupid. She knew going to see Miloslav at a location of his choosing was foolish. But she also knew that she'd beaten him, three to zero. And she wasn't letting him anywhere near Will this time.

"Yeah, right. Ivan told me what you can do with an apple tree. I'm staying on the Sirius peninsula. Great little gloomy corner of this sickeningly sweet island. There's this abandoned house with a red door."

"I know it," she interrupted.

"Come and find me," he said, then hung up.

Sage looked at the phone in her hand, then took a deep breath. It was time to have it out with Miloslav Stoch.

Chapter Twenty-Eight

Earth Witchery: a discipline based in a witch or warlock's connection to the earth. Part of the elemental branch with fire, air, and water witches, earth witches have an uncanny connection to the physical world. Soil, rock, wood—earth witches are intertwined most in solid substances found in the natural world. The earth witch is a rare breed. In the last three hundred years, only four lines of earth witches have been traced.

Allies: Earth witches are most often found in familial relationships with water witches, some even in the same exact bloodline. Less common are earth witches with siblings with air witchery tendencies and almost never do we find an earth witch and a fire witch in the same line.

Enemies: Like other elementals, earth witches often find themselves at odds with any who follow ethereal magic, such as chaos, blood, or celestial. Ethereal magic rarely affects earth witches, as they are so cemented in the natural world, though when an earth witch is in an unfamiliar place, she might find resisting chaos magic more difficult.

Will pulled his hand off the book with a start. He quickly flew through the pages, finding the exact place he was just reading. It was *The Elementals: A Magical Guide to Air, Earth, Fire, and Water Witchery.*

"Mom?" Will called as he landed on the chapter on earth witchery. "Do you know any earth witches?"

"Hm. I think Karen Liddy might have been an earth witch...but I haven't seen her since nineteen-ninety-two."

"Do you think Sage could be an earth witch?"

"An earth witch? I don't know. I thought she was a harvest witch."

"She is. But she said something once to me, about how she always felt closer to an earth witch than any of the other hearth and home specialties."

"Could be then. She would know better than anyone."

Will looked back at the book. It wasn't much, especially when going up against a chaos warlock, but it was something. "Hey, Mom? Are you sure you don't want to leave? I feel like..."

"Like what?" his mom answered. "Like I would abandon my baby? Absolutely not. Dad, Cate, and the kids are on the plane waiting for it to take off. John is picking them up at the airport. This Miloslav character doesn't know them. The plane will be fine. He may be a chaos warlock but I'm a storm witch. No one controls the skies like we do." His mom rummaged through her suitcase. "Now, I didn't pack all my supplies but..." She pulled out a jar of salt. "Aha! I did bring it."

"What is that?"

"Salt from the Pacific Ocean. And I collected some salt from the Atlantic two days ago. Nothing like a salt circle mingling two oceans to add an extra layer of protection." Will followed his mom into the kitchen where she grabbed another jar. Witches really loved jars.

"Miloslav Stoch, right?" His mom took a third empty jar and mingled the two salts together, then handed Will the jar.

"Yup."

"Keep that in your pocket. I'll make one for Sage too." She turned back to her work. Will walked to the dining table and pulled out a chair, then stopped.

"Why is this here?" Will asked. His mom walked over.

In the middle of the dining table was the Devil card.

"I...don't know." The two of them stared at it for a bit, neither reaching to move it.

"You know, modern interpretations really don't have the Devil as a literal devil," his mom began.

"Mhm."

"More of an inkling that the querent needs to let loose in life, enjoy some of the more 'devilish' activities Renaissance life looked down on. Or that there is something sinister within that needs to be excised. Or, you know, a shopping habit that needs to be quelled."

"Yup." Will crossed his arms in front of his chest.

"But you don't believe any of that?"

"Nope. Sometimes the Devil card means a devil is coming." Will pulled out his phone and opened his contacts to call Sage. His screen scrambled, then went black.

"Weird. Mom, can I borrow your phone?" He turned back to his mom, who was now staring at the door.

"Shit," she breathed. She grabbed Will's forearm and dragged him next to her. "Something's here. Guessing it's the chaos warlock."

The entire house seemed off. The clock on the wall lost its hands, the windows went black, like it was the middle of the night. Will's sensory perception of the world was shot.

"Tempestas," his mom called out to her patron. "We could use some help." She kept her hand on his arm, but Will could hear the storm raging outside.

His vision flashed. Lightning strikes intermingled with pieces of past lives. Miloslav as Lysander and the man on the plains. Other lives too. Will saw him in other skins, speaking different languages. Always alone. Never with a soulmate. Sometimes, he and Sage were there too. He saw visions of himself hidden until now; he and Sage must have lived a dozen more lives than they'd seen during the spell.

"Will!" his mom shouted. "Stay awake." Her voice commanded him, like a small child listening to a parent. He blinked his eyes open, and saw her, struggling to stay on her feet. "Do not lose consciousness. Hold on to this world."

"Mom," Will shouted back, his voice wavering. Fuck, he wished he was a storm warlock! Anything that could counteract a chaos warlock.

Then the door blew open, clear off the hinges, and in a flick, Will's mom fell to the ground.

"Mom!" he screamed. Will collapsed beside her, grabbed her shoulders, and tried shaking her awake.

"She's alive for now." Miloslav spoke as if he were commenting on the weather. "On your feet, warlock."

Will stared at the man in front of him. He could feel the power wafting off him like a bitter wind. This was the strongest male Will had ever been in the presence of. None of the warlocks he'd met at camp or since then had anywhere near the power Miloslav did. How did that happen? No warlock should be this powerful.

"What's your name this time?" Miloslav asked casually, leaning against the doorframe.

"Will."

"Okay, Will. That woman, who I believe is your mom since you screamed Mom like a toddler a few seconds ago, is fine. She's enjoying a bit of a mental trip at the moment, but nothing that will do any more damage than a night of heavy drinking. But she won't be fine if you don't get on your feet and come with me."

Will looked between his mom and Miloslav. Leaving with a chaos warlock felt like an unbelievably bad idea, but his mom was completely innocent in this. She wasn't in any of the past lives and had never met this rotten soul before. He couldn't risk whatever Miloslav could do.

"Fine." Will reached over and felt his mom's pulse. It was steady. "I'm coming." As he pushed to his feet, he checked that the salt jar was still in his pocket. It was. "Where are we going?"

"My place. It's perfect. You'll love it. Great atmosphere for two warlocks to fight over a witch."

"If you think I'm all that's standing between you and Sage, you haven't been paying attention the last few lives," Will mumbled. He hazarded a glance back at his mom. She looked peaceful now, like she had managed to fall asleep on the kitchen floor.

"How long will she stay out?"

"Hm, fifteen minutes? Long enough that she'll have no idea where the hell we are."

Will looked at Miloslav. "Why don't you ever leave us alone?"

Miloslav snorted and grabbed Will by the collar. "It's the bitch who doesn't leave it alone." He dragged Will down the front stairs and tossed him into a car, slamming the door behind him. Will frantically searched the horizon, unsure whether he wanted to see Sage or if he wanted her to be as far away as possible.

He didn't want to die today. But he also didn't want Sage to get hurt trying to save him. Or go to prison for murdering Miloslav. Which seemed likely.

He didn't add worrying about Sage dying to his list, because if there was one thing he knew about his soulmate, no one, not Miloslav, not Jonas, not Lysander, could take her out. She was pure power, and she was undefeated.

But she'd done some pretty insane things when he was in danger or when Miloslav's soul threatened her, which meant a lifetime in prison was definitely on the table.

Chapter Twenty-Nine

Sage stood at the meeting point, an empty house on Polaris. There were no tire tracks, no car, no footprints. Nothing to make her believe that Miloslav was there.

But that could be a trick. The wind whipped menacingly past her, a bitter chill coming off the ocean that rustled the oak tree beside her. She raced up to the door, crunching leaves underfoot, seeing no point in standing outside waiting for him to come to her. She burst into the house, knocking a bunch of spiderwebs astray as she did.

"Fuck," she grumbled. No one had been here in months. The floor was covered in thick dust, and there was nothing in the air that made Sage believe the chaos warlock was nearby. She rushed back outside toward her car and skidded to a stop.

Over the Centauri Peninsula was a crazy, isolated storm, spitting lightning like a hurricane.

"Oh no," she breathed. "Kelly." Sage sprinted to her car and threw it into drive.

Miloslav was with them.

Sage ditched her car outside the house and bounded up the front steps. The door was slightly ajar. She probably should have been more careful, took one moment to think of a plan before bursting into the house, but she didn't. Miloslav was here, or had been here. The air was thick and heavy with magic, crackling in every open space.

Kelly lay in the middle of the destroyed kitchen, curled in the fetal position.

"Kelly!" Sage yelled and dropped to her side. "Kelly, you have to wake up. Will!" she screamed, hoping beyond hope that he was somehow here, somehow unharmed.

"The chaos warlock took him," Kelly managed. Her eyes were still closed, but she tried to push herself to a seat. "He threw me into a dream world. But I could still hear them. As if any warlock could block the connection a mother has with her child."

Sage eased Kelly up and to the couch. "Do you know where?"

Kelly shook her head. "He said his place. Other than that, nothing. But they drove. I heard a car leave." Kelly sank into the couch. "I'm so tired. I don't think his spell has left me yet." She closed her eyes again. "Help Will. Please. I'll come when I can...oh...wait. Will asked me if you were an er..." and like that, Kelly was unconscious again.

Sage pulled a blanket over her and surveyed the damage. The house was completely trashed, as if someone had tried to knock everything off the counters and emptied all the cabinets. The books from the Bay library were shredded in the corner.

"Damn it!" Sage yelled. A chaos warlock had Will. The last time their souls had been together, they were Lysander and Ariston. She'd seen what he'd managed before. How he'd taken her soulmate away from her.

Sage got to her feet and rushed back to her car, grabbing her phone from the central console as it dinged.

Unknown: Now that I have your attention, about two miles east of the red door, there's an old fishing house. Come soon. I'd hate to get carried away with your man if you dawdle.

Sage: How do I know you are actually there? You could be on a boat to the mainland for all I know.

Unknown: You'll have to trust me, Sage. You've never wanted to trust me.

Sage: In my defense, your record in terms of trustworthy behavior is horrible.

Unknown: Says the woman who lured me into bed and slit my throat. Believe me or not, but the longer you take, the longer the two of us have to get to know each other. See you when we see you.

"Fuck!" Sage yelled. She threw the car into drive and pulled away. There were a couple old fishing houses on Sirius. How had she missed Miloslav when she drove to Kelly's? He must have taken the back roads. Which meant they hadn't been there too long yet. She still had time to get to Will.

She hoped.

A rush of memories flooded her. Watching him bleed out on the floor of Nemesis's temple. Clinging to him as they froze to death. She wouldn't let that happen again. They'd been happy in Baltimore, they would be happy again. One happy lifetime wasn't enough.

She raced down the streets, praying a cop wouldn't catch her. Because she wouldn't stop. And trying to explain magic to a police officer would be difficult. More difficult if all their brains were being addled by a chaos warlock.

Shit, she still didn't know how she was going to keep Miloslav out of her mind. She wished she had more time—that she could comb through the confetti of books and find something, anything, that could help.

But all she had was her knack for growing food, her blessing from Nemesis, and the hate in her heart toward Miloslav. That had to count for something. Laurel had the right idea cursing Morana for hundreds of years, dozens of lives. Sage should have thought of that. She should have bound Jonas to his grave three-hundred and some years ago when she'd buried him on the spring morning.

If she managed to get out of this one, she was definitely taking that sort of path in this life. Every curse available to her would be showered over Miloslav and any incarnation of him that came to be in the future.

The drive took longer than she'd hoped, with every single minute filled with everything that could have already gone wrong. Miloslav could have killed Will for all she knew.

She pulled up to the first fishing house and parked on the street. Before jumping out of the car, she opened the group text with her sisters and punched out a paragraph.

> Sage: Miloslav has Will, hurt Kelly. I am meeting with him. On Sirius. Stay away from the peninsula. I don't know if he's stronger with Laurel's blood. Or if he would be even stronger if he got mine. Keep yourselves safe. I'll check in when I can. If someone can go check on Kelly, she's passed out on the couch in their rental. Love you all.

Sage threw her phone on the front seat of her car before any responses could come through and ran to the house.

Chapter Thirty

Will had never been beat up before.

In other lives, yes. Physical violence was something expected in the Paleolithic period or Ancient Greece, but in this life, he'd spent his time avoiding any sort of altercation in which punches were thrown. Even his brother had refrained from really hurting him when they'd been kids.

But today, Will was experiencing getting the shit kicked out of him, and he didn't care for it.

When they arrived at the empty, derelict shack, Miloslav had immediately pushed him to the floor and kicked him in the ribs.

And that's where Will found himself. On the ground of an abandoned house, being kicked in the stomach by a man who had killed him before. It didn't bode well for this being a life in which he and Sage were able to hold on to their happiness.

Will tried to roll away, but Miloslav blocked his path, straddling him with a foot on either side of his hips.

"Hope your little soulmate gets here soon. You've never been a tough one, have you? Never a warrior or a soldier, never a mercenary or an athlete. It's crazy the fates have bound you to such a strong woman. You'd think she'd want someone with a little more grit. A little more fight in him. You've always been weaker than me. Every time."

Will grimaced and then grabbed Miloslav's ankle. Suddenly, he was in Miloslav's head, or his memories. He was searching throughout the world, over and over and over, coming up empty-handed. It was the ancient world with a bronze sword at his side...the Middle Ages and a pockmarked face... the wars of the twentieth century with a gun in his hand. Surrounded by war and violence in every single life. He was alone, always. Never finding his other half, never finding peace. No quiet lives by a lake with a small brood of children. No smiling brother chasing him through the woods on a summer day. A wisp of someone, never within reach. But Miloslav never turned toward her. He always moved with the darkness. Will held on as Miloslav searched, over and over again, never able to find her.

Miloslav had never met his soulmate.

He had heard of the mate-less. A cursed group of magicals who were destined to walk their lives alone, without finding the peace and happiness a perfect half could deliver. Will had thought it was a legend. After all, there had to be magicals who would much prefer a solitary life to a partner.

But this didn't feel like he was mate-less. This felt like he couldn't find the person. Like they were always too far away. Or he was choosing the wrong path over and over again. That something in time separated them, no matter what he did.

"You've never had a soulmate," Will sputtered as he released Miloslav's ankle. "You've never found them."

"Fuck you!" Miloslav shouted. "You...you don't understand. I deserve to find her. And if I don't get her, I get another witch."

"I saw it. She's always there, but you aren't on the right path. Maybe you'd find her if you weren't so obsessed with screwing up Sage's and my happiness. Leave us alone for a life and she'll fall right into your lap."

Miloslav kicked Will again, hitting him on the cheekbone. Spots like fireflies danced across the ceiling as he fell back. The stars shifted and turned real, glowing orbs bouncing around the building, until they broke through the roof and revealed a purple sky.

The world cracked open, and Will saw...everything. His past lives, Miloslav's past lives. He saw Sage in millions of different reincarnations. She fought in some lives, practiced magic loudly and in the open, lived quietly in others. But she was always her, always had the spirit of vengeance living softly within her until it was challenged and released. He walked beside her, every time, his eyes on her, as Miloslav stalked behind them.

His hands went up to his face. The world was spinning now, and he knew it was Miloslav in his head. The chaos warlock's magic made him feel like he was going mad. Will tried to calm his visions—chase away the demons who slinked on the sides and seek out particular things he wanted, rather than the muddled mess Miloslav pushed forth. He tried to keep Sage in his mind.

She would see him through it. Even if she didn't make it, if he went mad or Miloslav landed a kick against his temple and caused an aneurysm, he would find her again. He always did. They'd been together through pain, suffering, joy, and stillness. Sage was Will's and he was hers. No matter how many times Miloslav pulled them apart, they always found each other. He would find her again. No matter what.

Miloslav was so engrossed watching Will writhe on the floor, he didn't hear Sage enter. He didn't see her run toward him either, so when she punched him as hard as she could in the side of the head, and then quickly followed up with a punch on his kidney, he crumpled to the ground like a leaf. Sage didn't stop; she grabbed his collar and punched him again, and again, pounding against his jaw now. She put everything into it. All her pain of losing Ariston. All her fear in the Bay curse. Everything she felt when she saw Laurel in the hospital.

Miloslav would pay.

If this chaos warlock thought he was going to torture her soulmate and get away with it...he hadn't learned a thing from a single past life they had shared.

"Sage," Will mumbled. She glanced over her shoulder. Will was holding onto his ribs and pale as a ghost. In his other hand, he tossed a jar in her direction, which she grabbed.

"I'm—" She was cut off by Miloslav tossing her off him and into an errant table.

"Fuck," she grumbled, getting to her knees.

Miloslav stood, one hand toward Will, the other at Sage. "You, don't move. You," he said, looking at Will, "stay on the damn ground."

Sage did as he said and stayed put on her knees. She eyed the room. Other than a table from the 1940s and an overturned chair in the corner, this old shack held nothing but cobwebs. Nothing to use as a weapon. Sage had faith in her fists, and as much as she wanted it, she shouldn't actually kill Miloslav. But if she did, it needed to be with her own two hands so she could easily claim self-defense.

Sage locked eyes with Miloslav. "What happened to us meeting? Leaving Will out of it?"

"As much as you'd want it to be that way, he was always a part of it. The two of you are a package deal, and while I care little about him, I know the straightest way to you, is through him. You always come running to protect your little boy."

Sage tried to throw Will a look of strength, but she faltered. She couldn't see a path out of this that ended well.

"What do you want? What will it take to let Will walk out of this room?"

"Sage, no," Will interrupted.

Miloslav grinned. "And you asked why I picked him up on my way here. You are so much more compliant when he is concerned. I'm not an idiot, I know how to play my cards." Miloslav stretched his arms above his head and rolled his neck a few times. "Your blood."

"Fuck you," Sage answered.

"No," Will managed, slowly pushing up into a seat. "You cannot have her blood. Sage, listen to me for one moment. Chaos magic doesn't work on earth witches."

"Will, are you okay?" Was Miloslav addling his brain right now? There were no earth witches here.

"Oh, does the eternal boyfriend want to play?" Miloslav rolled his eyes. A flash later and Will was holding onto his head moaning. "What sort of excuse for a warlock are you this time? Nothing with real power, of course. No type of protector or warrior."

"You always were the superior warlock," Will began, as he panted, "but I'm confident I've always been the superior man."

Miloslav blew out a breath, then punched Will across the face.

"Stop!" Sage yelled. She couldn't watch Miloslav hurt Will again. She wanted to rip his eyes out, tear his hair off his head. She wanted that asshole to feel true pain. She wanted to rain down vengeance upon him. Give him everything he deserved.

Her hands shook, her fingertips tingled. She could feel her body becoming something else, not her own.

Nemesis.

In a breath, the goddess was here, populating every inch of Sage's body, flexing her fingers and toes, testing out this new body, and what it could do.

Miloslav Stoch, my sights are on you.

Chapter Thirty-One

It was not Sage's voice, but Will knew it all the same. The voice of the goddess.

He'd heard it before, when Nemesis crawled into the form of Callistrate over a thousand years ago. It was the last thing he'd heard as Ariston and unforgettable.

Like a voice from a cavern, a voice that gave you no option but to heed.

Instead of cowering, which Will definitely would have done if the goddess of vengeance spoke to him in such a tone, Miloslav's face split into a grin. He closed his eyes and shuddered, like he was slithering into a new skin. His trembling continued long enough that Will crawled toward Sage and away from him.

Hello, daughter.

Will snapped his head toward Miloslav. That voice was not his own. His face had changed too, almost comical in its twisting. His eyes looked red one moment, unchanged the next.

Erebus, Nemesis answered, her words like a curse. *Why are you here?*

I am not allowed to play? You play all the time. Your little devotees, rushing around this earth in your name. You jumping in and out. Killing in your name. Even one of mine.

You've never shown interest in him before.

Miloslav shrugged. *He never had it in him before. But now*—he smirked—*chaos bubbles within this child like a hot spring. Waiting to be tapped. His anger, his uncontrollable rage...it's delicious to live within. A treat for my old soul.*

Will glanced between the two, Sage and Miloslav. Nemesis and Erebus. Gods of Ancient Greece. From the pantheon he'd laid offerings at the feet of for an entire lifetime. Erebus was never one he'd paid particular heed to, a mess of chaos and darkness. He was shadows and terror, nothing any normal Greek gave reverence to.

And now the god stood before Will. On an island in the Atlantic Ocean.

You are not stronger than me, Erebus began.

Nor are you stronger than me, Nemesis countered. She cast her eyes upon Will. *Stand up, boy. I've killed for you before. You are hers and she is yours. Don't let yourself be cut down too easily. Grief is a powerful tool in vengeance, but it can often cloud the mind and depress the soul beyond retribution. Take care of her by taking care of yourself.*

Will got to his feet and looked at the goddess. It was such an eerie feeling, looking at Sage and knowing it wasn't her. Knowing she was aware of what was happening, but not a part of it.

Erebus, leave my witches alone. This one you claim as your own...he is a sorry excuse for a warlock. Using others' power as his own. Stealing from witches. He twists the world to serve himself.

As a true son of chaos would! Miloslav released a terrifying laugh, bubbling up like acid. *I am not done with this soul, as I assume you are not done with yours.*

She is mine. Hurt her and suffer the consequences, Father.

Shall we form a truce then? I will not meddle in the affairs of this witch, if you will not meddle in the affairs of this warlock?

Will watched as Nemesis narrowed her eyes at her father.

I will consider your offer, Father.

"Sage!" Will shouted. He grabbed her around the waist. "You are an earth witch. Chaos magic doesn't work on earth witches. Call to the earth below you. You are the caretaker of this island. You feed its people. You are the power of this place."

Miloslav grabbed Will's collar and threw him off Sage, then turned to her. "Go to sleep," he commanded.

Sage began to feel her fingers and toes tingle, but Will's words ran over and over in her mind.

She was an earth witch. The magic of Star Island was a part of her. Chaos magic couldn't hurt her.

"No," she said and took a step toward Miloslav.

"Go. To. Sleep."

"You heard Will. You think because you can throw a body across a room that makes you the stronger warlock? You don't even know your limitations." Sage took a deep breath and thought of every moment she'd spent tilling the earth on this island. She thought of every person on Star Island and beyond being nourished by her food. She called on Demeter and Pomona, the goddesses she gave heed to in this life.

She could feel the earth rumbling beneath her feet, and the door shaking against the hinges.

"I don't care if you are an earth witch, I can control you this time."

"You've never been able to control me, Miloslav. And you never will."

He flashed his eyes toward Will then ran at him, like a beast let loose from a cage. Sage dived after him, losing her concentration and attaching herself to his back, trying to protect Will. She lost all control she'd been holding in the earth, and the door blew open, a mound of soil coming with it.

"What the hell?" Sage mumbled. Had she done that? Did dirt listen to her?

In a swift movement, Miloslav pulled her off his back and pinned her beneath him. "Got you," he hissed, then stretched the neck of her shirt wide and bit her shoulder hard.

She yelled and writhed, trying to break him off her.

"Fuck!" Will shouted and tackled Miloslav. He pulled him off Sage and threw him to the other side of the room. He stayed on him, slamming his body over his. Swinging his hands at any piece of soft flesh he could find.

She felt like shit. The bite throbbed, nausea swept through her body, and she needed to get out of here.

"Will," she managed as she tried to sit, but crashed to the ground.

He left Miloslav in the corner and ran to her side. "Oh gods, you're bleeding." He pulled his sweater off and pressed it against her shoulder. "He bit you?" He turned to Miloslav. "You bit my soulmate?"

Suddenly, the world went hazy again, purples and blues crowded the room. Sage felt like she was a moment away from puking everywhere when Will stood up. She tried to stay connected to the earth, not let the chaos magic affect her, but she was so tired. She needed...

She needed Will.

She shifted to her back and watched as Miloslav wiped his hand across his bloodied face. "I got what I came for." He licked his lips again. "See you around." He backed out of the shack, then disappeared into the distance.

Will stood and started to run after Miloslav.

"Will! Come back!" Sage screamed. It was like Ariston all over again. She was going to lose Will. Miloslav was going to kill him again and this time she didn't even have the strength to go after him.

Sage rolled on her back and cried, falling into the deepest despair. Miloslav had gotten her blood. He was going to kill Will. Everything had been for nothing.

"I'm here. I'm not leaving." Will fell to the ground beside her and wrapped his arms around her. "He's gone. I've got you," he murmured. "I've got you."

Chapter Thirty-Two

Will helped Sage to her car—his arm around her waist and hers over his shoulders—once he was positive Miloslav was gone. He eased her into the passenger seat, took the keys, and headed to town.

"You didn't leave me."

"I'm not going to. Ever."

"But...before. Ariston left. And got stabbed."

"That is true. And I learned from my mistakes in that life." He glanced at Sage. She looked awful, but he was sure he did too. Facing Miloslav had been terrible, but they got through it. Together.

"Take me home," she groaned.

"Uh, hell no. You need a doctor. I'm taking you to the hospital."

She shook her head. "No. One crazy tourist biting a Bay sister is weird. One crazy tourist biting two Bay sisters is reason for an investigation."

"You need stitches."

"Laurel can heal me. She and Owen are pretty good at healing spells." Sage shifted in her seat and fished her phone out from the cupholder.

"Laurel couldn't heal herself," Will pointed out.

"I'm texting her now. If she can't heal me, I'll go to the hospital. I promise." Sage exhaled. "Your mom is okay. I found her. Rosemary texted that she is with her now. But you should call her and let her know you are all right. I'm just going to...I need to close my eyes," her voice drifted off.

"Sage. Stay awake." Will grabbed her thigh and shook it.

"I'm too tired."

"Sage, don't you dare fall asleep. You were bitten by a chaos warlock. He could have rabies."

Sage chuckled. "I don't think he's rabid; I just think that's his personality." She hummed again, like she was settling in to fall asleep.

"Talk to me. Come on. Hey, you want to hear something interesting?"

"Hm," she murmured.

"Miloslav has never found his soulmate."

"What?!" Sage sat up and opened her eyes. "Is he mate-less?"

"I don't think so. I saw a lot of the inner workings of his brain. It feels more like she's always out of reach. But he's been too focused on us, particularly you, to find her. And he talks about her like she exists." Will suppressed a shudder. "But what a terrible fate."

"Is it a punishment?"

Will shrugged. "Not one drawn down by us. But who knows which other deities might have it out for him. Nemesis isn't a fan."

"Could have been her. Maybe the cursed Bays were under her protection as well. He might have pissed her off on multiple fronts." Sage blew out a breath. "What a fucked-up life to live."

Will nodded in agreement. He didn't wish the Stochs anything but ill, and Miloslav could fall down and die as far as he was concerned...but he'd never heard of that before. Of the fates being so cruel to a soul. Never finding a soulmate, through multiple lifetimes.

"Do you think...Nemesis will come back? Or Erebus?"

"I'm not sure. She didn't say goodbye or anything, but she definitely didn't want to fight with Erebus. I get the feeling they are on the same team, on whatever plane they normally exist. For now, I think it is just us and just Miloslav."

Will pulled into the Bay cottage driveway, where Laurel, Owen, and Lavender were waiting.

"We told Rosemary and Verbena not to come. So, we aren't all together. Just in case," Lavender explained while helping Sage out of the car. "Oh, Sage." Lavender frowned. "That looks terrible."

"Thanks, it feels like shit." Sage leaned against her older sister. "In case of what?"

"In case Miloslav had stolen your phone and this was a ruse to get us all in one place. Now that he has both yours and Laurel's blood—"

"You and Verbena and Rosemary need to be extra careful. I can't believe..." Sage muttered before closing her mouth. "I could use some healing and a strong herbal concoction. Also, maybe three times the recommended dose of ibuprofen." She reached her hand out to Will. "Put me in bed?"

"Of course."

He followed her up the stairs, his hand on her lower back in case she stumbled, into her bedroom, and pulled back the covers for her.

"Normally, I'd ask you to join me, but Laurel and Lavender will be in here in a minute with all sorts of healing shit for me. I hope."

He pulled the blankets up to her chin and kissed her forehead. "I'm content to sit here and watch you heal." Will dragged a chair from the corner of the room next to the bed.

Sage nodded and snuggled under her covers.

Will tried to stay out of the way, and Laurel did seem to heal Sage, even if he would have been more comfortable with her at a hospital. But, watching her wound slowly stitch itself back together did make him feel a lot better.

After a healing session from Laurel and the greenlight to take a nap, Sage fell asleep immediately.

Will: I'm sitting right next to Sage, and she is asleep. How are you?

Mom: Yes! Oh, honey, I'm so glad to hear from you. Are you okay? Is Sage okay? Is that man no longer a problem?

Will: Sage and I are okay. She was attacked but is feeling better. I am pretty sore, but I'll be fine. I'm worried about you being alone though. Do you want to come to the Bay cottage?

A few minutes passed before the three dots appeared again, letting Will know his mom was typing.

Mom: I think we should leave, and I think Sage should come with us.

Will: We are easily google-able. He'd be able to find us in Ohio.

Mom: I don't think we should go to Ohio. I think we should go somewhere else. Some place we've never been. Did he get Sage's blood?

Will: He did.

Mom: Oh no. How soon do you think she'll be able to travel?

Will sat for a moment, looking at the question. He loved Sage. Every inch of her. And she loved her family. Miloslav was her enemy. He was as entangled in their lives as they were in each other's. Running away from him was never their style. They faced him, no matter the consequences.

Will: We're going to stay. This isn't the end of it, and I'm as a part of it as Sage is. We won't abandon everyone else or put you or Dad or John and his family in danger. This is going to be a battle, and my harvest witch and I are in it.

Chapter Thirty-Three

Sage woke up feeling much better.

She still felt like a chaos warlock had beaten her, bitten her, and messed with her head, but now she felt like it had happened a few days ago, instead of a couple hours earlier.

Will dozed on the chair next to her, a deep bruise blossoming on his cheek.

Miloslav.

She had wanted to kill him so badly. Every fiber of her being had wanted to. But Will was right. It wasn't Ancient Greece or early America. It may be a magical battle, but the rules were different now.

Plus, was she an earth witch? She literally called the soil to her. That was insane. She'd never done anything like that before. Sure, she could make branches on her apple trees move and stubborn plants grow in whatever direction she pleased, but that was on her own property, where the earth really knew her.

It seemed the entirety of Star Island had an affinity for Sage Bay.

"You're awake," Will said through a yawn.

Sage nodded and scooched over, then motioned for him to get in the bed next to her. Will slid beside her and pressed a kiss against her cheek.

"You look like you might need some healing too," she mumbled. She moved to hug him, but he winced under her touch. "Will! You should have had Laurel heal you."

"I'll heal. Probably a handful of broken ribs."

"Still. I don't like seeing you hurt at all."

Will shook his head. "Laurel was spent after healing you. I can wait." Will brushed his hand over her cheek. "I'm glad you are okay."

"I don't think we've seen the last of Miloslav. He's gotten blood from two of the five Bays. He isn't going to give up."

"I know." Will took a deep breath. "We need to talk."

Sage shifted uncomfortably. "Why does it sound like you're about to break up with me?"

"You're my soulmate, Sage. Breaking up isn't on the table. Ever. But..." He hesitated. "We need to talk about what happened. Before. When I said I couldn't wait to marry you."

Sage felt her cheeks go warm. So, this was going to be a big conversation. Though every inch of her ached to rush out of the room and away from having this talk, she stayed. Because she loved Will, and she owed it to him to hash this out.

"Do you want to be with me?" he asked.

"Of course."

"But you don't want to get married. Ever?"

Sage shrugged. "I don't know. Honestly, I never really saw the point of it. We're soulmates, bound by more than a legal document. I'm not really a white dress, big party kind of girl, you know? As long as I love you, what's the big deal?"

Will grinned a little and pulled her close. "You love me?"

"You know I love you."

"I don't actually," Will added. "You've never said it."

Sage pulled a face. "Words of affirmation aren't my strong suit. More of an acts of service girl. You know this." She chewed on her lip a moment, then released it. "I love you, Will Markham. I've always loved you, always will. In this life and those lives and every life to come."

"I love you, Sage Bay." He exhaled. "I would really like to marry you. Not today, not even this year. But in the future, I do want to get married. You don't have to wear a white dress, and it's obviously not going to be in a church." Sage laughed. "And we won't screw in the woods while our families hang out nearby. We can go to a courthouse. Or, you know, Tuscany."

"Tuscany?"

"I figure nothing can seduce a harvest witch like those wheat fields."

"That's a pretty good plan. But there's just...so much we still need to figure out."

He nodded.

"I feel really young," she continued.

"So do I. Let's seriously date until we feel a little older. I don't even have a job."

"That's another thing," Sage interjected. "People don't commute to Boston from Star Island."

"No openings at the public library at the moment?" Will asked hopefully.

"I doubt it. There are four employees, and they are closed on Sundays. And no one cares they are closed on Sundays." Sage sighed. "I don't know what we should do."

"Maybe," Will started. "Maybe we don't figure it out today. Maybe this is going to take us a little while for us to figure out. Like a year."

"Are we supposed to be apart for a year?" Sage didn't like the sound of that.

"No. I am unemployed at the moment, so as long as you don't mind me crashing with you for a little while, I can figure life out here as well as anywhere else."

"But what if you find a perfect job in New York City?" Sage pressed.

"I won't be looking for a job in New York City."

"What if you find a perfect job anywhere that isn't Star Island?" She paused for a minute. "I guess I could move."

"Your farm is here," he pointed out. "Can't really put that in a box and pack it."

"No," she answered slowly, "but I could start a new farm."

"Sage," he began.

"No, really. If you got a job in a more rural area, I could start a new farm. Not many twenty-four-year-olds have an established farm. I could start a new one. "

"I don't want you to give up your land. I'm not some human who doesn't get it. You are a harvest witch, and this is your plot. You are bound to this land, and it is bound to you."

Sage grinned. "I'm not bound to it."

"You're not?"

"No. You think when I was a recently orphaned eleven-year-old who had moved to a New England island from Ohio, I bound myself to my land? Hell, no. Until about four years ago, I dreamed of getting away from here."

Will moved his arm around her and drew her closer to him. "What did you dream of?"

"Hm. A place where my sisters weren't looking over my shoulder all the time. A place with real space. Five acres is great, but fifty acres...could you imagine? Room for everything I ever wanted to grow. Grains. Corn or wheat, stalks and sheaves blowing in the wind. Getting lost among what I had grown." She closed her eyes and pictured it. A place for her...and Will. Now, when she dreamed of that golden-lit place in her mind, there was a librarian on the porch when she came in. A pot on the stove simmering for them to enjoy. A bed to fall into at night.

"What about...a job at a big state university library? One that is surrounded by farms and fields. Most of the colleges in the Midwest are like that, after all."

"It's not something I could do right now," she admitted. "My savings are less than spectacular and running a huge farm takes a lot of money and..."

"It's a beautiful dream," Will interrupted. "I'm okay with us having a lot of dreams right now, and not much else."

"But each other?"

"Of course."

"And if I never want to have a baby?" Sage prompted. Marriage was one thing. She had no trouble imagining their relationship would basically be a marriage, but children were a completely different thing.

"I don't want to have a child until I am at least thirty, which is in five years."

Sage tossed it over in her mind. She had no idea what life would look like in five years. Hell, her entire family could be murdered by Miloslav tomorrow.

"Five years?"

"I'm not asking for a promise. Only that we can talk about it. In five years." Will ran his thumb over her chin.

"Five years," Sage repeated. "For now, you stay here. With me."

"I'll start applying for online jobs. You have good internet in this cottage? And an older sister who won't care I'm crashing here?"

"Yes, we have internet, it's not 1980. And I doubt Lavender will care. She's always wanted what was best for me, and it's easy to see that you are what's best for me." Sage planted a quick kiss on his mouth. "So. Do you have plans for Mabon?"

Chapter Thirty-Four

The sun rose softly on the autumnal equinox that year. Light filtered through the trees—their leaves kissed with hints of red and yellow—and speckled down on the Bay sisters. The men, Owen, Asher, Luke, and Will, would join them later. But for now, it was simply the sisters.

No one had seen Miloslav since he'd fled with Sage's blood, but he would be back. The Guardians had gotten back to Asher—both Morana and Ivan had been broken out of prison and were loose in the world. None of the Bay sisters were free from the Stochs. But today, they were safe, and the world was beautiful.

Sage's time was quieting. Soon, she would sleep more and more, and the harvest would go to bed. She may have awoken her connection to Nemesis, but this time, her soul was knitted to the earth through and through. She could feel its slumber coming, but not before it pushed forth abundance.

"Should we begin?" Lavender asked.

Sage stepped into their circle and knelt on the earth. She wore a skirt, the only one she owned for this solitary purpose. She flattened her bare knees and shins against the earth and tucked her toes and let her skirt billow around her in a circle. Her sisters closed their circle, their hands clasped together, as Sage pressed her palms into the ground. The dirt was cool, no longer the warm soil of summer.

And then she could feel it. All of it. The pulsing life within this land, within this world. Her soul entwined among it all. She pressed all of herself toward it—her power, her soul, all she had to offer. There was so much more she had to learn about her powers still. It was like opening a new book.

There was a time when she wanted to become part of the earth, leave all else behind. Not anymore. When nothing but tilling, planting, and harvesting mattered. Now, there was Will, and the lifetime they had to look forward to. Whether it be on Star Island or in Ohio or Idaho—wherever they made a home would feel like home because it would be something they built together.

Sage loved Star Island, but the grief she held on to here was not something she would ever be able to release. She knew herself too well for that. Thinking about home being somewhere else someday...it didn't scare her. Will was her home. As long as she had him, she was happy.

They concluded their ritual: more protection spells, a healthy harvest, a deep sleep for the earth come Samhain. The five Bay sisters standing hand in hand, looking out onto their land.

The fight wasn't over, far from it. The Stochs would return. Miloslav would try to steal their powers. The curse still hung over their line.

But they had each other, and they had their soulmates. Sage had every confidence the Bays would win this fight.

For the first time, Sage found herself rushing back inside, away from her precious land. She hurried up the stairs and into her bedroom.

"Are you finished?" Will asked. He lounged on the bed, book in hand. He still wore his pajama pants and bedhead. She brushed the dirt off her knees and climbed in next to him.

"I'll change the sheets later," she mumbled before finding his mouth.

"Don't we have celebrations to attend?" Will said between kisses.

"We have time," she insisted, slipping her shirt over her head and nestling against his chest.

"We have time," he repeated. "Forever."

One Week Later

Sage had never spent a full day in September in bed.

Yet here she was.

Four o'clock in the afternoon, not a stitch of clothing on her, not a spot of work done in the yard.

Sure, she'd had four orgasms since waking up, listened to her soulmate read her Emily Dickenson aloud, had a naked tarot card reading—which, of course, had given her the Lovers, the Two of Cups, and a very sexy-looking Knight of Pentacles—and only left the room to bring up food for Will and her, the remains of which sat on a tray near the door.

"Hm," Will mused. "I don't think I've kissed you here yet." He picked up her leg and pressed his mouth against the back of her knee.

"Will! I have to check the gourds. And the pots. It hasn't rained in three days."

Will's mouth moved up her thigh, nibbling against her skin. "Mhm," he answered, continuing his path.

"Don't you want to stretch your legs? Maybe go to the bookstore and grab—oh!" Will flipped her to her back and pressed a kiss between her legs. "Damn it, Will. I'm trying to talk to you."

He nibbled at her thigh. "You can keep talking. If you want to. I'll be busying myself in other ways." He grinned mischievously at her, then dragged his chin against her inner thigh until he settled at her core.

Fuck. Sage had so many things to say. So many excuses to make. The land. The butternut squash. The watering. She really should shower and get dressed and tie her hair in a braid and get the day going—

"Oh, fuck," she groaned.

Maybe it was good to have days off. Days like this. Will wasn't going to be unemployed forever. There would be years of nine-to-five jobs. Wednesdays filled with obligations to work and colleagues and the rest of the world. Today, none of those things existed.

"The squash can wait," Sage mumbled. She wove her fingers through his hair and surrendered.

Eventually, around six in the evening, Sage did make it outside to gather everything that needed picking, give the entire garden a thorough watering, and give a few squash bugs a serious talking to. It felt good to have a semblance of normalcy after weeks of anything but.

Sage had spent the majority of her time alone before now and was content with it. But now that Will was here, well, she liked spending time with him. She liked sitting with him in silence, eating her meals with him, just existing in the same space as him.

It was jarring but she was getting used to it.

"Hey," Lavender called. Sage switched off the hose and set it where she stood. "Is Will out here?"

"No, he's in the shower."

"Good." Lavender came close to her. Her face looked grim, like she was about to drop some very bad news.

"Oh no. Is Miloslav already back? Shit, I was hoping we had a little more time while he gathered his troops."

"That isn't it. Or at least, I haven't seen him or noticed any shift in the energy here." Lavender took a deep breath. "You and Will can have the house."

"What?" Sage must have misheard Lavender.

"The house. You and Will should take it. Owen is building a house,

Rosemary and Asher bought a house, Verbena lives with Luke next door. You and Will should live here. You've spent years cultivating the yard. All your work is here. Your livelihood is here."

Sage stood dumbfounded. "Lavender, the house is yours. You deserve it. You raised us here."

"I know, and I can't live here without all of you. If you and Will leave—and I know you will eventually if I'm here—I'll hate it. It'll drive me crazy."

"But your soulmate—"

Lavender put up a hand and stopped her.

"Sage." She exhaled. "He isn't coming. I know him already. It...didn't work out. The prophecy is already complete. It's a huge house, a huge yard. I can't take care of it alone. You and Rosemary always did the whole yard. And I'll be so sad." Lavender shook her head. "I can handle being alone in my life, but not here. Not surrounded by all the memories. I need to move. I can't..." her voice trailed off.

"Lavender, are you all right?"

She nodded vigorously, as if she was trying to convince both of them. "You don't have to stay here forever. There'll be a whole new generation of Bays before we know it. Someone will always live here. But you're only twenty-four. Your soulmate is between jobs. The two of you need this. Let me do this for you."

"It's too big."

"It's not. You didn't go to college, you never traveled. You've done nothing but financially support your family since you turned seventeen." She paused. "I rented a place in Solaris. I'm moving out tomorrow."

"Tomorrow?!"

"Yup." Lavender smiled. "Now, you and Will can make the house yours. And for heaven's sake, get at least a full-size bed. You're too old to be sharing a twin. It can't be good for your backs." Lavender squeezed her arm and turned to leave.

"Thank you," Sage called. "You were a great parent."

Lavender stopped but didn't turn around.

"You were a great kid."

Lavender stood on the threshold of her new apartment. Everything was moved in, the kitchen was already set up, and sheets were on her bed.

It only left her, and her brand-new kitten, Erie, to move in.

"What do you think?" she asked her mewling cat, smoothing her cheek against his fur. He answered with a definite "meow" that Lavender interpreted as, "walk in the apartment."

So she did.

She set Erie down and left him to explore his new house and put her keys on the kitchen counter. It was a nice place, newly renovated with that white-everything feel. It wasn't necessarily her style but...

But she couldn't stay in the Bay cottage anymore. She'd been a mom there, as much as she had tried not to. She firmly believed in the word "guardian" in terms of her relationships with her sisters. But that didn't stop her from scheduling doctor's appointments, and keeping the fridge full of food, and making sure everyone had a haircut before school started. She had conferences with teachers, even with Laurel's when she was a senior in high school and barely passing her classes and Lavender was only a twenty-two-year-old still reeling from the death of her parents. She brought baked goods in for fundraisers, took the ferry to Sage's softball games on the mainland, made sure the house had enough pads and tampons and Advil and Band-Aids. She memorized her sisters' allergies, knew which kids were bad news in high school, which parents didn't care if kids were drinking and driving, and which ones were good people. She took the stares and the "are you sure you can handle this" and the "you're doing your best" comments from nearly everyone.

And now that part of her life was over.

Her children were grown. Her little sisters were now adult women with soulmates of their own. Partners to live out their lives with. No matter what the Stochs threw at them, Lavender had faith. She had never let anything happen to them, and she wasn't going to start now. Miloslav—Jonas, Ariston...Charles—no matter what he called himself, Lavender would stand between him and her family. Because that was her calling this time. She was the protector. It was her job, alone.

She turned the lights on in every room of the apartment, not caring that her electric bill would be astronomical. Nothing like some warm light to turn an apartment into a home.

She was alone and would remain so. There was no soulmate coming for Lavender Bay. She had made sure of that thirteen years ago. Some hurts didn't heal, no matter how much space she managed to slip between that day and today. No matter how often he snuck into her dreams, unchanged. Still a twenty-one-year-old with the world in his eyes.

It was okay. They'd find each other again, in another life, when things weren't so complicated. When Lavender knew better than to try out spells in college dorms and reap consequences that were far too great for her to handle.

Erie wandered back over and rubbed against Lavender's leg until she picked him up. She cradled her cat against her chest and rocked side to side.

"All right, Erie. You're a witch's cat now. Let's see if we can make a cake that can bring down a chaos warlock."

Lavender nodded once and got to work.

Thank you for reading! Did you enjoy? Please add your review because nothing helps an author more and encourages readers to take a chance on a book than a review.

And don't miss more from Colleen Delaney's *The Witches of Star Island* series, coming soon.

Until then, discover PINK GUITARS AND FALLING STARS, by City Owl Author, Leslie O'Sullivan. Turn the page for a sneak peek!

You can also sign up for the City Owl Press newsletter to receive notice of all book releases!

Sneak Peek of Pink Guitars and Falling Stars

BY LESLIE O'SULLIVAN

You only get one parachute. There's no point packing two for a B.A.S.E. jump since you'll be pavement art before the second chute blossoms.

"Justin!"

Startled by a bellow from my jump leader/uncle, Timmer MacKenzie, my toe jerks to a stop half an inch above the trigger pedal of my launcher. Is his gray matter shredded, distracting me during a safety check? There's no chute on my back. One accidental tap on the business end of this launcher, and I'll be eye to eye with the flock of seagulls patrolling the Hollywood skies. I retreat onto the non-ballistic end of my perch. Peering over the edge of the Rampion Records Tower, I analyze the antics of the wind.

"Join us," Unc calls, teeth clenched in a P.R. smile. He hosts a cluster of reporters near the center of the circular roof. "Meet the rising star of the Slinging Seven."

Their faces morph into a collective portrait of panic as I leap more dramatically than necessary from launcher to the terra firma of the rooftop. After a salute to the Hollywood sign, a photo op my uncle will appreciate, I join the party. Pre-jump interviews are not my happy place, but keeping a smile on Timmer's face is essential. He leads our B.A.S.E. jump troop, giving the green light for my carcass to launch off skyscrapers, bridges, and cliffs in a wing suit.

"This Rampion Records Tower may rival Mount Olympus for

acceptable jump altitude," Timmer tells the press jam sandwich. "Even so, I believe in enhancing the safety zone for my lads."

I sweep an arm across the roof. "Thus, the launchers."

"Your latest exhibitions of low altitude B.A.S.E. jumps have raised serious concerns," says a fresh-out-of-journalism-school reporter. He rocks a Channel Six pin on the lapel of a blazer clearly tailored for someone else. We get his type all the time: low man on the news roster, usually stuck with covering mudslides or C-list celebrity screw-ups.

I grunt at the question. Timmer's a walking archive of aerodynamics. His B.A.S.E. jump designs adhere to a superhuman canon of safety. Even Unc can't control the wreath of clouds descending on the tower. Humidity makes trickier conditions. My bangs congeal into a sweaty clump. Twenty-three is too young to die when you have plans, and I have plans.

"To you, B.A.S.E. jumping is an extreme sport. To me, it's a science." Timmer slings an arm around my shoulder. "Would I risk my own nephew's life?"

A grandfatherly dude slides square-framed sunglasses to the end of a nose in serious need of a good hair plucking. "Come on, Mr. MacKenzie, that kid can't be eighteen."

I wince at the familiar speculation my youthful image always dredges up. Satan's roadies have prepped a new circle of hell for Timmer's perpetuation of the lie about me being eighteen. My B.A.S.E. jumping talents at twenty-three are PDG – pretty damn great—but a fresh out of high-school dude rocking my moves is prodigy wonder boy territory, great P.R. fodder.

I keep my lip zipped over the deception. I'm not going to lie, it does not suck being a prodigy wonder boy.

Unc spins me to display the product emblems plastered all over my banana-colored wing suit. "Endorsements like these don't come from launching children into the sky. Justin jumps one-hundred percent legally."

The reporter's skepticism settles at the edges of his mouth. Metallic coating on his sunglasses turn my gray eyes silver as I catch my reflection. The gloaming breeze plucks strands of my tawny mane free from the generous layer of product I always apply before a jump. I'll have to re-tame those suckers to restore my roguishly hot vibe instead of the young and soft look Timmer prefers. I'd give my right nut to have a growth spurt on the spot. Sadly, thanks to MacKenzie short man genes, there probably aren't any in my future.

A gust of wind blows the press a tiptoe closer to the curved edge of the roof. Timmer and I hold our ground with matching "no big thing" expressions.

A babe in a raspberry-colored lady suit pushes toward me, eyes bulging with concern. Twitchy fingers alight on my shoulder. Next to my banana wingsuit, we're a fruit salad. Here comes the *concerned auntie* vibe.

"Justin, why take risks B.A.S.E. jumping with the Slinging Seven Troupe even for someone as enchanting as Zeli?"

I bite back a groan at the mention of the pop queen.

"Is glorifying her platinum record worth your life?"

Truth rumbles in my throat. *Yes, ma'am, B.A.S.E. jumping is worth the moon. It got me to Hollywood, the land of my music dreams. Dreams that will free me from Timmer's whims so I can make my own destiny.*

Timmer's glare scorches a hole in my suit, cueing the trained monkey answer he expects.

I open my arms to the clouds. "Who doesn't want to fly?" Every person on this roof does. I see it in the way their eyes brighten.

My stomach loops into a knot. Unc may piss himself when his prize canary asks to go AWOL. I've jumped off everything Timmer asked of me on our jiggy pathway around the country to make it here. My gaze drifts to the Hollywood Sign as I press toes into the roof of Rampion Records, the touchstone by which all music greatness is measured.

Tonight, this bird will fly off the Rampion Tower. Tomorrow, I dive into the audition for Rampion's annual singing competition, The Summer Number One. It's the U.S. Open of music, amateurs vs. pros, where Rampion Records dangles a chance for nobodies like me to go mic to mic with their current stable of rock stars. According to the Rampion P.R. machine – *Even the little people in this world have a shot at the Summer Number One dream.* This ammie is going to kick some serious pro ass and score a Rampion Records contract. I've got everything I need for the audition: demo tracks, my guitar, ass-hugging black jeans, and a sexy aviator jacket.

For the last five years, in every crappy rent-a-room the Slinging Seven have crashed, I've done dozens of online music courses. I study. I practice. I'm ready.

Unc laughs at one of the reporters he's chatting up, and I see Ma's smile here on the rooftop. Our signature MacKenzie smile packs serious wattage. I should know, I've busted it out often enough to sway, play, and dazzle females of the species.

Once I grab the top spot in the Summer Number One, my pile of gold for winning will be enough to snag my own digs here in L.A., the last place I remember Ma smiling. The cold burn of loneliness flares when I think of her and wonder if she's safe.

Clouds thicken as I watch the sun dip into the Pacific Ocean. I ignore a stitch of concern at the base of my neck as the jump difficulty ticks up a notch and think in my language of future Justin merch.

T-shirt moment: Music Dreams Sucker Punch Death.

Channel Six pushes in front of his colleagues. "Justin, does Zeli have a lock on the top pro spot in the Summer Number One?"

Lady Suit bumps her shoulder into mine. "Is Zeli your dream girl?"

My lips twist into a frown. Zeli is my nightmare.

Timmer digs his fist into my back, my cue to fix my pissy face. I manage to upgrade to a grimace dressed as a smile. By their winks and snickers, the reporters take my tension as embarrassment. I'd like to water cannon them all off the roof. I'm entitled to a dream girl, but it will never be the plastic diva with her bubblegum diluted pop crap. That chickadee is an affront to everything I love about music.

Unc hasn't run out of bluster. "It's an honor for the Slinging Seven to be part of Zeli's platinum record celebration."

My temple throbs. I'm more than half nuts to risk a concrete sandwich for that over-hyped female commodity with a pink guitar.

Don't miss more from Colleen Delaney's with *The Witches of Star Island* series, coming soon, and read all her books at www.colleendelaney.com

Until then, discover PINK GUITARS AND FALLING STARS, by City Owl Author, Leslie O'Sullivan

Zeli's signature pop diva sound and image are nothing short of magical—literally. Her fame comes with hidden costs, a curse that could ruin her voice forever.

Aspiring indie musician, Justin MacKenzie, is determined to kick it to the top of the Rampion Records' Summer Number One professional vs. amateur singing competition.

The favorite to beat in the annual televised contest is none other than the label's smoking hot superstar, Zeli, whose crazy extensions flow the length of a football field. Those ridiculous extensions, coupled with her bubblegum brand of pop, are an affront to everything Justin loves about music until a stolen kiss blazes into a romantic encounter.

Once inside Zeli's world, Justin discovers things are not as they seem. In their quest to allow the real Zeli, to step into the spotlight, the pair must confront the mysterious force behind the dazzle of Rampion's success. If these star-crossed lovers can't rally their own magic to defeat the darkness, they will lose everything—including each other.

Please sign up for the City Owl Press newsletter for chances to win special subscriber-only contests and giveaways as well as receiving information on upcoming releases and special excerpts.

All reviews are **welcome** and **appreciated**. Please consider leaving one on your favorite social media and book buying sites.

Escape Your World. Get Lost in Ours! City Owl Press at www.cityowlpress.com.

Acknowledgments

Sage Bay was a beast of a main character to get onto the page. After three books in the background, I worried endlessly over how I would actually do her justice. So, I cannot help but begin by thanking my author friends who held my hand through the writing of this book. To Jenifer Lynn, who gave me the best compliment about this book when I finally handed it over to you (shaking in my boots as I did). I went from "no one is going to like this book," to "wait, are people going to love this book?" I'm so glad we met.

To Hadley Grey, Olivia Malo, Janine Amesta, and Natalia Williams, who listened to me day in and day out while I complained and cried over what a hard time I was having with this book compared to the others. Thank you for your friendship.

To Tee Tate, my amazing editor. You make my books SO GOOD. Also you have the enviable ability to respond to my panicked emails in a way that instantly calms me down. It's a gift.

It's my first time being able to write this...thank you to my ARC team! I sincerely appreciate all of you for taking a chance and joining—I hope you loved *Warlocks Get Witched*!

To the Dark Tomes and Tombstones Book Club: I cannot wait to meet up with you all and talk about Sage and Will. I hope you loved every moment of her vengeance ridden heart and his book organization skills.

And lastly, to my family. The mister and the four kiddos who make my life as full as it is. I love the five of you with every inch of my being. I hope we're tied together in every lifetime.

Now, I have to dash...Lavender Bay is about to be very busy.

About the Author

COLLEEN DELANEY is an author, librarian, gardener, and occasional baker. She likes being outside in every season except winter, which she prefers to enjoy from a window. She currently lives on the shores of a Great Lake with her husband and four time-consuming children.

www.colleendelaney.com

instagram.com/colleendelaneywrites
x.com/cdelaneywriter
tiktok.com/@colleendelaneywrites
youtube.com/@ColleenDelaney
threads.com/@colleendelaneywrites

About the Publisher

City Owl Press is a cutting edge indie publishing company, bringing the world of romance and speculative fiction to discerning readers.

Escape Your World. Get Lost in Ours!

www.cityowlpress.com

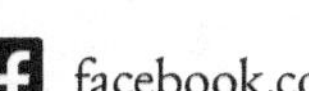
facebook.com/CityOwlPress

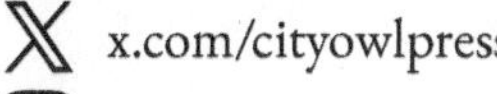
x.com/cityowlpress

instagram.com/cityowlbooks

pinterest.com/cityowlpress

tiktok.com/@cityowlpress

www.ingramcontent.com/pod-product-compliance
Lightning Source LLC
LaVergne TN
LVHW091043080826
845145LV00002B/599

* 9 7 8 1 6 4 8 9 8 5 7 7 5 *